STEEL VENTURES

STEEL CHRISTMAS

WHEN GRUMPY MEETS SUNSHINE

○

C C GEDLING

To Mum, who is sad that the Steel series is ending, despite being expressly told not to read the first book. xx

Cover Designer – CC Gedling (ebook and paperback wrap)

Beta readers – Nina Fiegl (original novella) and Allie Bliss of Blissed Out Editing (latest version)

Proofreader –Chloe L Proofreader

Previous publishing –Part of Steel Christmas featured as a novella in 'Twas The Night anthology published December 2023.

Ebook ASIN - B0DJPHHTFQ

Paperback ASIN - 9798343283020

AUTHOR NOTE

The first Steel Ventures series book was dark romantic suspense, and the second was less dark. While this third and final book (which can be read **stand-alone**) is mostly a Christmas rom-com, there are content warnings. *Take care of your mental health.*

It is written in British English (BE) because Zoe is British, and the rest of the series is set in the UK, despite Theo being American. Embrace the slang, and something you think might be a spelling mistake might just be BE.

Content Warnings

Explicit scenes, grief (off-page but significant theme in book), pet illness (no loss), height jokes, family drama, sexual assault (attempted), on-page violence, homophobic behaviour (side characters/back story)

1

Zoe

The street bustled with people, and I sidestepped someone to avoid getting trampled. My insides vibrated with energy as I fought towards my prize – the corner of the street and my first New York breakfast.

Pain burst through my shoulder as a guy smacked into me forcing me back a step.

"Watch it, shortie," he complained as if he hadn't nearly knocked me into oncoming traffic.

I rubbed my arm. No matter, I was nearly there. A few more steps, and I could tick the first thing off my Big Apple bucket list.

My phone buzzed as the surly street seller handed me my salty, baked goodness. I beamed at him and handed over my dollars.

"Howdy!" I said in my best American accent as I answered the phone to my best friend.

"Happy freaking first day!" Elle screeched down the phone.

I grinned like a lunatic. "Got my first pretzel."

"For breakfast? Wait, it's not lunch there, right?"

"Nope. This is an authentic New York breakfast."

"Are you sure they eat those crusty things for breakfast? Like, have you asked an actual local?"

"Don't burst my bubble. An authentic pretzel is the first item on my list."

"You and your lists."

"They keep me organised." I shuffled my big bag on my shoulder, reassured my heavy planner was in there.

Many people like digital, and I did have an e-calendar, but I loved my trusty Filofax.

"Have you met your new boss yet? I googled him, and holy Batman, he's a fittie."

I rolled my eyes. Elle thought half my clients were *fitties,* but rich men didn't interest me, especially not the arrogant ones I had to wrangle.

"I flew in yesterday. I've not even shopped for food, let alone met my client. I'm on my way there now."

"That guy won't know what hit him when the *CEO Whisperer* arrives."

I groaned at the nickname my brother had recently coined. Mind you, it was better than "short stack" or "shorty bum-bum" that my brothers usually called me, so I'd take it.

"Let's go over the plan."

"Sightsee the pants off New York, shop till I drop, and demonstrate my ability to style across continents."

"And win that prize!"

"Sure, maybe."

I was up for Best Image Consultant in an award ceremony held by Stylz, a UK-based fashion magazine I sometimes guest blogged for. One of my co-writers nominated me, and the ceremony was in the New Year. Elle reminded me that international image consulting jobs would impress the judges.

"It's a shame there's not a huge cash prize." I sighed.

"Or a holiday. We could jet away to somewhere exotic like Hawaii to sip cocktails on the beach," she replied.

The award came with a big feature in the magazine and could significantly boost my business. Maybe even one that would allow me to take on some junior image consultants and stylists to expand my brand.

"You assume I'd take you then?" I teased.

She scoffed at that remark, not even bothering to answer. There was literally no one else I'd take but Elle.

"Just don't fall in love and move to New York. I couldn't bear it." She fake-sobbed.

I sidestepped a couple arguing on the pavement – wait, they called it a sidewalk here.

"That's not going to happen. I'm professional with my clients, nothing more. I swear you're convinced I'll fall in love with every CEO I meet."

My job meant I had met a lot of powerful men and women and each time, Elle predicted I'd be married with babies within two weeks. She was a dreamer, and I might consider a version of that dream myself. Obviously, not with one of my clients, but maybe with someone special.

At twenty-nine, I wasn't getting any younger. I'd built a successful business doing what I loved. Image was everything, and helping people improve theirs was my passion, but I sometimes missed that deeper connection. In my experience, having a successful career hadn't proven conducive to a successful love life, although training and taking on junior stylists could ensure my business in the future without me being the only one working.

"To cheer myself up at the devastating loss of my bestie for weeks on end. I've booked a table for us at Cassidy's. We are going out Christmas Eve-Eve in style."

I was due to fly back just before Christmas, which would fit perfectly with dinner and dancing. Elle always made a big thing about the day before Christmas Eve, like she created a whole new day to celebrate.

"Good thinking."

"I miss you. Is it Christmas yet?" she whined.

"It's four weeks. It's not that long," I reassured her.

"Yeah, but all our December traditions can't be done with you halfway across the world."

"Don't be so dramatic." I rolled my eyes.

I loved it, though. Elle was my favourite person.

"I've got to go. My lunch is almost over. Miss you, boo."

I said goodbye and refused to feel sad that I wasn't back in the UK. I freaking loved Christmas, and although I was giving up my December back home for this job, which was a favour for my brother-in-law, being in New York was a dream come true. Everywhere was decorated for the festive season. All the shop windows twinkled with lights, and everything seemed much bigger and bolder here.

Munching on my pretzel, I followed the map on my phone to the giant high-rise where my new client's offices were. The bite of chill in the air had me fastening my red scarf tighter around my neck.

My latest client was why I was here, getting to tick things off my New York bucket list. People booked image consultants for a variety of reasons. Most commonly, though, it was to change their style. This often included improving their public facing image, especially on social media. Theodore Kelly, however, had not chosen me. His business partners from back in my home city, Sheffield, had arranged for him to see an image consultant. He was a renowned tyrant, and the company staff turnover was terrible. I was likely to receive a hostile reception.

Growing up with my grumpy dad and eldest brother trained me perfectly for this role. I specialised in grouchy CEOs and couldn't wait to get started.

My phone vibrated.

David: Knock 'em dead today, tiger.

I chuckled, imagining David, my brother-in-law, doing cat claws in the air. He was the PA to Mr Reid, one of Mr Kelly's business partners, and was always a little extra.

I realised I had a barrage of texts on my family thread. Usually, I muted it, as it could get manic.

> Mum: Good luck today, sweetheart. Send me some pictures of your pretzel. Bowser says hi.

My heart leapt at the picture of our beloved family dog my mum attached. He was a big old boxer with slobbery jowls.

> Dad: Show those Yanks how it's done.

My brothers all messaged words of good luck except for Isaac, my eldest brother.

> The Old Bill: Make sure you have pepper spray and an alarm. Remember the instep, nuts, solar plexus, and nose.

I rolled my eyes. All my brothers were protective, but Isaac was a police inspector and was big on personal safety.

I scrolled to the top of the thread. One name there never replied anymore. I clicked it to bring up a new message, and a string of one-sided texts popped into view.

> Me: First day across the pond. New client today. I wish you were here. Love you always. Xxx Tink.

As I arrived at the glass entrance, I blinked away tears and swallowed my final mouthful of pretzel around the lump in my throat. *No sad feelings today.*

Carefully, I extracted the two velvet bags from my handbag and pulled out my shoe-babies, their red bottoms glinting in the light. I slipped off my ballet flats to put them on and immediately went up a few inches. Those inches were needed when you were under five feet.

Brushing the pretzel crumbs off my scarf, I tucked it away and used the window to check my pixie cut to see if it was still in place.

Cool air rushed underneath my fitted black jacket with its red piping. The bright red belt accentuating my waist was just enough Christmassy shine to lift the tailored black dress. Taking a deep breath, I readied myself.

The shared lobby looked fit to host Saint Nick. I loved it. A massive Christmas tree rose in the central area that was vaulted and airy. The main desk had gold plaques behind it stating the businesses within the building. Each of them was trimmed with tinsel – all but one of them. *Steel Ventures New York* didn't have any bling around it. I wondered if it had fallen off.

Smiling widely, I approached the security guard whose nameplate read 'Bill' and introduced myself to him.

"What's the weather like down there?" Bill joked, and I resisted rolling my eyes at his unoriginal short-person joke.

He couldn't, however, find my name on the list. I glanced around at the fashions while waiting for him to call the offices. Grey and black dominated the sea of people as they walked by.

I did a few breathing exercises, visualising a successful conclusion to the job and reminding myself of my capabilities. It was my ritual.

Bill eventually got hold of Mr Kelly's PA. She was coming down to meet me to verify who I was. I didn't mind waiting; I loved people-watching, speculating who the people were and what they were doing, so I leaned back against a pillar and breathed it all in.

A lady in a tweed skirt and white blouse with a cute silver broach bustled over.

"I'm so sorry, dear. I'm Carol, Mr Kelly's PA." Her grey hair was pulled up into a tight bun.

"I'm Zoe." I shook her hand. "Don't worry, I didn't mind waiting."

"David said you were coming, but I swear it said tomorrow on the schedule. Anyway, you're here now. Let's get your security passes. You've had all the pre-checks, so you'll have full employee access."

"Don't be a stranger, little lady." Bill winked at me.

"Keep your eyes to yourself, Bill," Carol said sharply, leading me to a bank of elevators.

"You have your work cut out for you." Carol grimaced as the doors closed on the lift. "Theo... Mr Kelly is a complex man."

Her words didn't frighten me; if anything, a tingle of anticipation rose with the challenge.

The doors opened, and the sleek white corridor stretched ahead. The space looked barren in comparison with the seasonal lobby.

"You haven't decorated for Christmas yet?"

Our heels clacked against the floor as I walked alongside Carol.

"Mr Kelly forbids Christmas decorations."

I stopped mid-stride, alarm bells ringing. "What?"

"He doesn't like Christmas. Don't be surprised if he doesn't like those." She gestured to my candy cane pin and my red nails with presents painted on them.

"Don't tell me he's a total Grinch?"

Carol laughed. "Sweet thing, Theo Kelly makes the Grinch look like Santa's little helper."

I giggled. "Oh dear. I do have my work cut out."

"That you do, dear. That you do." She kept walking.

I sighed, adding *Get Christmas decorations put up* to my mental objectives list.

2

_____

Zoe

Most of the harshly white spaces we passed were meeting rooms. An open-plan workspace near the end of the corridor was again void of decorations, even in individual cubicles. The staff here were a mix of people from mid-twenties to late fifties. Carol introduced me, and the reception was frosty at best, making me wish I'd left my scarf on.

She led me into her office, which adjoined Mr Kelly's. The room smelt delicious with hints of a woodsy aftershave, much better than the lemony chemical smell on the rest of the floor.

I moved to the window to admire the impressive view across New York City.

"I will let him know you're here," Carol said, sitting and tapping on her computer. She cleared her throat. "Er... it seems he's been called into a last-minute meeting. Are you okay to wait?"

My name was not on the list... The boss had an "emergency meeting" his secretary knew nothing about...

Well, well, Mr Kelly, are you trying to avoid me?

"Not to worry. I'll grab a drink from the break room you showed me. Would you like one?" I said.

"Oh yes, please, I'll have a chamomile tea. There are some in the cupboard and there's a hot water boiler. Mr Kelly had it installed just for my tea."

I walked back along the corridor to the airy break room. Of course, the kitchen was made for giants, with cupboards set at the height for basketball players. I reached into my bag past the Filofax and pulled out the slim but sturdy plastic step I took everywhere. *God bless Ikea.*

"What is she doing?" a voice whispered behind me.

I clicked the step out and stood on it to reach the cupboard.

"Standing on a step," another voice said.

I spotted the chamomile tea and decided I might have a cup if Mr Grinch-Kelly wanted to play games. Ignoring the whispering behind me, I snapped the step flat and stuffed it in my bag.

"That freaking bag is like Mary Poppins' case," the first voice said as I turned around.

A woman and a man were leaning against the table, watching me.

"Hi, I'm Zoe," I said as I added boiling water to the teabags.

"We know. I'm Taylor, and this is Ben," the girl with curly blonde hair said. "We wanted to say hi because you'll probably be gone tomorrow."

"What makes you say that?" I asked, studying her face.

Her tone wasn't malicious, just factual.

"Carol introduced you as a consultant. The previous two lasted less than twenty-four hours."

"Why was that?"

She glanced around. "Let's just say the boss doesn't take too kindly to outside interference."

"Yeah, and no offence, but if you need a step to reach the cupboard, then *Theozilla* will eat you alive," said Ben, smoothing his artfully styled hair.

He wore a colourful tie with his dress shirt, and it was possibly the first pop of colour I'd seen in this dreary officescape.

Taylor smacked him in the gut. "Shh. Don't call him that. His spies might hear."

Spies huh?

I ignored their assumptions that my height made me incapable of dealing with grouchy CEOs. People frequently underestimated me.

"What's it like working here?" I asked.

"Bonuses are great if you can survive the *Wicked Witch of the West*," Ben said, widening his eyes dramatically and earning another smack in the gut.

"Someone worse than Theozilla?" I asked, intrigued by the office politics already.

"Theozilla's henchwoman," Ben whispered conspiratorially, but Taylor began pulling him out of the break room, hissing about using their nicknames out in the open. "See you around, shortie," he called as he disappeared.

I rolled my eyes. People needed more original nicknames, but I had received valuable intelligence. My job was primarily to work on my client's image, but it was helpful to assess their work environment. I already knew Theo – Mr Kelly was known for being an unpleasant boss, but now I needed to find out who this witchy person was because I doubted it was Carol.

When I returned, she was grateful for her tea but looked uncomfortable when another "urgent meeting" came up. Mr Kelly was pulling out all the stops. I hoped he had a private bathroom for his bladder's sake, or any potted plants would end up overwatered.

ᒥ°▲▦✿○ᒧ

My stomach rumbled as I typed the finishing line on an article for a fashion magazine. I had a semi-regular slot, and with the speed at which the fashion world moved, it wasn't something I could do more than rough out ahead of time. Glancing at the clock on the wall told me it was after twelve.

"I'm going to grab some lunch. Would you like me to bring something back for you?" I asked Carol.

"I usually order for Theo and me, but I'm not impressed with the quality lately. If you can find somewhere better than Carsons, then let me know. However, I might start bringing sandwiches from home again. I know Theo enjoyed those." She dropped her head back down, returning to her furious typing.

I nodded at her as I gathered my big bag. If I planned to play Mr Kelly's waiting game, I'd do it on a full stomach. My curves were all bought and paid for in cake and not maintained by skipping meals.

Returning down the gloomy corridor, which would look stark anytime of the year, I shook my head at the distinct lack of Christmas cheer, imagining how a few well-placed trees and some garlands would pop against the white walls.

The lift filled as we descended the floors. A mousy girl clutching her bag like a lifeline entered and immediately glued herself to the back wall. A rowdy pair of suits joined, talking loudly about markets, and the girl shrank further against the wall. The doors opened in the lobby, and I waited for the finance bros to get out and turned to her.

"Hi, I'm Zoe. It's my first day here. I'm from the UK, and I wondered if you knew somewhere to get lunch."

"Oh." The girl blinked, as if surprised anyone would speak to her. "Your accent is nice. Er... yeah, a little deli opened a few weeks ago. It's hidden away, but it does the best subs."

"That sounds perfect. I knew you'd have a great recommendation." I grinned at her.

She blushed, glancing away.

"Could I tag along?"

"Er... okay. I'm Brandy. Are you new at Steel Ventures?"

"I'm an image consultant working with Mr Kelly."

She nearly tripped over from gaping at me as we joined the busy street outside.

"What does an image consultant do?" she asked breathlessly.

"It's a blend of a few things, and I've learned to be flexible over the years. Some jobs are purely new wardrobes to maximise a person's shape and appearance, and others are about coaching out a whole new image on social media or in the workplace."

"And you are working with the big boss?"

I will be.

"Yep. How about you?"

"Wow. I'm a junior analyst. I've been at Steel Ventures for six months." She tucked her flyaway hair behind her ear as we moved through the crowds of people. "I couldn't find anything affordable in the city, so I commute from New Jersey."

"Awesome," I said as we reached our destination.

"Not as awesome as your job. I'd love to work for myself one day."

"You can do it. You must have faith in yourself and stick to your guns."

"I need to get better at that. But I couldn't imagine working with CEOs like Mr Kelly all day." She shivered, fiddling with her bag strap.

We joined a long queue that snaked out of a small doorway inside an alleyway. You would have missed it if it weren't for the people milling about outside eating large, overfilled subs.

"The trick is to remain pleasant but firm." My stomach gave another grumble.

My brother might have jokingly named me the CEO Whisperer, but I was hella proud of the business I'd built. My reputation was hard won, along with my repeat client list.

"He's so scary." She gulped.

"I've heard rumours of some people who are worse," I whispered, digging for more information.

She glanced around furtively. "Yeah. Working there is intense."

"What makes it intense?"

"You won't quote me?"

I made a cross sign over my heart sign.

"It's just the culture. Everyone warned me corporate America would chew me up and spit me out, but I thought things might be different."

The line moved swiftly, but with some more digging, I gleaned that it was more than the usual metric-driven corporate culture; it was outright bullying that even HR was involved with.

"You shouldn't have to stand for that, Brandy." I touched her arm.

She gave me a half-shrug. "It'll toughen me up, I guess."

"That's not how it works."

We reached the front of the line.

"Let me get these." I added her sub and drink to my order and chose a sub for Carol and Mr Kelly.

"Say tomato again." Brandy giggled, slurping the milkshake I passed her as we turned away from the serving area.

"Toh-mah-toe."

"I've never had a friend from England."

"Consider me your first."

We perched on stools, watching the view of the busy street at the end of the alleyway as people bustled by. I kept our conversation light after the heavy chat in the queue.

We were fast friends when we parted ways in the lift. I had her number and agreed to take her shopping to help her pick clothes to suit her figure. Her mousy look begged for a Zoe-over. Elle's name for my makeover shopping trips.

Carol gushed and simpered over the subs, insisting I take the cash for hers and Mr Kelly's. She looked more than a little guilty on behalf of her boss, though I doubted he felt even a little bad for his avoidance tactics. Some might have thought it was weird bringing food to a man who was being rude, but my mum always said, "You shouldn't change yourself just because someone is unpleasant." Plus, everyone knew the way to a grumpy man was through his stomach.

Listening to Brandy over lunch and hearing from Ben and Taylor in the breakroom, it was apparent Mr Kelly needed an image upgrade, but it wasn't his only challenge by far. I wrote up everything in my growing report and quizzed Carol. She thought the sun shone out of Mr Kelly's backside and was oblivious to office politics.

Five o'clock rolled around, and the city had darkened outside the window. Christmas lights twinkled from neighbouring offices. I added a bullet point to my physical objectives this time about getting the Christmas decoration ban reversed.

"Mr Kelly said he's very sorry. He needs to rearrange for tomorrow," Carol said, grimacing.

I noticed she didn't give me a time for tomorrow.

"I'll wait. I doubt he leaves the office at five. This is the only way out?" I gestured to the inner door that had remained firmly closed all day.

Carol blinked and sputtered. "Yes. He barely leaves the office at all. I'm sorry..."

She trailed off, unwilling to point out her boss's childish behaviour.

"It's no bother. I am here because Mr Kelly's business partners in the UK requested it. I didn't expect a warm welcome."

At six, I "left" just before Carol did. However, I went to the toilet and looped back to wait in her office once she was gone. Technically, this could get me into trouble, but security probably wouldn't throw me out as I had full employee clearance. My instructions from David's boss, Mr Reid, were clear. "Don't let him weasel out of this." So, I was determined to see Mr Kelly today. If I let him avoid me, it would give him the upper hand.

I drafted a post about New York fashions for my image consulting blog, reassuring myself that I could see the tree at the Rockefeller Center any day.

My stomach rumbled, and I clicked out of my social media planner, realising with a jolt that it was nine o'clock. Carol's office was filled with shadows, illuminated only by the desk lamp beside me. The light flicked off in the inner office, and Mr Kelly's door opened.

A massive man emerged wearing a suit stretched to capacity over his broad frame. A thick brown beard covered his lower face, and equally wild-looking dark hair covered his head. I drank in the sight of him in the dim light, and an unexpected shiver ran through me. His full lips settled in a grim line as his fiery gaze bore down on me, doing nothing for the unwelcome sensations that cascaded through me.

Oh, this wasn't good.

"Who the fuck are you?" his deep, masculine voice rumbled.

3

This was a hostage situation. How did cops last on stakeouts? Thank fuck I had a bathroom in my office. My business partners in the UK had tricked me into this charade, but I didn't need her or the other two business consultants they'd sent me. Just because I wasn't cheerful didn't mean there was something wrong with my image. I expected a lot from the staff here, but if the team didn't want to work that way, then good riddance. Steel Ventures wasn't a place for slackers.

The worst joke was she was supposed to improve my portrayal in the press, but those parasites could go fuck themselves. My public persona was decimated when my poisonous ex used our relationship like a sideshow to gain publicity. But what did I care?

The board cares. A small voice scratched at the back of my mind, and I tugged at the collar of this uncomfortable shirt, squeezing my old, worn-out stress ball.

Forcing my focus back to work, I reached the end of my email list and rechecked the market movements before kicking back to stare out over the city.

Being trapped in my office had some benefits, allowing me to keep clear of employees keen to waste my time. I trusted a handful of people, and the rest were best avoided. They wouldn't stick around when the chips were down, so superficial friendships were pointless.

My phone rang, and Abe's name flashed on the screen.

"Brother?" I answered.

"The sale of the final hotel location has closed. I need you to look at a new proposal for me."

Abe, my younger brother, was easygoing and cheerful, but he was always serious about business. We'd been in partnership for many years, but I'd taken more of a back seat as a silent partner since I took this role. Hospitality ran in his blood, whereas I was far less social and preferred figures.

"Inks barely dry, and you're already after something new," I ribbed him.

He'd sold off some hotel locations in the Canaries that we'd deemed were dead wood. I knew he'd been champing at the bit to get moving on a new project.

"Of course. Onward and upward."

"Onward and upward," I echoed him.

That was our motto, after Dad disowned him for coming out and we became a team.

"Send me over the figures. I'll have them ready by Sunday."

We always caught up on Sundays over a game. More often than not, it dissolved into business discussions, making his long-suffering husband grumble.

"Thanks, bro. Anything going on your end?"

"Nothing much." I glared at the door, reminded of my siege situation.

We chatted for a little longer, before I hung up.

When I closed the files Abe had sent me, it was dark outside, and my back was killing me, so I reluctantly shut my computer down.

Usually, I took a walk around mid-afternoon to loosen my muscles, but today, I was confined to my office jail, pacing and doing stretches. I shook out two Tylenol from the bottle in my top drawer and swallowed them dry. One got stuck, and I coughed it back up, accidentally breaking the capsule, making the bitter taste explode across my tongue. Digging in my drawer for a water bottle, I rinsed the nasty taste away. Standing, I stretched, making my spine crack and pop.

Fuck me, some days, thirty-four felt more like eighty-four.

My stomach rumbled. Carol brought me a delicious sub earlier, but now I was ready for more food. Often, I would remain in my office until late, but I'd waited until long after Carol left to ensure the image consultant menace was gone. Hopefully, she got the message, or I would eventually need to be blunt.

The clock read nine as I flicked the light off and wrenched the door open, noticing a light remained on in the outer office.

My eyes snapped to a woman in the visitor's seat. What the fuck was going on? Did we have no security in this building?

"Who the fuck are you?" I growled.

Papers surrounded her, and a tablet screen illuminated her heart-shaped face framed by short hair. The hairs on the back of my neck rose.

A smile spread across her face, and she bounced off the seat, scattering documents in her eagerness to get to me.

"Mr Kelly. Pleased to meet you, finally. I'm Zoe Barnes. Your new image consultant." Her British accent rolled over me as she held out a small hand.

I glared at her. The image consultant – had she waited all this time? My jaw ached as I clenched it.

"Not a shaker. Okay." She dropped her arm.

"I told you I couldn't see you today." My voice came out gruff as I studied her.

At first glance, she looked far too young, but her curves and manner told me she was older than her height implied. Christ, she was tiny.

"Your secretary told me you had emergency meetings. I guess that they occurred for the same reason I was not on the visitor's list this morning." She blinked at me, still smiling pleasantly.

It took my brain a moment to reconcile her sly dig with the bouncy, cheerful bundle of energy she portrayed. My blood heated.

"You are a busy man, Mr Kelly. I was happy to wait."

"I don't know what you hope to achieve this evening, Ms Burns."

I deliberately messed up her name, aggravated at being cornered at this late hour.

"I wanted to meet you and let you know that you'll have to get up earlier and stay later to shake me off, Mr Kelly." She gave me another sugary smile. "I'll see you tomorrow."

She spun away and bent over to retrieve her papers, treating me to a view of her ass. I gripped my briefcase at her blatant challenge wrapped up in a courteous tone. Worse still was the burst of lust that blasted through me at the sassy words coming out of her pouty mouth. I forced my eyes away from her curves, because I did not need to be attracted to this tiny menace.

"What if I'm busy again?" I taunted, well aware I was being an asshole.

She ignored me as she stuffed items back into her massive bag. I watched, fascinated against my will, as she took off her spiked heels, descended closer to the floor and pulled on some flat shoes. She wrapped a red scarf around her neck and turned to me with fire in her dark eyes.

"If you think you are the first reluctant client I've worked with, you are very wrong." She breezed past me with her rosy perfume, leaving me to gape at the dark doorway, and it took more minutes than I'd ever admit to unstick myself. However, I'd faced much bigger opponents in the past, so if she wanted to play, then game on.

4

Zoe

Oh my gosh, it's incredible here! It was nearly eleven at night, but people milled about near the gigantic Christmas tree outside the Rockefeller Center. I should be bone tired, but a lightness filled me, making me want to squeal. *The freaking Home Alone tree!* I leapt about and snapped a million selfies with the tree in the background.

Satisfied, I sat on a nearby bench to balance my part-eaten hotdog on my lap and sip my warm cider while I uploaded pictures to my social media with the tag "Loving New York at Christmas."

My phone buzzed straight away.

Elle: I'm so jelly. You know I love Christmas.

Me: You mean you love Santa. 🎅

Elle admitted while drunk that she'd love for her boyfriend to dress up as Santa and sneak into her room to tell her she'd been a bad girl. Unfortunately, the numpty she was with dumped her shortly after she shared that kink, so she hadn't gotten to live out her Santaphilia dreams.

Elle: You are supposed to take my secrets to the grave!

Me: And I will.

Elle: Have you had a hotdog yet?

Me: Hotdog 80% consumed.

Elle: I miss you. How was the CEO fittie?

Me: A work in progress! Why are you up so late?

Elle: Up early. I'm meeting a big new client today and couldn't sleep. Your social post popped up, so I knew you were awake. This time difference thing is weird.

It was strange to know it was the next day in the UK. We continued to text during my return on the subway when the signal allowed. The assignment came with a generous living allowance, and David, my brother-in-law, had offered to sort out my accommodation, but I found a cheap apartment in Astoria as I heard it was a safe neighbourhood for single women. Safer possibly, classier definitely not, but the extra money would be handy for sightseeing and shoes, obviously.

Dumping my heavy bag and stretching out my shoulders, I flicked the light on in the apartment. The damp smell lingered underneath the perfume I'd sprayed. The space comprised of a sparse main room with a kitchenette, a small table set, a single bed with a massive TV on the wall, and a boxy bathroom with a shower and toilet.

Nevermind; I was in my dream city and it was nearly Christmas.

I had unpacked yesterday, and my travel Christmas tree, Bob, twinkled on the kitchen counter, making it feel more festive, but I needed to get groceries and more decorations.

My thoughts turned to today and my latest client. No one could say I didn't like a challenge. Theodore Kelly wouldn't be the easiest nut to crack, but the prospect excited me. He was gorgeous, which shouldn't have been a shock as David's boss was also hot. My initial attraction to him wasn't ideal. His jerky behaviour would likely put me off once we started working together, but it didn't matter as I always kept things professional. When previous clients asked me out, I politely declined. A woman's success was so often undermined by suggesting they slept their way to success, and that wouldn't be me.

My eyes were on that award prize and expanding my business. Grumpy Americans wouldn't stand in my way, no matter how huge they were. And good lord, that man was massive.

After removing my make-up and clothes, I turned the shower on, stepping inside with a small shriek as the freezing water wasn't warning up. I grabbed my shampoo, vowing to email the leasing company, but looking on the bright side, my hair would be nice and shiny. Once dry, I got into my reindeer onesie and snuggled under the covers. My American adventure was truly underway.

I placed the cheesecake wheel on the break room counter and smiled as whispering started behind me. Taylor and Ben appeared right on cue. *I love it when a plan comes together.*

"Did you bring a whole cheesecake to work?" Taylor asked.

Today, she wore a pink pantsuit, which actually worked with her hair.

"Not a whole one. I had a slice for breakfast," I said.

Ben chuckled and held his hand up for a high five. "Breakfast of champions."

"It's bribery for information." I dived straight in with the truth.

"I'll consider cake-based bribery." Taylor flicked her long hair and slid the cheesecake wheel over to her side of the counter.

Ben gaped at her.

"What? You told me if she lasted more than a day, we should tell her the truth," she said to him.

They grabbed slices each and settled into the comfy chairs around the edge of the room.

"Hold up." Ben held up his hand, then hastily scribbled a note.

He stuck it to the outside of the door and closed it, locking it too.

Taylor giggled. "What did you write?"

"*Flooded. Do not use.* We need privacy if we're spilling the tea to Little-Miss-Cheesecake." Ben flopped down and scooped up a big bite of the dessert.

"What do you need to know?" Taylor asked, crossing her legs.

"What do people think of Mr Kelly?"

"What part, aside from him being *Theozilla* – Terror of New York?" Ben said around a mouthful of cheesecake. "Well, let's see, worka-holic, high standards, grumpy, unapproachable, and either a total douche or…" He hesitated. "Clueless."

"Ben!" Taylor whisper-shouted, tugging on his sleeve. "Go easy, or you'll get fired."

"If I go, I go. It's time to speak my truth." He smoothed his hand down yet another brightly coloured tie.

I stifled a snigger, and Taylor rolled her eyes at him.

"Why clueless?" I asked.

"The real 411 around here—"

"No one says that," Taylor interjected.

"It's a retro phrase. I'm bringing it back." Ben pouted.

These two were like a comedy double act.

"This place can't keep staff because of the *Wicked Witch of the West*. But the real question is." He leaned forward conspiratorially. "Is she his lap bitch, or is he unaware of her campaign of terror? Hence clueless."

"Who is she?"

"Vanessa," he hissed her name quietly and glanced around. "Plus, she has an evil bitch team. On the surface, they all act nice but rule like queen bees. They have bullied plenty of people out."

"Why hasn't anyone told him?"

"Approach Theozilla and tell him his managing director, who is also a board member's niece, is a raging bitch? Er, no," Taylor said, her manicured eyebrows disappearing into her curls.

"What about HR?"

"The HR manager is one of her minions."

Oh dear. It would make sense for a bully with that much reach to be high up and connected.

We chatted longer, and they gave examples of the harassment ex-colleagues endured until Ben declared they had to get to work.

I returned to Carol's office with a slice of cheesecake for her and Mr Kelly.

"Thank you, dear. I'll take it home and share it with my husband. You know what they say, cholesterol shared is cholesterol halved."

I wasn't sure anyone said that, but I smiled at her.

Her bright expression faltered. "Mr Kelly is quite busy again today. I'm unsure if he'll have much time to see you."

"It's fine, Carol. I have plenty of work to do. Although I have some more questions for you."

"Shoot."

"What keeps you working here?"

"Theo – Mr Kelly might seem stern, but he's got a heart of gold. He loves his brother and sister and would do anything for them. How a man treats his family means a lot in my book. He's big on charity, but he doesn't like people to know. That evil woman ruined him, dragging him through the press. He didn't deserve that."

"The evil woman being his ex-fiancée, Savannah Cristo?"

Carol pursed her lips and nodded curtly.

Theo came from a famous sporting family. It was well known that he had a high-profile relationship with an actress that turned into a celebrity sideshow. Most of his altercations with the press and social media spats were about that, despite them breaking up a few years ago.

"Thank you, that's helpful," I said.

"He's a good boy, really. I hope you can help him." She stared briefly at the door before returning to her work.

She certainly painted a different picture of Theo than his other employees. Although, I suspected he possessed some redeeming features to retain Carol.

For the rest of the day, I visited various departments and scoped out Vanessa's queen bee team. I'd yet to meet the woman, but her reputation certainly preceded her. The lower floors were filled with fearful, unfocused employees, and the blank walls and lack of Christmas cheer didn't help. This issue was clearly affecting Mr Kelly's image negatively, and I needed to find out if he knew about it.

Carol left around five, and I repeated my trick with the bathroom, but I didn't have to wait as long tonight. At eight, his door opened, and he groaned before emerging.

"Why are you still here?" A muscle ticked in his cheek above his beard.

He was five years older than me, with deep creases in his forehead, but even that worked for him. His hair remained thick and dark brown, although it needed a trim.

"Waiting for a gap in your schedule. And I got one an hour earlier today. That's a win in my book."

"Your bar must be very low," he grumbled, fine lines appearing around his eyes.

"I like to celebrate incremental improvements." I gave him a sunny smile that made his frown more profound.

His gaze flicked over my outfit, and heat sizzled through me, reminding me we were alone. I shook that thought away, focusing on my task and ignoring the unwanted burst of attraction.

"I know a tailor here in New York. He's an old friend. He needs a bit of notice, but we can visit him to get to work on your wardrobe," I said.

Theo drew himself up to his considerable height. "I don't need to go shopping and certainly don't have time."

I eyed the stain on his shirt, likely from the Tex-Mex sub I bought him for lunch. His entire outfit didn't fit him well. The suit was expensive, but it wasn't made for him. His shape and height needed proper tailoring, not just adjusting something off the rack. As CEO of the company, his image mattered. His scruffy beard and overgrown locks didn't help, even if they looked perfect for running my fingers through.

Where had that thought come from?

"Clothes are part of my service," I said.

"I don't need that particular service," he drawled, making it sound dirty.

"We'll see." I turned and packed up my things.

"How are you getting home?" he bit out.

"The subway."

His face scrunched. "It's too late for a woman to travel on the subway. You'll take a cab."

Ignoring him and taking my time, I replaced my shoe babies, returning them to the soft cases David bought for me. We shared a special love for footwear. I wiggled my toes in relief before finally turning around.

"The subway is fine. Public transport is better for the environment."

"You'll ride with me then."

"No, thank you. I don't require that *particular service*."

Walking from the office, I swore I heard a muttered "Touché" before the door closed.

Maybe he did have a sense of humour, after all?

5

Z

On Wednesday morning, the break room was empty. I grabbed my step and unclipped it, reaching for the chamomile tea. I'd begun to enjoy a cup daily and bought a packet to replace Carol's box that was running low. A tickle chased up the back of my neck, alerting me that I was no longer alone, and my peripheral vision caught on a slim, feminine figure.

"Would you like a cup?" I turned to face the woman who leaned against the table with her arms crossed.

The houndstooth skirt paired with a bright yellow jacket and silk shirt made for an impressive combination; her dark hair was swept up into a sleek roll, and her heels were from the latest line at Dior.

Her lip curled minutely. "I don't drink tea."

"Okay. I'm Zoe, you are?"

Although I knew who she was. After conversing with Ben and Taylor, I studied her picture on the website.

"I heard you are here to whip our industrious leader into shape." Her smile didn't reach her eyes.

"I'm an image consultant."

"Fascinating what some people do for work."

"It is fascinating," I agreed, pretending not to hear her disdain.

"How does one end up doing such a thing?"

"University and on-the-job experience." I shrugged, not inclined to share my qualifications with her.

"And a dash of nepotism. I dare say."

I blinked at her hinting at knowing my connection to the founders via my brother-in-law. How on earth did she even know that?

"I think knowing people is always an advantage in business," I replied with a smile.

"Indeed, I hope that you are successful. Theo is such a valuable asset to the company."

At that, she smirked and left without another word, her heels clicking back along the corridor.

So that was the infamous Vanessa. She hadn't sounded like she thought Theo was much of an asset.

I returned to Carol's office to mull that over with my calming tea.

The office door clicked open at seven-thirty, and I smothered a grin. The grumpy behemoth that was Theo Kelly emerged, and his hair and jacket were unkempt. I was beginning to think dishevelled was his signature look. My fingers ached to straighten him up.

He froze in the doorway. "What are you still doing here?"

I stretched my back, not missing Theo's slow perusal of me, which caused prickles to wash over my skin. It was a problem every time I saw him, despite his behaviour. Perhaps having a grumpy dad and brother helped attitudes like Theo's bounce off me, leaving only my libido to have an opinion.

I grabbed the Liquorice Allsorts packet from my bag and popped one in my mouth. The sweetness burst across my tongue. Theo stood clutching a folder and staring at me.

"Why are you eating candy in the office?"

"They're super yummy."

"Ridiculous," he replied gruffly but watched me eat another.

The grumpy man could do with something sweet to cheer him up.

"They are a mix of liquorice and soft candy. They're the king of sweets." I offered the packet to him.

Theo's brow furrows deepened. "I doubt that somehow."

His reluctance forced me to hold out a black and white striped Allsort. The look on his face darkened, and for a few moments, we came to a stand-off. Grumbling under his breath about this being ridiculous, he snatched the sweet and shoved it into his mouth.

"Hardly king of sweets. More like the court jester," he scoffed.

"You liked it, though."

"I didn't spit it out."

"Would you like another?" I waved the bag tauntingly.

He reached his big paw out, and I snatched the packet back.

"I propose an exchange."

"You're bribing me with candy?"

His frowny face was back. Not that it ever left. Nor did it detract from his hotness.

"Let me do your colours," I hedged.

"What the fuck is that?"

"It helps with your styling."

"I told you I don't need a stylist."

I looked down at his outfit, noting each crease and even a snag in the shirt that had pulled a small hole. Unfortunately, the assessment backfired as I ended up staring at his quads, which stretched the suit's material to capacity. The sight dialled up the previous heat inside me, but I shook off the unwanted attraction.

Don't ogle the client.

"You finished?" The corner of Theo's mouth tipped up.

A flush rushed through my body and up to my cheeks.

"I haven't even got started," I shot back.

"Keep your weird British candy and your style advice." His eyes found my candy cane brooch. "And your Christmasness."

"Is that a term?"

"Newly coined," he deadpanned.

I snorted. The grump had all the jokes.

"Okay." I held up my hands in mock surrender. "I can tell candy-based negotiations are a hard no."

He bared his teeth. "You'll find me very difficult to negotiate with."

The growl in his tone sent a thrill through me.

"We'll see," I replied nonchalantly.

Turning away from his enticing aftershave, I gathered up my things. I'd already told him he'd need to work harder to shake me off. *Mama didn't raise a quitter.* Plus, if anyone needed my skill set, it was this man.

"Don't underestimate me or my Christmasness." I grinned at him.

Theo folded his arms. "Sure."

I gave him a cheeky salute as I pulled the bag onto my shoulder.

"Are you going straight home?"

"What, after being released this early? Most definitely not. Lots to see and do." I smirked, and Theo opened his mouth and closed it again, scowling.

He had different levels of scowl to go with his frowns, and we were only in the mid-range.

"Goodnight, Mr Kelly."

"Menace," he grumbled under his breath.

⁘ ⌢⌢⌢⌢⌢ ⁘

I tore my eyes away from Theo's door for the millionth time today, refocusing on the notes I'd made so far on Steel Ventures, compiling them into a summary. The new sofa that appeared in Carol's office this morning was so comfy that I'd taken off my shoes and curled my legs beneath me.

A noise inside his office forced my eyes back towards it, but I glanced at my watch. It was only seven pm Thursday evening. Was the grumpy bear emerging from hibernation early?

The door flew open, and he looked even more ragged than usual, his tie askew and deep rivets in his hair where he'd been no doubt tunnelling his fingers.

"Don't you have things you want to do in the city?" he snapped, folding his arms across his chest.

The flex of his biceps underneath his rolled-up shirtsleeves caught my eye. Why did he have to be so hot?

"I've ticked seven things off my New York bucket list." I jumped off the squashy couch.

"How long is your list?"

"Twenty-eight items. Tonight, I'm going skating in Central Park."

"Can you skate?" he scoffed.

"I can skate great. Low centre of gravity." I slipped my flat shoes back on and gathered my things.

His grumpy gaze tracked my movements just as it had the other four nights this week. Each day, I looked forward to reminding him he couldn't ignore me out of his city, but it had become more than just a battle of wills. Despite barely spending time with him, my body was very aware of his presence. I'd had several very inappropriate daydreams about him ending our evening chats by grabbing me and silencing me with his full lips. It was becoming a serious problem.

Get a grip, Zoe!

"You're going alone?" He pulled what I decided was his papa bear face, which was kinda endearing.

"Yep."

"It's not safe in the city for such a tiny woman."

"This *tiny* woman can look after herself," I bit back with a smile.

He scoffed again, but I ignored him because he didn't get to avoid me, then boss me around. I slung my bag over my shoulder, staggering slightly.

"Jesus Christ, what's in there?"

"Just essentials."

"Essentials?" Theo glared at my bag. "It's almost the size of you."

"Not everyone can be a giant among men, Mr Kelly."

"Theo," he snapped.

I grinned big. "There you go. We *are* friends. Have a great night, Theo."

He looked like he wanted to say more but watched me go without a word. Why did bantering with him energise me after a long day? I wondered how long he thought he could dismiss me.

At the outdoor ice rink, the skating was cold but so fun. The bite in the air as it rushed by me added to the magic of ticking this off my list. Despite my self-professed low centre of gravity, I had a wet bum from falling over. Once off the ice, I sipped my hot chocolate, watching everyone skate by. The seasonal spirit was high, and I loved it. It was everything I dreamed of doing at Christmas, aside from a pang that went through me, watching the couples skate holding hands. It would be nice to have that someday, but experience told me having a successful career wasn't conducive to having the same in a relationship.

In the meantime, I had a job to do. The *CEO Whisperer* wouldn't put up with being made to sit in Carol's office for another week. I had prepared my case with evidence of what was going on at the company, and tomorrow, Theo Kelly would see just how good my negotiating skills were.

6

*T*HEO

I clicked out of the social media site and crossed my arms. *Who goes ice skating on their own?* Why did I care? And more importantly, why was I stalking my image consultant's social media profile? She was a distraction.

The video conference reminder flashed on my screen, and I clicked it to open my morning meeting. My two British business partners appeared on the screen in what appeared to be Liam Reid's home office.

"Theo, my man. How is it going with your new image consultant?" Oscar Russell asked in his posh "Prince Harry" accent.

My chest tightened, and I shifted in my chair.

"Fine."

"I'm looking forward to the progress report," Liam said, his dark eyes glaring across the video feed.

"I'm sure the financial report is more interesting," I countered, shifting in my seat.

"I can read a financial report in my sleep. A report on your grumpy arse is what I am looking forward to."

"Pot calling the kettle black," Oscar coughed under his breath, and Liam punched his arm.

These two jokers were the founders of the most successful investment firm in the UK, yet they bickered like an old married couple. Liam was brooding and snappy, and Oscar – Sir Oscar – because he'd recently inherited the title of baronet, was the pleasant, friendly one.

Years ago, I became fascinated by their meteoric ascent when one of my international business study lecturers quoted their early success. They were only five years older than me, but they'd made waves in the UK right from the get-go. Of course, I'd never tell them I greedily watched their careers like a fanboy. But fate placed us on a path together, eventually leading us to strike up an unlikely friendship that spanned the Atlantic and, ultimately, resulted in me heading up the flagship American branch of Steel Ventures.

My respect for Liam and Oscar and the fact I always honoured a wager left me in my current predicament. I bet against them on an investment outcome, which wasn't a good call in hindsight, but it was supposed to be a sure thing. Losing to them gained me the little menace staking out my outer office.

"What's she like?" Oscar asked after he finished shoving Liam.

"She sure is something," I muttered.

My bid to avoid her had confined me to my office for five days. Her tenacity knew no bounds.

"I heard she's small but mighty. Trevor at Maximum Consulting credits her for turning his entire image and life around after his messy divorce. We thought the company might go to the wall."

"Yeah, we could have got it for a song," Liam groused.

Something flickered inside my chest at the thought of her working with this dude, Trevor. Had she waited outside his office in those fitted dresses?

Get a grip.

Our meeting finally turned to actual business, and we signed off on the hour mark with more than a little light-hearted ribbing.

I rubbed my temples. I'd run out of time. If they had Zoe on weekly reports, I'd have to meet with her this afternoon and set things straight. She had nothing to offer me. I would come to an arrangement with her about check-ins and let her enjoy her time in

New York. Ignoring the knot in my stomach, I typed an instant message to Carol.

Tell the image consultant I have a slot for her at two. And could you bring me that pastrami on rye again?

Carol was a sweet lady until you crossed her, then she'd stab you in the hand with a pen while still smiling. She was unerringly efficient and a little too doting. At first, she made me homemade sandwiches with enough butter to put me in an early grave. We eventually agreed to order lunch, but this week, she'd bought the most delicious subs I'd ever tasted.

Carol knocked on the door and poked her head around it.

"Zoe's getting the subs right now. She found a new deli nearby. I'll tell her you will see her at two."

"Why's she getting the lunch?"

"She's been bringing us all lunch since Monday."

The woman I'd been avoiding and goading each evening had brought me lunch every day? Why the hell had she done that? The weight in my stomach intensified. I shrugged the feeling off because she was probably poisoning me in revenge. Carol's expression as she closed the door told me that maybe I deserved it.

Fuck.

Today's sub had chicken with mustard mayo filling, and it was almost as good as the pastrami, but it didn't seem to fit in my stomach next to the stone lodged there. The clock told me I had one more minute before Carol let her in.

"Ms Barnes for you," she said, opening the door.

Zoe walked in with her gigantic bag hoisted onto her shoulders. She wore a dark green skirt which reached up to her ample tits that her fitted shirt barely contained. I tore my eyes away. Her scent still reached me and today, it had a distinct cinnamon hint, almost like gingerbread.

The door closed, and I heard her take a seat. Unwillingly, I focused back on her. My lip curled, noticing the faint holly leaf pattern on her shirt. She was a fucking Christmas elf sent to torture me.

"As you can see, I'm a busy man. I'll be frank with you. The truth is I lost a bet with my business partners, and they thought it would be funny to send you here. I don't need an image consultant and don't wish to waste either of our time. Instead, I propose you create adequate progress reports for my business partners. In exchange, you can be free to sightsee."

Her expression hardened, and the silence stretched between us. Sweat prickled the back of my neck as we stared at each other.

"I have an hour. No..." She paused and checked her watch. "Fifty-three minutes of your time?"

I nodded, unsure where she was going. I watched as she pulled a binder filled with paper from her monstrous bag and flicked it open to the first page. The rustle of documents was the only noise.

"I'm here because of a bet," she repeated, and I winced at how it sounded. "So, I'm not here to help you improve your image?" She laid out newspaper articles and screenshots from social media. "Or to tackle this thirty-eight percent staff turnover that the board is trying to attribute directly to you?"

My blood pressure rose and a pulse thumped in my temple.

"How can it solely be my fault?"

"It's rarely one person's fault. However, your closest competitors have much lower turnover rates; some even have it below twenty."

"Do they have our profits?" I snapped.

"They don't need your profits if your overheads continue to rise. Do you know replacing an employee costs around fifty percent of a person's annual salary and up to double for more senior positions? And it often takes at least two years to become most efficient at their job. Your employees frequently last less than twelve months. This is hurting your bottom line."

Did she think I was a naïve little boy? I knew these things. Blood rushed in my ears.

"I thought you were an image consultant?" I glared at her.

"My role is many things; unfortunately, I haven't had access to my client – unless you count late-night snarky remarks." She flashed amused eyes at me, and I felt the urge to spank her ass.

Get a grip!

"I have been investigating the only place that I can. On the ground with your employees."

"You've no right to interview my staff," I said, torn between being irritated and impressed.

"I didn't interview them. Friendly chats over coffee aren't the same thing. Leaders of companies would do well to listen to the employees. But if you prefer that I work purely on your image, then you'll have to stop hiding in your office."

I glared at her, and she smiled widely.

"If that's your company assessment, what's your summary of me?" I asked, almost against my will.

"Your suits don't fit you, and you often have food stains from eating at your desk and staying too late. You are overdue for a haircut and a beard trim. Most of all, you would do well to keep your mouth shut rather than give the press unsolicited sound bites, especially regarding your ex-fiancée, Savannah Cristo."

I scoffed.

"Tell me about her." She blinked calmly at me, and my blood pressure rose to dangerous levels.

Grinding my jaw, I debated what to tell her as the silence stretched.

"When we met, she was an aspiring actress. Unfortunately, she never aspired to much, some small-time reality television gigs and flashing her tits on social media. She is like a bad smell I can't get rid of."

"If she is in your past, why are you still arguing with the press about her?"

"Because she's constantly doing things to provoke me."

"Unfortunately, when you throw mud, you also get covered."

"You expect me to keep quiet in the face of her fucking lies?" I squeezed the chair arms.

Savannah was like a noose around my neck, and it made my skin crawl that I ever got involved with her in the first place.

"There are better ways to get even than the front of a tabloid."

"That's another reason we can't work together," I scoffed.

"Nope. That's just a difference of opinion. It doesn't matter in the long run."

"Why doesn't it matter?"

"Because my clients always end up listening to me," she said brightly.

I balled my fist. She was an infuriating bundle of sunny confidence.

"None of this is new information," I ground out.

Delivered in a deceptively cheerful manner by a woman I'd barely given the time of day to was pretty galling, but none of the facts were new to me.

She pulled out a single sheet of paper covered in garish-coloured highlighters and swirly diagrams. Moving the other documents, she looked up at me.

"I won't lie about being here. If you want to fire me, that's fine. But I won't be filing false reports. I'm not that kind of person. If you refuse to work with me, I will apply to cancel our agreement. I do not wish to be paid for work I'm not doing." She levelled me with those fiery eyes.

So few people looked me in the eye at work, and a begrudging respect rose inside me.

"You don't have to listen to anything I suggest, but you should pay attention to your staff. They are fearful and unhappy. The culture here isn't good." She paused as if gathering herself. "I'm not looking to get into slanderous claims, but many people allege Vanessa, your Managing Director, and several other high-level employees are using bullying tactics. It's far more than office gossip and hearsay, although you'll need to look into it yourself. Modifying your image will only go so far in the face of this. Especially if you condone it." Her eyes bored into mine.

What? Vanessa? My MD?

"What the fuck?"

Was that true? Hang on, did Zoe think I knew?

Zoe dropped her eyes and cleared her messy papers off my glass desk. My skin tingled with discomfort. She stood up, turned around in that infernal Christmas blouse and walked away. The woman was the queen of having the last word, which drove me nuts. But she wasn't getting away with it after dropping that bomb.

"You can't drop an accusation like that and then run off." I leapt up from my seat, my back protesting the sudden movement.

I was across the office in a flash, my hand closing on the door handle before she could reach it. She blinked up at me, so close that the heat from her seared me through my shirt. I noticed her brown irises were, in fact, pixelated and scattered with green. My body reacted to her as my agitation gave way to a much baser set of emotions.

"I said you can't walk away after dropping that bomb. What kind of evidence do you have?" My voice came out gravelly as I fought with my body's reaction.

She sidestepped me, and, letting go of the door, I moved with her. I didn't miss the hitch in her breathing as she craned her head back to look up at me.

Jesus fucking Christ, she was so tiny.

"Nothing that would hold up in a court. I'd be happy to discuss what I found, but I won't waste any more time if you do not want me here." The fire in her eyes reminded me she might be half my size, but she was feisty.

"I've got time now," I gritted out.

I burned with the desire to seize her and slam her against the wall and fuck the sassy look off her face. But I wasn't a caveman and didn't need a lawsuit.

"Unfortunately, I haven't got the time. I have a date."

A date!

"Who with?" I exploded.

"None of your business."

"The workday isn't finished."

"I am freelance, contracted for up to fifty-six hours per week. I passed that total two hours ago."

"It's only Friday afternoon," I snapped.

"And someone kept me late each day." She tilted her chin up even further.

"You are infuriating," I said, curling my fingers into a fist.

"And you are grumpy and avoidant. We all have our quirks." She winked at me.

My blood pressure spiked again. This woman was trying to kill me!

"Go out with me instead. I need to know all about these so-called reports," I demanded.

"No can do," she said in a singsong voice.

I stalked forward, backing her up against the wall again, despite knowing I shouldn't. Her pupils dilated as she looked up at me.

"You haven't even been here a week. How can you have a date already?"

Was she going out with one of my employees? Did someone need to be fired?

Her smile faltered briefly. "I guess there's one American that has seen my worth."

With that, she slipped under my arm, darting for the door and disappearing.

I leaned forward, resting my forehead on the wall, my pulse still thundering in my ears, and reminded myself that who she dated was none of my business.

The office grew dark around me. I'd stewed all afternoon, her words tumbling through my mind. More than once, I almost pressed the buzzer to tell Carol to summon Vanessa. But I needed more answers, and that infuriating elf had them.

Zoe had me by the balls. *Damn it.*

I'd have to track her down because I couldn't wait all weekend. I clicked on the file I needed, ignoring the voice inside my mind whispering about the invasion of privacy and abuse of power. But I needed answers damn it. The idea of confronting her outside of work sent a buzz through me, and I tried hard to ignore how my heart raced at the thought.

The woman was driving me insane.

7

*L*ights from the TV screen danced over my new Christmas garlands, and the gooey, cheesy Italian dish perfectly complemented a cold beer and a festive movie. The only thing missing was Bowser lounging on my bed and finishing my crusts. Jeez, I missed that big furball.

Did I feel bad about misleading Theo into thinking I had a date with a guy when I meant a yummy pizza? *Maybe.*

He hadn't reacted well to my assessment of the culture at his office, and it was evident he had no clue what was happening, but that information needed to be shared, especially if he planned to kick me out. Plus it served as my hook. In my experience, you had to create a sense of FOMO for reluctant clients and make them believe you had something they wanted. *Let him stew over the weekend.*

Although I almost bit off more than I could chew. Up close, looming his big body over me, my underwear was toast. Why did he have to smell so delicious? Even with his messy beard and stained tie.

Elle: I signed us up to a new dating app.

I groaned and wiped my greasy fingers off on a napkin. What was Elle up to now?

Me: Shouldn't you be asleep?

Elle: Can't sleep. I am searching for my soulmate.

Me: You'd be better off sleeping.

Elle: This new app has a 95% matching success.

Me: Why did you have to sign me up?

Elle: Because you need a soulmate too. Then we can double date.

I rolled my eyes. Elle constantly ramped up her dating in the run-up to Christmas if she was single. I was more of a girl who lamented her status in the New Year, because I didn't need a man to enjoy the festive season.

Me: I've not got time for a soulmate.

Elle: You'd make time if you found him.

I sighed. It was true, but Elle's half-baked plans never boded well.

While I loved work, the slow march of my thirties was exerting pressure to find someone special in recent years, but I didn't think having a successful career was compatible with having a relationship. Work consumed my life, and my career put off many of the men I dated. Plus, how the hell was I supposed to fit in having babies around styling clients?

Me: I'll bite. What's the app?

She sent me a link, and I downloaded the app. It asked me to sign in, and I added my email and the password that I knew Elle would have used. This time, my groan was audible.

> Me: Why on earth did you use that photo?

> Elle: You look hot. Guys dig that classic pin-up style.

She'd used a picture from a fifties-themed ball we went to last year. I was wearing a red polka-dot dress and had big hair.

> Me: My boobs are hanging out.

> Elle: Exactly, it's totally hot.

> Me: It'll attract the pervs.

I clicked through, and sure enough, five dick pics were in the private message already. I deleted them all.

> Elle: I'll set up double dates for when you get back. If we need to ditch them, we'll be together.

There would be no fighting her. I chucked the final crust back into the box.

> Me: Okay. Choose wisely.

> Elle: I'll start sorting through them first thing tomorrow. I'm going to bed now.

I sent her a goodnight message and flopped back on my bed. It was time I started dating again. An image of Theo's brooding face swam into my head, but I firmly batted it away. I did not sleep with clients, no matter how attractive I found them.

Theo beckoned me over to his desk.

"Now," he growled.

Light twinkled in the city behind him as he leaned back in his chair, sliding me in front of him. His big hands trailed up the sides of my skirt, and my breath hitched. Desire curled through me, and I waited for him to say something, but he lifted me to the edge of the desk. The heat of him through his suit seared my inner thighs as he pressed me backwards onto the desk. The look on his face sent a shiver through me. The darkness of the room pressed on me as his finger slipped beneath the edge of my thong. My skin tingled as he pushed it down my thighs. Bristles from his beard scraped across my oversensitive skin, and I gasped as his lips found my centre—pressure built as he devoured me, masculine grunts falling from his lips.

The orgasm woke me with a jolt. My heart pounded in my chest, and I blinked around in the dimly lit room, arousal still simmering through my body. *Oh, my gosh!* These dreams were getting out of hand. Heat infused my cheeks. Holy heck. Theo wasn't grumpy in the dream. No, he was growly and dominant in a very different way.

Aaand it's time for a cold shower.

A loud banging startled me, and I screamed.

8

"Zoe?" Theo's rumbly voice cut through the flimsy door. *Motherfudger, did I shout his name in my sex-addled unconscious state and conjure him up?*

My heart pounded as I fought with the tangled sheet to release me.

"Shizzle-sticks!" I leapt off the bed, sending the pizza box and crust flying.

I must have fallen asleep last night without clearing up. Crumbs decorated my onesie, and my hair was probably stuck up in a million directions. I scrambled about, snatching up pizza debris. Powerful thumping rattled the door.

"Wait a minute," I said, shoving the box into the small bin, but it got jammed, making the crust fall everywhere. "Motherfudger."

Slowing my breathing, I smoothed my hair down. What the hell was Theo doing here?

I unlocked the door and yanked it open. Theo stood there in another suit; his eyes looked bluer than usual, and his hair looked like he'd been running his hands through it.

"Morning, Mr Kelly. To what do I owe the pleasure?" I said, attempting to project professionalism in my reindeer onesie.

Then I blushed because it sounded dirtier than I intended. *Stop thinking about sex!*

"Is that the only lock? The security in this building is a joke," he grumbled.

"How exactly did you know where my building was?"

He glared at me, knowing he didn't have a defence for that. He must be desperate to learn more about what I said yesterday to have looked up my information.

"Did Christmas throw up on you?" His eyes ran down me.

I burst into laughter. Gosh, he was extra frowny this morning.

"Maybe. Do you want to come in?" I left the door open and headed to put on a pot of coffee. The clock in the kitchen said eight as I mentally pulled myself together.

"How do you take your coffee?" I called as I heard him close the door.

"Black."

I smiled at the machine as I turned it on.

"Did you bring all these Christmas decorations from the UK?"

Theo turned, slowly taking in my shiny streamers and tiny Christmas tree. He looked oversized in the small apartment, but his look of contempt helped me settle back into our normal roles.

"Bob came with me. The rest I bought here."

"Bob?"

"The Christmas tree. Normally, I bring him to my workplace at Christmas, but a certain *evil overlord* forbids Christmas decorations, so he's had to stay home alone. Fitting for New York."

"Evil overlord." Theo's mouth twitched as if he might smile.

I took it as a win.

"Now, said overlord is here at the crack of dawn in my apartment."

"No one speaks to me like that." He stalked closer.

I shrugged and turned my attention back to the coffeemaker, reminding myself I was playing with fire. Flirting with your client went against my code of conduct.

Mental note, I need to write a code of conduct.

"I don't work for you. I work for your business partners. And you wish to end that arrangement. So does it matter?" I shrugged. "You've looked up where I live and invited yourself over. I'm going out on a limb and assuming you want to talk to me about what I told you yesterday."

His frown was something to behold as I passed him the coffee. I sat down at the small table. He glared at the cup, then at the tiny seat opposite me and gingerly settled into it with a creak.

"This neighbourhood isn't safe enough."

"I researched it, and it's perfectly safe. David signed off on it."

"It's miles from the financial district. Who is David?"

"David, you know him. Mr Reid's personal assistant and my brother-in-law."

"Liam's PA is your brother-in-law?"

"Yes. He suggested me to Mr Reid and Sir Oscar."

Theo grumbled and sipped his coffee. I added some gingerbread cookie syrup to mine, which I'd found at the corner store.

"How can you stand that sweet shit in your coffee?"

"How can you stand it all bitter and black?" I arched a brow at him.

He fell silent, glaring across at Bob as if the tree had personally offended him.

"What evidence do you have on Vanessa, and how did you acquire it?" he asked, setting down his mug.

"The thing about being short is that people often overlook you. Sometimes, they can't even see you in an office cubicle or assume you are young, dumb, and insignificant."

"I don't think that."

I smiled at him. "Thank you. I expected a lot of size jokes from you. Although you've not spoken to me much, maybe I've avoided them."

"I call you elf in my head if that helps." His voice was still grumpy but with a hint of amusement.

My grin widened, and something warm flicked in my chest. "You gave me a nickname. It's sizeist yet Christmas-themed. I'll allow it."

"How was your date?" Theo frowned.

"My date?" My eyes flicked to the pizza crusts on the floor around the bin. "It was great."

Theo grunted, squeezing his cup.

"Work with me for a week, and I'll tell you everything I know," I said, anticipation running up my spine.

His head snapped up. "You're blackmailing me now?"

"No, I'm negotiating." I smiled, and he shifted in the chair, making it creak again.

"Then let me take you on a better date next Friday," he countered, a steely look in his eyes.

My mouth hinged open. "I don't date my clients."

"I don't like being blackmailed." He grinned savagely, and suddenly, it felt too hot in here.

"Why bother taking the *elf* out?" I asked, aiming for nonchalance.

"Because I like to win. I'll blow last night's date out of the water."

"So it's a competition date. Like, I rate whether you did better than my last date?"

"Sure."

"Providing it's not a romantic date." I narrowed my eyes at him.

"Fine," he huffed.

"Okay. But I must tell you I only date well-dressed men." I pressed my tongue into my cheek, knowing I was pushing my luck.

Theo scowled. "You're unbelievable." His jaw worked. "Let me guess, you have a solution for my fashion-challenged case."

"Of course, let me sort something." I stood up and grabbed my phone, ignoring Theo's impatient noises.

I dialled my friend's number, hoping he was free. A short conversation later, we were all set for today, and excitement thrummed through me.

"Who the fuck is Juan?" Theo said, looking thunderous when I returned to the table.

"You'll see," I said as I pulled my Filofax out of my bag and sat back down.

My onesie wasn't precisely business attire, but that was Theo's problem, not mine. He came here uninvited.

"None of the allegations I gathered would hold up in a court unless we could get individual employees to make a statement, which I doubt they'll do." I shuffled my notes as I set them out on the table. "It seems Vanessa has a team, including your head of HR, and I suspect someone influential in PR. My impression is that their mission is to make the workplace miserable. I'm unsure why, but it seems more than petty power plays. Worst-case scenario, it's an attempt to get you removed."

I'd spent time considering their possible motivations, and from what David told me, Theo had been sent two business consultants by the board before his boss albeit tricked Theo into allowing me to come over here.

"This all sounds like hearsay."

"That's why you'll want to investigate it. Like you said, this isn't technically my job. You have the potential to be a well-liked boss. Many employees are big fans of the NFL team your grandfather and uncle played for. More than once, I've heard people mentioning the connection. That kind of support can't be manufactured in the work-place. Sure, you undermine it with your draconian policies on Christmas decorations, for example, but you could easily gain popu-larity if you chose it."

He leaned back, making the chair protest as he contemplated my words.

"I don't use my sports connection. I lead the company based on my business prowess. It's not a beauty pageant or a popularity contest."

"How much longer will you lead the company, though?"

Theo's eyes widened, and I doubled down.

"Mr Kelly…"

"Theo," he gritted out.

"Theo, there is a rampant bullying culture at Steel Ventures New York, and many employees assume you either support it or ignore it. Neither of these assumptions is good for your image. The negative work environment affects the morale and productivity of your employees. Do what you like with my information, but I'm here to help you. I'm in your corner." I touched his hand without thinking, and sparks tingled under my fingertips.

He glanced down at my hand as if it were an alien ship.

Reluctantly, I pulled away. "Now, you have your half of the bargain to uphold. I will shower and change, and then we have a date with Juan."

He blinked at me. "A date with Juan?"

"Yep." I skipped off, grabbed some clothes, and headed into my tiny bathroom before he could quiz me.

Twenty minutes later, I was dressed and ready to go after an express shower and makeup application. Theo remained where I left him, scowling at his phone.

"I can't be long. I have work to do," he said.

"You can work afterwards."

"There's a car outside." He stood towering over the small space.

I grabbed my purse and led Theo out of my apartment as he grumbled about poor security.

Theo's driver easily cut through Saturday morning traffic, and we pulled up in front of the men's clothing shop. Theo muttered under his breath as we got out.

Juan came out dressed in a houndstooth check suit jacket, a khaki cravat, and deep purple trousers, which complimented his dark skin. Clearly, houndstooth was making a more significant comeback on the New York scene than I realised. I made a mental note to add that to my blog.

"Sweetie. It's been too long." He enveloped me in a hug.

"Thank you for fitting us in."

"Anything for you." He air kissed my cheeks.

He turned to Theo, who was scowling and looming over us. Juan was five-nine, but he looked tiny in comparison.

"What a canvas." Juan rubbed his hands together as he raked his professional gaze over Theo and motioned us towards the shop.

"What are we doing here?" Theo asked, falling into step with me, his large palm between my shoulder blades.

The warmth of his palm did funny things to my body.

"Makeover time."

"Have you done his colours?" Juan asked as he led us through the bright white shop and around dummies wearing designer suits.

"He's been reluctant. But I can do them while you measure him."

Juan hummed and went to collect his supplies.

"How do you know this guy?" Theo asked.

"I know Juan from years back. My best friend Elle works for a fashion house, and they worked together when he came to London for a while. I lived with Elle while I did my course at the London Image Institute. We all used to hang out a lot. He came back here to open his shop. His fittings have a six-month waiting list. But he agreed to keep a last-minute slot for you."

"I already have suits."

"Not like Juan's. He is a master. He sources fabrics from around the world sustainably and only employs the best tailors. Then he creates a style wardrobe, not just a selection of bespoke suits."

Theo rolled his eyes, but Juan reappeared and ushered us into his fitting area. He gave Theo a long spiel about his brand and mission statement. Theo just stood with his arms crossed.

"Right then, big man, let's get you stripped," Juan said.

Theo raised a brow at me in challenge, and I shrugged, but clearly, I hadn't thought this through because watching his strong fingers unbutton his shirt and bring his toned torso into view had me wondering if Juan's heating was faulty. I batted away images of him from my dream last night and tried not to squirm.

Theo smirked, and the effect was devastating. He clearly didn't have body hang-ups as he exposed more and more golden skin. It was a battle to remain professional and hold in the drool as he dropped his trousers.

Motherfudger.

He looked like he'd stumbled in from a Calvin Klein underwear shoot. I clutched my colour swatches as my breathing hitched.

Juan, ever the professional, flitted around and began measuring him, but Theo's eyes remained on me like a predator sensing its prey. He knew he was having an inappropriate effect on me.

I was sweating through my fluffy Christmas jumper. Clearing my throat and giving myself a mental shake, I moved closer. I held colour swatches against him. Oh, so much skin on display and so warm.

Focus!

"So this is the full image consultant package?" His voice was low, and his eyes gleamed down at me.

It was the first time I'd seen him being anything but grumpy. I resisted the urge to fan myself like some Victorian maiden. He was handsome in his ill-fitting suits, but holy hotness out of them, my underwear was toast. My reaction and thoughts were highly unprofessional; worst of all, he knew it.

I worked silently for once, not trusting what might come from my mouth. I'd never felt this way about a client. It's like he was a magnet, and I was a hapless piece of metal drawn to him.

After finishing the colours, I discussed fabrics and styles with Juan. He would work on it and send us some sketches and swatches in a few days. Sadly, Theo redressed while we conferred, but I felt the weight of his gaze on my back.

"How's Elle?" Juan asked.

"Causing mayhem. She's signed us up for a dating app, so I'll be subjected to a million dodgy double dates when I return."

"Omigod. I want a full report on each. It'll be hilarious. You remember that date we all went on with those triplets?"

I groaned, remembering the total disaster that was Elle's idea of a triple date.

"It was fine until you stole them all for yourself." I nudged him.

"That was a great night." Juan winked at me, and I rolled my eyes, giggling.

Theo cleared his throat and brought us out of our reminiscing.

"Where do I pay?" Theo asked, his face pulling into his signature scowl.

"I'll invoice Zo—"

"No, invoice me directly," Theo snapped.

"Okay." Juan steered Theo to the computer and gave him a business card.

"Let's catch up for drinks. Text me," Juan called as Theo hustled me out of the shop, crowding me with his firm, delicious-smelling body.

My phone buzzed as I got back into Theo's car.

Juan: Grumpy Hottie is a ten.

The image of Theo in boxer shorts came to mind, and I had to agree with Juan.

9

Glaring at the side of Zoe's head as the car moved away from the sidewalk – the desire to both wring her neck and kiss her senseless warred inside me. The sensation was as infuriating as the tiny menace herself. Watching her giggle and talk with Juan had me fuming. *A dating app*. She'd just been on a date last night. The only good thing was that she was in her own bed this morning.

Not that it matters to me, of course.

Why had I demanded a date with her instead? I was a fucking idiot. I didn't know why I thought that was a suitable counter-negotiation. Perhaps it was my competitive streak coming out.

"That wasn't so bad, was it?" she asked me, putting her phone away.

"I didn't appreciate being paraded around like a giant Ken doll."

She giggled.

"We'll see when the suits arrive," I sniped, trying to pull my usual sternness back around me.

However, it seemed this annoying attraction went both ways if her reaction in the shop to my half-naked body was anything to go by.

"Oh ye of little faith."

"What are you doing for the rest of the day?"

"Ticking things off my New York bucket list."

"Like what?"

She pulled out a scrappy bit of paper from her giant bag and smoothed it out. I peered over her shoulder at the handwritten checklist.

"You've put 'eat a hotdog from a street seller' on your list?" My eyebrows practically hit my hairline.

"Sure. That's totally a thing."

The colourful scrawl had a key, and some items had top priority.

"Hockey game at Madison Square Garden. Why the hell would you want to go there? Why aren't there other sports on there?" I bristled.

"I always fancied seeing an ice hockey game."

I grunted, disgusted.

"Can you drop me off at the Winter Village? Someone said there were these igloos and amazing hot chocolate."

I opened my mouth to tell her I'd come with her, but then I shut it again.

"Why do you love Christmas so much?"

She turned her pixelated eyes on me. "Why do you hate it so much?"

I clenched my teeth. "Bad memories."

She nodded and didn't press for more.

"Bad memories can be turned around," she said and pain flashed in her eyes. "I love Christmas time. You could do a lot for morale by allowing decorations and having a Christmas party."

"I'll take it under advisement."

She sighed. "That's a no then. Maybe I'll have to incite a rebellion."

"You'll do no such thing." I leaned down, barely holding back from growling a threat about spanking her ass if she started undermining me with mutinous decorating.

The image of her curves laid across my lap in the office made me jam my hands in my pockets to avoid embarrassing myself.

We fell silent, but against my will, I wanted to hear more about her, especially the pain I heard in her voice earlier.

It's none of my business.

In the end, I said nothing, and the Winter Village appeared. She gathered her large bag and thanked me.

The return to the office felt dimmer without her. I threw myself into work, but my focus was shot. Images of the way Zoe licked her lips when I stripped down floated through my mind. I stayed in shape, and I knew she appreciated what she saw. It was highly inappropriate, but damn.

Stop thinking of the elf!

I dialled Liam's number, knowing he'd likely be in the office.

"If you're calling to bitch about your new haircut, then save it." Liam's growly voice came on the line.

"No one's cut my hair."

"They ought to, and that monstrosity you call a beard. A whole family might live in there, and no one would know."

I ran my fingers through my beard, which was getting unruly. Zoe said it needed a trim, so I ignored his jab and told him about Vanessa.

"She's Frank Cubit's niece?"

"Yes," I said, squeezing the stress ball my brother bought me.

I explained the plans I'd put in motion.

"Let us know if you need help. We chose you for a reason, and it wasn't to have you replaced in a coup."

Something settled inside my chest. I wasn't short on confidence, and my work ethic was solid. It always was, whether I was throwing a ball, running a line, or chasing corporate goals, but after the injury took me down, it was all on me to turn things around. Having business partners with faith in my abilities and genuine support in my corner meant a lot. The Steel Brothers might be many things, but once you were in their inner circle, you had their support one hundred percent.

I'd give this image coach thing a chance. Zoe had already proved to be useful in a more tangible way than redressing me. The guys had faith in me, and they had my back. I ought to follow what they were trying to do. It felt easy to be the villain – a role that my ex painted for me in the media and that I played into. But Theodore Kelly wasn't afraid of hard work.

It was late when I left the office. My back reminded me I'd been sitting in a chair too long. I wondered what else Zoe had checked off her ridiculous list today.

> Jackson: Don't forget the game next weekend. You promised Lucas you'd be there.

I groaned as I looked at the message. Jackson was my only friend if you didn't count my siblings or the Steel Brothers across the pond. He was an NFL quarterback and a prodigy of my grandfather. We grew up together, even though Jackson was a few years older. Unlike me, he still played but was nearing retirement from the sport.

> Jackson: Are you bringing a date?

No. Maybe.

Zoe could attend an NFL game rather than watch pretty boys with wooden sticks skate about. She deserved to see the best American sport in action. As a rule, I avoided attending games in person for many reasons, not least of all the press, but Jackson's son, my godson, Lucas, guilt-tripped me into it. That little dude was as wily as his old man, and I was a sucker for him.

> Me: Yes.

> Jackson: Holy shit! Tell me she's not a wannabe actress.

I winced.

> Me: Nope.

Jackson: I like her already. I'll see you after the game.

Me: Is Lucas okay?

Lucas's health varied. He had cerebral palsy and was prone to infections in his leg after an operation that went wrong.

Jackson: Yep. See you there.

10

Theo 🏈

*M*onday morning dawned bright and early, and I glanced at the clock, waiting for her arrival. Would she be wearing something annoyingly Christmassy again today?

I'd been thinking about her the rest of the weekend, even while watching the game at Abe's. I found myself thinking of things to say to her to incite a sassy response. How had I become addicted to her infuriatingly cheerful personality so quickly? She was like a combination of crack cocaine and cat nip. It was insane how far she'd burrowed under my skin in no time. That said, I'd never had such a strong, visceral reaction to anyone that seemed beyond mere attraction.

I left a message with Carol to send her in as soon as she arrived, but I was agitated by ten in the morning. Using the number I pulled off her file, I called her.

"Hello?" she answered.

"Hello? Hello? Where the hell are you?"

"I had breakfast with a journalist."

Hairs rose on my arms as I strangled the stress ball. The plastic split and gloop exploded over my desk.

"Fuck."

"It was just an informal meeting over coffee."

"You're dating a journalist on company time?" I growled, wiping stress ball guts off my hand.

"No, silly. I was trying to get a handle on your media image. The PR department isn't on your side."

"Tell me you didn't tell a journalist that?"

She snorted. "Thanks for crediting me with a single brain cell. No, Theo, I didn't tell them that."

My name on her lips had me gripping the phone.

"You should have told me."

"We haven't exchanged numbers. We aren't even working together."

"We had a deal, a deal you blackmailed out of me. I need you back here. And you need to attend an event this weekend as my date. You can see your first NFL game, the far superior American sport."

She went quiet for a minute. "If we're going out, you'll need more clothes."

"I have clothes!" I tossed the saggy stress ball at the wall.

"And a hair and beard trim. Don't worry, I'm on it."

She hung up before I could say no. I rubbed at the throbbing in my temples. This was going to be hell.

Zoe breezed in forty-five minutes later, wearing a fitted dress that drew my eyes to her ample curves and a tiny red jacket. Mercifully, there wasn't a Christmas print in sight until I noticed the candy cane lapel badges.

"Do you know what time it is?" I growled at her, annoyed at my annoyance.

She placed a bag on the desk, and the warm scent of baked goods wafted up.

"You might need a bib, but here's a pastry to cheer you up."

I swiped at the bag and rounded the desk to loom over her. The little pint-sized menace just placed her hands on her hips and stared up at me.

"I'm sorry if you expected me here at a certain time, but all of last week, you didn't grace me with your presence until after seven in the evening."

Fuck, this little cheeky elf. She loved to call me out on my shit with a smile on her goddamn face.

"We are working together now," I gritted out, stepping far too close to her.

"Since when?"

My palm itched to connect with her backside or, better yet, put her sassy mouth to use somewhere else. Blood rushed south as my body began reacting to her nearness, so I stepped back.

"Since Saturday. You blackmailed me into a week. But I want the full treatment."

Shit, that sounded dirtier than I intended.

"I'm delighted you finally saw sense." She walked around me and sat down in my visitor's chair.

I blew out a breath and tried to get my raging body under control.

"Tell me more about your ex, Savannah." She clicked a pen and opened her infernal binder.

The mention of Savannah effectively killed my boner. "I'm sure you've heard plenty."

"I know what the press says, but it's a skewed view."

I made a disgusted sound in my throat and returned to my seat, crashing down heavily. Stalling for time, I devoured the bear claw she bought me before reminding myself that I didn't shy away from hard things.

"I thought we were in love. It was fun until it wasn't, and I realised how incredibly vain she was. My family name and business success made me famous enough for her to use it to begin her social climb. When it wasn't enough, she began manufacturing attention. She enjoyed picking fights in public places. At first, I couldn't understand why. But I began to suspect she staged things because the reporters appeared like magic every time. She turned our relationship into a sideshow, especially after she appeared on a reality show. Even our breakup was messy and public." I clenched my teeth tightly, glaring out at the city skyline. "Unfortunately, she has an uncanny knack for knowing just what buttons to press."

"What buttons are they?" Zoe asked, staring at me with an infuriatingly cute face.

"So that you can press them too?" I glared back.

"No, so we can work on them."

I huffed, discomfort coating my tongue. "Football. My family."

Zoe blinked back at me, and I swallowed.

"My dad believes I'm a failure and a quitter for not returning to football after my back injury. I broke my spine before the draft after being identified as a top pick. He can't accept that I lost my chance at the NFL. His whole life revolves around football. Savannah liked to remind me of that, among other things," I choked out.

This wasn't shit I ever shared, and I had zero clue why it came out so easily with her.

"You broke your spine. Can you even return after that?" Zoe raised her eyebrows.

"It's been done, but the doctors told me not to. The combination of fractures left my spine vulnerable. One more bad tackle and I might not walk again."

"And you still have pain," she said.

How did she know that?

She shrugged. "You chew through painkillers and are grumpier when your back is stiff."

I opened and closed my mouth a few times. She wasn't wrong.

"Do you still do your physio?"

"I still exercise. You saw me in my boxers," I deflected.

She shuffled her file about. "That's not what I asked."

I blew out a breath. "No."

"Why not?"

"Busy."

"Bullturd."

"Bullturd? Is that even a word?"

"Sure. Want to know what I think?"

"No," I grumbled.

"I think you like the bad-guy role they've cast you in as it keeps people away. And maybe you think you deserve the pain."

"I think your psychology degree fried your brains."

"Ten points for reading my CV. But tell me I'm wrong." She tipped her chin up defiantly.

"You're wrong."

"Bullturd. Why not let people have Christmas decorations?"

"What the hell do Christmas decorations have to do with anything?"

"It's part of the bad-guy mythology you've built for yourself."

I snorted. "No, it's not."

"Then reverse it."

"No."

"Then it is." She jutted out her little chin.

"No, it's not," I gritted, my temperature rising.

"It's okay. It'll be our little secret."

Argh! She was so annoying.

"Fine, decorate the place. I don't care." I threw up my hands.

She smiled widely, and it punched me in the chest. I didn't even feel mad that I'd been played.

"Wonderful." She made a note on her pad. "Why do you hate Christmas?"

Fuck me, she was on a roll. Going for the jugular every time.

"Because I spent a miserable Christmas in traction with a fractured spine while my father reminded me what a failure I was. And every year, I get a repeat performance of that speech on Christmas day for the sake of seeing my mother, who won't leave his miserable ass.

"Because that same Christmas, my father found out my brother was gay and kicked him out. So, on top of everything, I had to organise somewhere for him to live and spend Christmas without him. Years after that shitshow, Savannah begged me to go out. 'You never take me out to celebrate Christmas,'" I mimicked her high-pitched, whiny voice, my vision blurring with the ugly memories.

"The woman picked a fight on Christmas Eve in the middle of

Times Square, and it made the front page." I finished my rant, panting.

Zoe's arms encircled me, and shock rang through me. I hadn't noticed her moving, lost in my memories of why I hated this cursed season gushed out of me. The misery of being back home instead of helping my team to the playoffs was fucking torture. Knowing my football career was over amidst excruciating pain and difficulty pissing. Worse than that was the fear for my brother, Abe, and the scramble to make sure he was safe physically and mentally. All that bullshit with Savannah barely registered, but it reinforced my hatred for the season. That and the humiliating lengths I went to, to make something one-sided work.

Zoe's cinnamon scent filled my lungs, and I breathed deeply. It chased away some of the resentment, and my heart rate slowed. I focused on the candy cane pins on her jacket and the soft feeling of her against me.

"I'm sorry you went through that." She stroked my back. "But no man is an island, Theo. Sometimes rewriting happier memories over bad ones can help."

Against my better judgment, I shoved my chair back and hauled her fully onto my lap. I needed to feel her against me to feel something other than those ugly images of the worst period of my life. She fit perfectly there. Her curves pressed against me as I took more deep breaths of her scent. A groan fell from my lips as she tunnelled her fingers through my hair, scratching my scalp and soothing me on a level I'd never experienced.

We stayed like that for a while until Zoe shifted, and I groaned for another reason. She must have felt what her body did to mine, and yet she remained there. I wasn't alone in this crazy attraction. I lifted my head, and her face was closer than I expected.

Her beautiful smile was something I craved. She licked her lips, and I tracked the movement of her little pink tongue. It was a bad idea for many reasons, but before I could overthink, I pressed forward. Our lips met, hers soft and pouty under mine, and heat burned through me. I cupped her cheeks and licked at the seam of her mouth. She sighed, and our tongues entwined as I deepened the kiss. Her short hair was soft under my fingers, and my heart thudded.

She pulled back, her pupils blown and panting.

"Theo... I..."

For once, I'd rendered her speechless.

She cleared her throat. "I'm sorry, this isn't professional."

That pissed me off. I didn't want her professionalism. I wanted her moaning and writhing underneath me, stretched out across my desk.

Back it up, Kelly.

I reminded myself I didn't do romantic entanglements.

"Is this a new technique to ensure client compliance?" I drawled, attempting to bring my body under control. "I can see why it works."

She paled and scrambled off my lap, leaving me with a raging hard-on, tenting my suit trousers and a cold space where she'd been. The look on her face told me I'd fucked up.

"I'll go..." She straightened her dress and cleared her throat. "I need to sort out the Christmas decorations."

I watched her round the desk and snatch up her things before scampering out of the office. Groaning, I leaned my head on the desk.

Fucking hell.

11

onight was game night. Apparently, they didn't always play on a Saturday, but before Christmas, it was practically a whole day affair. I pulled my Christmas jumper on and smoothed it over the skinny jeans that made my butt look great and dug out my knee-high boots. The heels were almost pointless next to Theo, but they might mean the difference between watching someone's back throughout the game and seeing the ball. Was it called a ball or a pigskin? Jeez, I knew nothing about this sport, and Google was just confusing. My second eldest brother, Dylan, said it was like rugby while wearing twenty pounds of padding. He said it like an insult, so I had yet to mention it to Theo.

Flopping down on the bed to wait, I looked at my messages from Elle.

> Elle: Why can't you bang him?

> Me: Because he's my client.

> Elle: Cancel the contract, then bang him.

> Me: How would that look to the Stylz judging panel?

> Elle: I hate it when you argue with logic. You could bang him secretly.

That was not the advice I wanted. I had kept things professional with Theo this week after that incredible kiss. *Best freaking kiss of my life.* And the most inappropriate. It was partly my fault for hugging him or, at the very least, not scrambling off his lap when he pulled me there. He looked so sad I couldn't resist. I could still feel his beard tickling my face. Did his grumpiness improve his kissing abilities?

After his douchy but accurate comment about professionalism, I feared it might have ruined our working relationship. However, everything appeared to have stayed the same. We'd made progress in the office, and it now had a warm Christmassy feel. I had him work on meditation practice and a calmness anchor. Plus, he had an appointment with his back specialist and physio. I'd done some online shopping for a more casual wardrobe for him based on Juan's measurements, and Juan's barber did a stellar job cleaning him up. Mind you, the look on Theo's face when the guy suggested using beard oil could have stripped the paint off the wall.

My phone buzzed again.

> Elle: I might have found someone to fulfil my Christmas fantasy.

> Me: Tell me, he's not from that dating app.

> Elle: No, it's a forum for that kind of thing. A client mentioned it.

> Me: Is it safe?

> Elle: Yep. Got to go. Speak soon. Make sure you bang him.

I rolled my eyes. Who knew what she'd got herself into? And I certainly would not bang Theo, even though my lady parts were totally on board. I'd have to be dead not to have felt his arousal pressing against me during that kiss, and I'd be lying if I didn't want to know what it felt like.

Nope! No salacious thoughts. It was bad enough that I'd had at least three sex dreams involving Theo. I wasn't *that* image consultant that banged her client.

A heavy pounding on the door made me jump. Rushing over, I yanked it open, revealing a frowning Theo. He filled out the New York Giants jersey perfectly, and his new hair and beard looked great.

"Is that for me?" I pointed at the top, gripped tightly in his hand.

He grunted and thrust it at me. It was blue and gigantic. I spread it out. It had an enormous number twelve on the front with Coby on the back.

"What does yours say?"

"The same. They are Jackson's jerseys, but..." His expression was difficult to read, almost like a pained scowl.

"But what?"

I pulled off my jumper and put the jersey over my vest top. It drowned me. The irony of wearing something that said giant wasn't lost on me. I knotted it at the waist to stop it from looking like a potato sack.

"You'd look better in one of my old ones," he mumbled.

"I doubt the size would be any better."

"I don't play anymore," he said gruffly.

"Do you miss it?"

"Sometimes. I miss my teammates. But it was always my dad's dream, not mine." He avoided my eyes, and it told me more than his words.

From what he'd already said, his dad was a real piece of work.

"It must have been conflicting to strive for something you didn't want but then have it taken away anyway."

He grunted again. The look in his eyes told me I was close to the truth. Theo still carried a lot of pain from that time, and I hoped he would eventually deal with it. Stupidly, I wanted to be the one to help him despite leaving in a few weeks. There was more to this guy than his grumpy exterior let on.

The drive to the stadium was quiet, but when we arrived, the place was heaving with a sea of blue and white. The atmosphere was charged with excitement. Theo showed special passes, and they escorted us up to a box.

"Can I get nachos in here?" I bounced on the balls of my feet.

"Nachos?" Theo's lip curled.

"Oh, it's on my list, along with beer in a plastic cup at a game. Do they only sell them at ice hockey?"

Theo scoffed and steered me to the rear of the box, where there was a bar with drinks only. He ordered me a beer. Sadly, it wasn't in an authentic plastic cup but tasted hoppy and cold, which was nice.

"Teddy!" a voice shouted, and then a tiny figure collided with Theo.

He picked up the slender girl who wasn't much taller than me and pulled her into a bear hug. A hideous feeling burned through my chest. Was this his girlfriend? No. He never mentioned a girlfriend. A fuck buddy? Her long dark hair was in a ponytail, and she wore the same jersey as us.

"Pipsqueak," Theo said in a voice I'd not heard him use.

The beer soured in my mouth as he set her back on her feet.

"I don't even want to introduce the two of you," he groaned, glancing between us.

I hitched a smile onto my face, unsure what to make of it and mortified at my internal reaction.

"Did you bring a date?" The girl stared at me with a shocked look.

"No, I'm Zoe, his image consultant."

"Image consultant!" Her eyebrows shot up.

She glanced back at Theo, who ran a hand down his face. Suddenly, she burst out laughing and doubled over.

"Zoe, this is my little sister Georgina. George meet Zoe," Theo grumbled, shoving her lightly.

Relief flooded through me – his sister. I looked at her closer and realised they had the same shade of eyes and a similar hair colour.

"Are you the one that finally persuaded him to get his beard trimmed? He looked like Robinson Crusoe." She set off cackling again.

"I'm going to say hi to Jackson's mom," Theo said, stomping off towards an older lady standing with a boy of about seven, who I assumed was Lucas.

He wore leg braces and was all decked out in number twelve gear. Theo told me Lucas was his godson.

"Come on." George hooked her arm around mine and steered me towards our seats.

"Nice to meet you. Theo didn't tell me his sister would be here," I said.

"Typical, Theo." She rolled her eyes as we sat down. "Tell me all about you. You've achieved the impossible with him."

"Trimming his beard? Because that was the barber."

She giggled. "No, he looked happy. I saw it across the room."

George quizzed me about the UK for a while. She was bubbly and fun, the exact opposite of her brother.

She leaned in conspiratorially, "Are you sleeping together? Will you fulfil my dreams of having a niece or nephew?"

"No!" My stomach dropped out at her words.

"Shame. I mean, I didn't want to think of my brother having sex, but I'd like a cool sister-in-law like you. Not like that ice queen he was engaged to."

She wasn't just shipping us; she'd married us off with babies!

"He's my client."

"There's nothing professional about the look he's giving you," she said slyly, and we glanced over at Theo, who looked away quickly and back to his godson.

I shivered in response, diverting George back to what to expect from the game.

The pregame got underway, and it all seemed larger than life, even from the height of the enclosed box. Screens flashed, and drummers appeared on the field.

"When are the cheerleaders coming on to throw each other in the air and make pyramids?" I asked George.

She snorted. "NFL cheerleaders are more about the boob shaking, but The Giants are one of the teams without a cheer squad."

I felt bad some of my online research was off base.

"Fair enough. I'd take my eye out doing some of those moves with my boobs."

George fell about laughing.

"Tell me you are coming over for Christmas dinner?" George asked when she recovered.

"I'll be back in the UK by then."

"Shame."

Theo settled into the seat next to me at that moment. There was a big advantage for a short girl like myself to this box as there were no people in front of me to try and see around.

"You're going to have to explain what's going on," I told him.

As the game began, I was on the edge of my seat. Theo explained what was happening, like my personal commentator. I was able to follow the game to a point, although there were more rules than I could keep up with. I learned and promptly forgot the difference between a sack and a tackle, which players were offence and which ones were defence. Of course, I heard all about Jackson as the quarterback since that was who Theo paid the most attention to. Jackson was easy to spot on the field with his number twelve jersey, and I cheered each time he had the ball. But I winced when the players tackled each other, and I could see why they wore so much padding. It was a slower game than UK football, though, because they were stopping all the time. I mentioned that to Theo and received one of his deeper scowls along with a scoff.

At half-time, he had someone retrieve nachos and a beer in a plastic cup for me. Between that and watching him interact with Lucas, something expanded in my chest.

The second half was just as pulse-pounding. Theo shouted things at the refs, who looked like mint humbugs on legs in their black and white striped shirts. We jumped up when the team scored, almost losing my nachos. It was addictive, almost as much as the feeling of sitting so close to Theo. Dragging my focus from his warm body, I watched Lucas instead as he shouted for his dad and waved his big foam pointer around.

Jackson's team won, and we all jumped up cheering. Theo high fived Lucas, then threw his arms around me, lifting me clean off my feet. George caught my eye with a knowing look when he set me down. He seemed like a different person, surrounded by his friends and family.

After the game, Jackson was due to meet us here after he'd spoken to the press. We tucked into the delicious buffet, and I chatted with George. She wasn't impressed with the food. It turned out she owned a catering company.

"Just give me a minute. I've got to take this call," she said apologetically after fishing her buzzing phone from her pocket. "This client is a nightmare."

"I know all about those." I winked at her.

She answered her phone and moved to the back of the room. I watched as she spoke animatedly.

"What's the matter?" Theo drew level with me, his eyes on his sister.

"A tricky client. It's tough when they give you a hard time." I elbowed him lightly, and he smirked.

It was like all his cocky business persona coupled with this sporting one combined to create a devastating effect.

"Fuck's sake!" George appeared looking close to tears. "The fucking audacity."

"What's the matter?" Theo asked, tensing.

"This client has been a nightmare. Now they're cancelling. It's just over seven days, so they'll get fifty percent back."

"I thought you changed that in the terms and conditions," Theo snapped.

"I haven't done it yet. Anyway, they booked ages ago. They've been making my life hell for months. It's almost worth the loss in money, but I feel bad for my team. They rely on the pre-Christmas gigs." She threw up her hands and sank into a nearby seat.

"What was it for?" I asked, perching on a chair next to her.

"A big office party. I'd accommodated loads of extra requests too."

"Bill them," Theo barked.

"It doesn't work that way," George snapped back.

I seized the opportunity to fix two issues. "You could book her for an office holiday party instead. It's very last minute, but think of the morale-boosting effects. Everyone loved the decorations."

Theo glared at me.

"Wait, you got him to allow Christmas decorations at the office?" George's mouth hung open.

"She blackmailed me," Theo argued.

George let out a watery laugh.

"You couldn't organise a party at such short notice," Theo said.

"Wanna bet?" I said, excitement sparking through me. "If we have a caterer, that's half the battle."

"Where are we holding this party that isn't happening?" Theo deadpanned.

"At Steel Ventures. There's plenty of room. We can decorate. How many were you catering for?" I asked George.

"One hundred and fifty."

"Great."

George and I simultaneously turned puppy dog eyes on Theo, who quelled under our joint stare.

"Looks like you are in trouble, man," a deep voice behind Theo said.

We turned to the speaker. He was an equally tall, stacked guy with dark skin and a deep grin. Lucas hung off one of his arms, and Lucus's grandmother was tucked under the other. His suit was tailored to his enormous frame, and his dark eyes sparkled with mischief. He dropped the arm from around his mother and embraced Theo with a back slap.

"Thanks for coming, man."

"Great game. You carved up their defence like a fucking Thanksgiving turkey. And that hit from Cramer. Was it as bad on the field as it looked up here?" Theo asked.

They dissolved into game speak before Jackson turned to us.

"George, looking fine in my shirt," Jackson greeted Theo's sister and then turned to me. "Who is this beauty wearing my number?" He extended his hand, but Theo slapped it out of the way.

"That is Zoe."

"Pleased to meet you, Zoe. Your man is possessive of you already."

"Oh no, I'm not with Theo."

Jackson smirked at me before his son claimed his attention.

"So, will you save my bacon, big brother?" George batted her eyelashes at Theo.

"If you can both pull it off, then fine," he grumped.

I squealed, and George and I high fived.

Jackson ended up doing the rounds talking to people, and I could tell that Theo grew tired of being dragged into conversations with random people. He called it and suggested George get a lift with us.

We left the stadium, and Theo tensed as a group of reporters spotted him. He hustled us towards the car. My pulse spiked as I picked up the pace. Theo wasn't ready for a live lesson in front of multiple press members.

"Mr Kelly, Theo, what did you think of the game?" one guy shouted.

"Theo, who is with you? Are you building a harem?"

"Ignore them," George said, grabbing Theo's arm.

"Savannah has a new man. Is this payback to show her you've moved on?"

Theo growled at that and shoved his sister into the waiting car.

"Which one are you banging, the fat one?" A sneering male voice hollered from the crowd.

Theo wheeled around, but I caught his arm. He twisted back to me, anger painted on his face. I had to calm him down.

"Ignore them. Use your calmness anchor," I said, grabbing his hand.

My touch seemed to draw out some of his anger as he focused on me.

"I won't let them speak like that," he gritted.

"As sweet as that is, I don't matter. Everything I'm doing here does.

This won't be the only time they ambush you," I pressed, breathless in my urgency.

"You do matter."

The press shouting continued as our gazes magnetised, and the rage in his eyes transformed into a different kind of heat. The mob shouted more things, but the noise dimmed as the sound of blood rushed in my ears.

"It doesn't matter. They are doing it to get a rise out of you," I whispered, licking my lips.

He hunched over protectively, bringing his face closer to mine. His eyes fell to my lips, and I knew what he would do before he moved. The first press of his lips switched my brain off.

Frantically, I grabbed his cheeks, and he pushed me back against the open door, his mouth moving against mine. Cameras flashed, but I was lost in a haze of lust, savouring the scratch of his beard and his closeness.

Theo pulled away and placed his forehead against mine. "Get in the car, elf."

I was dazed for a few seconds, then mortified when I realized the cameras still flashed, and the reporters had pressed closer.

"Come with me. Please," I begged, dragging his arm into the car.

He hesitated but followed me inside. I let out a relieved breath at having gotten him away from the press. The door closed on the shouts, and my cheeks blazed as I caught George's eye, realising we'd had more than one audience. She bit her lip and turned away, smiling. We pulled from the curb, and Theo clutched my hand in his. Lightheadedness washed over me. What was I doing?

12

T H E O

I concentrated on not crushing her hand, fuming over the press invasion and still painfully aroused from that short but soul-sucking kiss. Why did I do it? I avoided public displays of affection, especially in front of the vultures like that. A small savage part of me enjoyed claiming her lips publicly, but the sensible part of me didn't agree.

George shot me surreptitious looks, unable to hide her smirks. Fucking hell, my brother would be calling by the time I got home.

The car pulled up in front of George's apartment, and she exchanged numbers with Zoe. Unfortunately, I had to let go of Zoe's hand. But it was for the best, as I was getting too attached to this woman, and I was reasonably sure I'd developed a severe case of blue balls.

"Bye," I called belatedly to my sister as she skipped to her apartment door.

Zoe pressed against me as she waved at George. I adjusted myself in my seat, painfully aroused by the closeness of her inviting curves. After breaking up with Savannah, my sex drive went into hibernation, but since the elf appeared, it had come raging back. Normally,

I'd consider contacting an old hook-up, but the only person I wanted to work this lust out on was next to me. Maybe if we slept together, I would get her out of my system. Then, I only needed to resolve this Vanessa situation to return to normal.

"Theo?" Zoe called my name, and I pulled back from my thoughts. "This is me. Thank you for taking me to the game. It was fun." Her mouth twisted. "I know you needed a distraction, but the kissing can't happen again. I'm not that kind of woman. My work with you needs to remain business-like. My professional reputation could easily be damaged, and that would be devastating for more than just my client base." Her lips twisted down.

Frowning, I was torn again between arguing with her and agreeing it was a bad idea. George was always reminding me of the double standards between men and women in the press. Despite Savannah's best attempt at making me look like a beast during our breakup, there was far more support out there for me than her. This worked for me back then, but not with Zoe.

She held out the jersey to me, and my eyes fell on her thin-strapped vest that strained over her ample chest. Before I could stop myself, thoughts of how unprofessional I could get with those breasts flooded my mind.

What was the question?

"I..." I shook myself. "Sorry about the press. No more kissing." I managed gruffly.

Her expression was unreadable.

"I agree. Keep practising that meditation and calm anchor. It's worse if they see they are getting a reaction out of you."

I grunted. She handed me the still-warm jersey. I exited the car and jogged around to her door. Opening it, I helped her out. She shivered in the biting wind, and I pulled off my jersey and covered her in it.

She giggled again. "I just took one off. Mmmm, this one smells nice." She buried her nose in the material.

Fucking hell, why did I like that?

"Keep it. It's cold out here," I said.

"I'm only walking to my apartment, which is just there. I come from Sheffield in the UK. I'm used to the cold."

I grunted. Why was I allowing her to leave again?

"What are you doing tomorrow?" I asked.

"I tried to get tickets for the Top of the Rock, but they didn't have a time slot near sunset, so I think I'll visit the Botanical Garden."

"I can get tickets," I said without considering the logistics. "I'll pick you up at three."

"Really?"

"You owe me a date."

The grin froze on her face. "I thought today was our date?"

Technically, it was, but I decided against my better judgment that I wanted another.

"That was your induction into America's best sport."

"So, Top of the Rock is the competition date?"

I nodded, not trusting my voice.

"Okay. Will we grab some street food?"

"We're not having hotdogs."

She smiled. "What should I wear?"

Fucking hell.

Her lips made me want to kiss her, but if I did that, I'd end up dragging her upstairs and fucking her six ways to Sunday. *No kissing, that's what I agreed.* Jesus, this woman was like a drug.

"It's time to show you the real food this city offers. Wear a dress." I returned to the car, leaving her on the sidewalk.

It was my turn to have the last word.

My phone rang before I even got back to my penthouse in Tribeca.

"Abe," I answered.

"A little bird tells me you took a woman on a date. A normal woman, to a game, no less. Spill the details," Abe said without preamble.

"George is a menace."

"But she's right. Why am I hearing this second-hand? I called you two days ago. We watched the game last Sunday." The pout in his voice was evident.

"Zoe is the image consultant. I told you about the bet I lost with the Steel Brothers. She is my penance."

"George said you were tongue fucking your penance in front of the press, so I'm guessing she's not exactly an albatross around your neck." There was hurt behind his words.

My throat tightened. We'd been a team for a long time. But I hadn't even told him Zoe had arrived, letting him fill our time with football and business. I wasn't sure why.

"It's complicated. I'll catch up with you later in the week. I can't make it tomorrow."

He usually hosted a dinner on a Sunday after we watched the game.

"Going out with your penance, I suppose? George says she is catering for your Christmas party. Who are you, and what have you done with my brother? You better be ready to spill your guts when I see you."

I rolled my eyes. Then I remembered I had to find some sold-out tickets.

"Abe, you know that ticket guy you know?"

Abe wasn't happy that I was blowing him off and asking for his help, but he came through for me and I would be grovelling for a while.

Sunday morning crawled by like a snail despite forcing myself to work. At five to three, I pursed my lips outside Zoe's flimsy apartment door. This place wasn't good enough for her.

But when she opened the door, her face was puffy and red as tears streamed down her cheeks. Seeing her in distress was like being hit by the whole defensive line.

"I-I'm sorry... I forgot the time." She finished with a sob.

"What's wrong?" I muscled into the small room, scanning for threats as I hauled her against me.

The one bed apartment looked as empty as it did last time, nothing to clue me in. She clutched my dress shirt, tears dampening the material at my mid-chest. I wanted to smash something, anything. Who made my happy elf cry?

"Tell me, and we'll fix it," I barked.

She shook her head. "It's Bowser."

"The Mario character?" I asked, confused.

"No, my dog."

My heart sank.

"What's wrong?"

Tell me the dog isn't dead.

"He broke into the pantry and ate a whole tin of cookies. They had chocolate and raisins in them. Mum didn't realise at first until he got sick. They've taken him to the out-of-hours vets to see if they can pump his stomach." She gripped me tighter, tears streaming. "I can't lose him. He's all I've got left of him."

I didn't understand what she meant, but I steered her over to the bed as there wasn't a couch, and I was certain those spindly chairs at the tiny table wouldn't hold us both. I sat down, pulling her against me.

"When was the last update?" I clenched and unclenched my fist, feeling useless.

"Half an hour ago. I'm waiting for my brother to call. He met my parents at the vet's."

"Do you want to go?" I asked.

She lifted her head. "What do you mean?"

"I could get a jet. We could be there by the early hours."

She blinked at me. Despite the crying, she was still the most beautiful woman I'd ever seen. I meant it. I'd move heaven and earth to get her back to her dog.

She shook her head. "Thank you. Let's wait. I don't know if I could face seeing him if he..." She hiccupped and buried her face in my shirt again.

I felt powerless. I'd only been here five minutes and hated the waiting.

The phone rang, and we both jumped. She scrambled off my lap to reach it. The caller ID said *The Old Bill*. A nickname, I assumed.

"What's happening?" Zoe answered in a frantic voice.

I couldn't hear the words, just the deep base of presumably her brother's voice.

Zoe burst into tears again as the call ended. I took the phone from her, but it rang again with an incoming video call. I clicked it on, and a scowling guy appeared on the screen. He was older than me, but definitely not her dad.

"Who the fuck are you?" he barked. "Where's Zoe?"

"She's crying. What's happened to Bowser?"

"He's here." Zoe's brother panned the camera to a sleeping dog in a cage. "He's sleeping it off. The vet said he's going to be fine."

"Zoe, look." I nudged the phone closer, and she pulled her tearful gaze up to the screen.

"My poor baby boy." She stroked the screen, and tears fell onto it.

"He's going to be fine, Zo," her brother said gruffly. "Why is there a man sitting on your bed?"

I couldn't help smirking at him despite the circumstances.

"We were going to the Top of the Rock. Theo got tickets," Zoe said shakily.

"My offer to fly back to the UK is still there," I said.

"Fly you back, huh?" her brother said. "Don't be stupid, Zo. The dumb mutt just ate something he shouldn't."

I tensed, and Zoe swiped at her tears.

"You know why he means so much." She straightened. "Thank you for video calling me. Let me know any updates."

She clicked the call off before he could say bye.

"Jeez, he's such a jerk sometimes." She threw the phone onto the comforter.

"He shouldn't tell you off for being upset."

"That's my brother. Isaac doesn't handle emotions very well. He's a police inspector and is used to being a jerk when dealing with criminals. He forgets to turn it off. Him being at the vets meant he was just as worried as me. He just made less of a scene." Zoe sighed and dabbed her eyes. "You must think I'm crazy."

"Oh, I know you're crazy, but not because you care for your dog." I nudged her lightly.

She grinned weakly at me. "Was that Theozilla making a joke to cheer me up?"

"Hey, what's that nickname?" I asked, frowning.

"It's one from the office." She shrugged.

Huh? My employees call me that? I didn't know what I thought about that.

"The look on your face." Zoe smiled again and rubbed her cheeks. "Wow, I bet I look a mess."

"You look fine."

"I'm sorry I freaked out. Bowser was my twin brother Jacob's dog... Jay died in a motorcycle accident seven years ago, and..." She swallowed. "I can't bear to lose Bowser too... I know it will happen sometime, but..." She trailed off crying again.

My chest cracked open, and I pulled her onto my lap.

"I'm so sorry. I couldn't imagine the pain of losing my brother."

"It's awful." She shivered in my arms.

We sat for a while until she hiccupped to a stop. My throat felt thick, but I didn't bother to try to settle her. I couldn't comprehend that kind of grief. The need to take her away from this unsafe apartment and tuck her away at mine clawed at me.

"I'm sorry I've ruined your shirt and our competition date." She wiped a hand down my shirt, making my abs jump at the touch.

"Why don't we go to my place and order a pizza? I saw 'loaded hot chocolate' on your list. I'm positive I can do that," I offered, knowing my space was better equipped to help her feel better.

She gave me another weak smile. "It's already better than last week's date."

Wow, that bar was low. He must have been a total loser. My chest puffed up in challenge.

Zoe looked exhausted and admitted her crying had brought on a headache. I grabbed a glass of water and gave her some Tylenol, then I steered her to the door.

13

Zoe

My head thumped as I shuffled into Theo's vast living space. I liked this modified version of him. It was like something snapped, and he'd gone into caretaker mode. Part of me knew I shouldn't be here, but my capacity to care about it was shot. My eyes ached from the crying. The thought of losing Bowser just wrecked me, and it brought back all the ugly grief over losing Jay. If it was unwise and selfish to take advantage of Theo's concern, I'd deal with that later.

Theo's apartment was immaculate and less harshly masculine than I imagined. Abstract art with soft swirling pastels broke up the technology. The couch had textured cushions in muted colours, and a fluffy throw draped over the back made it look inviting. When he caught me staring, he told me his brother designed everything.

He wrapped me up in a giant hoodie that smelled of him, and I wilted onto the couch. He covered me with the fluffy blanket. My fingers smoothed over the soft throw as I stared out the window at the high rises and listened to him move around the kitchen. A knock signalled the pizza's arrival and roused me from my stupor.

"Is it okay to eat here?" I asked, clutching the blanket as Theo appeared with the box.

"It's fine." He sat down and put his feet up on the coffee table. He didn't turn on the TV, and we munched on yummy cheesy pizza in silence.

"Would it upset you to tell me about your twin?" Theo asked me once he cleared the box away.

I inhaled a deep breath. It still hurt to talk about Jay. The kind of deep longing that never truly went away. Losing my twin was like losing a piece of myself, but I wanted to talk about him. I never wanted to forget him. I shuffled my phone out of my pocket and unlocked it.

"I text his old phone every few days. Even though I know the phone is in my wardrobe at home."

It was such a stupid habit but one I'd never broken in the years since we lost him.

"It helps me feel closer to him, even though I know he'll never text back." I swallowed around the constriction in my throat. "He hit a patch of black ice on his motorbike. Spun out on his way home from a New Year's Eve party. He wasn't drunk," I said hastily. I always felt I needed to clarify. "Jay wasn't a big drinker. He loved that bike."

I closed my eyes against the tightness in my chest, and Theo's warm hand closed over mine, giving me silent strength.

"For a long time, I hated it. Whenever I saw a bike, I wanted to scream at the rider to get off."

Rage and fear would swarm me when I saw a guy Jay's age on a motorcycle.

I lost my words for a few minutes, remembering it, and Theo rubbed circles on my hand.

"But in the end, Jay wouldn't have been my brother without his bike. It was like an extension of himself. It wasn't fair that we lost him."

My tears started again under the force of my sorrow. I leaned into Theo's silent strength as he tucked me under his arm. He didn't interrupt me, just let me cry as he stroked my arm. The comfort of leaning on him allowed me to focus on sharing countless memories of growing up, being the only girl with four brothers. Jacob was my twin, but we were very different. He was a free spirit and did what he wanted. He was the baby of the family. A whole five minutes younger than me.

My throat ached when I finished talking. I had shown Theo a million pictures of Jacob and Bowser on my phone. Silence fell, but it didn't feel strained. My eyelids drooped, and my body felt drained. *I should go home.*

"He sounds like an incredible guy," Theo said.

"Yeah, the bestest." I nodded sleepily, losing the fight with a wave of tiredness.

I woke up with a start. It was dark and I was moving. Where was I? Turning my head, I realised Theo was carrying me through a hallway.

"Need to go home," I mumbled.

"Shhh, it's late. I'll put you in the spare room." His voice rumbled through his chest next to my ear.

"I'm too heavy."

Theo chuckled throatily. "Elves don't weigh anything. Go back to sleep."

He set me down on a cloud, and I was gone.

The bright light made me burrow further into the covers and against the warm heat source at my back. The warm heat source? Then it flooded back to me, and I froze, realising I shouldn't be grinding against Theo, who was snug against my butt. His unique scent surrounded me. I wiggled, and he grunted, bucking his hard cock against me. A flurry of heat rushed through me, chased by a wave of self-consciousness.

Theo's heavy arm trapped me. It was suddenly too hot as I realised I still had his hoodie on.

"Morning." His voice was thick with sleep, and it made me shiver.

"Hi," I squeaked.

He froze and then disentangled himself.

Oh my gosh! Had I really cried all over him and then fallen asleep last night? I couldn't get any more unprofessional. *Except maybe grinding against his dick this morning?* a nasty voice in my mind said. I resisted retreating under the covers.

"I'm sorry. I only meant to settle you back to sleep," he said gruffly.

I blinked around. The room had floor-to-ceiling windows and was decorated in dusky pinks and greys.

"This is my sister's room when she stays. I put you to bed here, but you woke up screaming, and I came to calm you down, but I fell asleep. Sorry."

The regret in his voice made me wince.

What was I doing here? What were we doing, kissing, sofa snuggling, and pouring my heart out? This man was my client, not my boyfriend.

"I'm so sorry you had to deal with that last night." Rolling over, I couldn't meet his eyes. "I'll get up and head home."

"It's fine," Theo said gruffly, and the bed dipped. "Take your time."

My gaze flicked up in time to see his gorgeous arse in boxer shorts heading out the door. *Holy hot butts.* The view temporarily robbed me of my ability to move.

Blinking rapidly, I sat up and took stock. My phone was plugged into a generic charger on the side of the bed. Isaac had texted me a picture of Bowser back home at my parents' house, awake and looking fine.

He captioned it. **"Tell Zoe I'm okay."**

My relief over Bowser did nothing for my general mortification. There was an ensuite, and I bolted inside. I winced at my reflection. My short hair stuck up at odd angles, and my face was still puffy. Cleaning up as best I could without a hair or toothbrush, I pulled up Theo's hood and crept out into the main room.

"Sit," Theo barked as I attempted to skirt the main room, thinking I could call a rideshare in the lobby.

The island had various breakfast foods on it, and I eased myself onto a stool and grabbed a pastry. Tearing it up, I stuffed it in my mouth, not tasting anything but the bitter taste of mortification. Theo seemed to be faring no better, slamming things around as he scrambled eggs.

My stomach was full of rocks by the time he sat opposite me with his plate, avoiding my eyes.

I wanted to say something to cut the tension, but each time I opened my mouth, I closed it again.

"Thank you. I'll call a cab." I moved to put my plate in the dishwasher, but Theo swooped over and grabbed it.

"There's a car outside," Theo muttered, still not looking at me.

Shame burned up the back of my throat as I said goodbye.

Staring out at the city as I headed home, the heavy weight on my chest didn't lessen. What the heck was I doing, crossing all these lines with this man?

14

The physical therapist, Garth, packed up his travelling bag of torture devices as I hobbled back behind my desk. Sweat lined my brow, and my spine burned like he had jabbed me with hot pokers.

"Ice and painkillers for the next few days. It wouldn't be so bad if you'd kept up with the exercises," Garth said with a look that said I told you so.

I grunted and waited for the sadist to fuck off out of my office. He always was a pain in the ass, but he was the best PT in New York, and he travelled to his clients for the right price. Which just meant I'd paid a premium price for the torture he called therapy.

"I'll see you next week."

I grunted again, easing myself into the padded chair with a wince.

I'd seen my spinal surgeon, and after a scan, he told me my metal-work was fine, but my back was stiff, and the reason for my pain was a lack of physical therapy. Garth was a smug bastard when I rang him.

A knock at the door sounded just before the elf slipped inside. It seemed she no longer needed to wait for me to reply.

"Are you okay?" Her eyes filled with concern, raking over me.

It was the most attention I'd had from her all week. Aside from the necessary, she'd avoided spending time alone with me since we shared a bed. My feelings were a mess. When I woke that day, the dread in my gut about letting another woman close was overwhelming, and her reaction seemed to confirm I had made the right call. However, this distance between us didn't feel right anymore.

"Garth is well trained in the art of pain."

"I thought he was a physiotherapist?"

"It's the same thing," I growled.

She clicked her tongue, rounding my desk. "Have you taken some painkillers?"

"I was working up to it."

"What else did he say to help recovery?"

"Ice packs."

"Do you have any?"

"Sure, I've got a stash under my desk," I grumbled.

The pain was making me even more irritable than usual.

Zoe huffed. "Where is your medicine?"

I indicated the bottom drawer, and she pulled out the bottles of anti-inflammatory and Tylenol.

"Take your usual dose, and I'll find ice packs."

"You don't need to."

"I do. You need to be better for your interview this afternoon."

I groaned – that damn interview. I hoped to impress the elf with my progress when I agreed to it, but scheduling it after torture master Garth seemed like a disaster waiting to happen.

I leaned forward, stretching my spine out, waiting for the meds to kick in. I hated this pain. It reminded me how fucking broken I was. My back was eighty while the rest of my body was in its thirties. Garth had banned me from working out in the gym to ensure I remained focused on the exercise he'd given me. Where would I blow off all this pent-up lust the elf stoked in me?

The door clicked open, but I didn't bother to look up. I jolted painfully as something cold connected with my lower back.

"Where does it hurt worse?" Zoe asked.

"Where did you get ice packs? Is your magic bag part freezer? Is that why it's so large?"

She smacked my arm, her eyes twinkling. "No, I'm resourceful."

"You sure are *something*," I muttered.

She smacked my arm lightly again. I blew out a breath; between the ice and the drugs, the pain was receding.

"Let's go over some points for this interview." Zoe perched on the edge of my desk, and I fought the urge to drag her into my lap.

She grilled me and discussed possible questions. I listened to her advice and studied the curve of her full lips.

"Did you even hear what I said?" She frowned.

"Yes."

"What did I say?"

I scanned my memories, pushing away the thought of her lips and where they really should be.

"Discussing challenges that sports stars face after an injury?"

"We talked about that five minutes ago." She pouted.

"I'm ready. I know how to handle the media."

"Yes, but you have a hot temper, and they know the buttons to push. It's better to over-prepare. Remember the saying, 'Fail to prepare—'"

"Prepare to fail," I finished the saying, rolling my eyes.

"Exactly." She stood and took the ice away. "I'll go get the subs for lunch. You need to change."

She headed for the door, and I shamelessly checked out her ass before it disappeared. Groaning, I got up and headed into my office bathroom to get clean and change.

⁘ ⸎⸎⸎ ⁘

The reporter looked around twelve. His spotty face gave away that he was barely out of his teens. I ground my back teeth in annoyance.

The magazine had sent their work experience boy. Either that or they were hazing a new recruit.

Zoe smiled at him and fussed over his seat. He gave her a smarmy smile, and I didn't miss the gaze he sent down her body. I sat up straighter despite the ache that shot through my back. As if this man-child could handle a woman like Zoe.

"Would you like a drink?"

"Sure, I'd love a latte."

Hell, if I was going to let her get him a drink while he stared at her ass. That was for my eyes.

"Sit," I barked at her and pressed the intercom. "We need a latte, a water, and..." I looked at Zoe expectantly.

"Chamomile tea."

I relayed that to Carol and clicked off the intercom.

"Mr Kelly, may I call you Theo?"

"No."

Zoe cleared her throat and widened her eyes. I sighed, swallowing my ire.

"Sure."

The chump smiled like a douche. "I'm Zane. Do you mind if I record this?" He waved his battered smartphone, setting it up next to his tablet without waiting for my reply.

Aggravation licked up my spine, but I took a deep breath and blew it out slowly. I caught Zoe's eye, and she rewarded me with a dazzling smile. Something warm moved through my chest at the idea that she was proud of me. For that reason alone, I got through his first round of inane questions. Her continued approving glances became a mini high to chase.

The chump shifted in his seat, and I sensed a change of pace coming.

"How do you feel about how things played out in the press about your relationship with Savannah Cristo?"

Zoe shifted in her own seat as if she sensed my irritation rising again. I knew he'd bring this shit up.

"How should someone feel about their personal life being printed for other people's amusement?" I barely managed to keep the growl from my voice.

He was no doubt aware of my punching one of his peers.

"I'd imagine it was hard. Emotions ran high." The douche licked his lips, leaning forward.

"I'd imagine you're right. That chapter of my life is over."

"Mr Kelly supports a number of charities, including one improving access to sport for children with disabilities." Zoe spoke up, interrupting the chump.

I blinked over at her, shocked she knew about that as it wasn't common knowledge.

"Sure," the chump muttered, but my gaze was locked on the elf, who made a shooing motion with her hand, trying to get me to focus back on the reporter.

"Did you have anger management?" he asked back on his bullshit.

I shook my head in irritation that he was even here.

"It's public record that I was required to do that," I deadpanned.

"I think you have plenty for your interview, Zane." Zoe stood and drew his annoyed glance.

No one threw that look at my elf on my watch. Standing abruptly, I towered over him.

"Indeed. I have a meeting I need to prepare for shortly. I'm grateful the Gazette could spare one of their *top people* for my interview." My looming forced him to scramble and grab his things.

"I still had a few questions."

"Then you should have asked those first," I growled.

"Eat the frog and all that," Zoe said briskly, helping him gather things as I crowded him toward the door, blocking her from touching him and sticking out my hand.

"It was a pleasure." I crushed his tiny, smooth hand below my rough palm.

He whimpered and nodded, backing away.

"T-thank you."

I grinned at him. It was the same look I used to give the opposing team at the start of a game – it promised pain. He shrank visibly into himself and scampered away.

"You did well," Zoe said as the door clicked closed.

"Little douche."

She hummed. "They certainly sent their youngest-looking reporter. I almost asked if his mama knew he was out."

I laughed, and Zoe blinked like I'd grown a second head.

"Smiling suits you, Theo." She smiled back, our gazes magnetising. "I'm proud of you."

Words hung unsaid between us, and I flexed my fingers at my sides, suppressing the desire to snatch her up and kiss her silly at my victory.

Fuck, she was gorgeous.

"Let's see what the little fucker prints before we celebrate," I said, breaking our moment to prevent me from grabbing her.

"True." Zoe laughed and gathered her things.

I watched her tempting ass disappear out of my door and swiped a hand down my face. I was so fucked.

15

itting the street outside Steel Ventures, I moved into the crowd on the sidewalk towards the deli for an early lunch. It was the most I'd seen of New York this week. Working with George was a whirlwind, and there was so much to organise for the Christmas party that my sightseeing was on a hiatus.

I loved event planning, though, and I didn't often get to do something so big. Bringing Christmas to the Scrooge-ified employees of Steel Ventures New York was a spectacular turn of events I couldn't miss out on.

I checked the time and saw a text from Mum with a picture of her and Bowser. My heart leapt seeing his cute, jowly face. I missed my boy. He had to return to the vet because his tummy was still playing up. It made me nervous, and my desire to go home to him was strong.

Elle's name had a message icon, and my pulse leapt as I read it.

Elle: SOS, call me

I rang her number, calculating the time in the UK to be late afternoon.

"I can't speak for long," Elle whispered.

She must be at work.

"You sent an SOS!" I hissed, sidestepping someone who'd stopped for their dog.

"I've got a date tomorrow night. A date with a man in red."

"You've found your Santa? Is it the guy from the forum?"

"Yes." Her breath hitched.

"Do you know him?"

"We've chatted online."

"Where are you going? Are you safe?"

I didn't want Elle's endless quest to fulfil this fantasy to endanger her.

"Totally safe," she said breezily.

"Seriously, you don't always think these things through."

Worry tightened my throat at the idea of her meeting some weirdo who had agreed to dress up as Santa for her. She wasn't known for her careful planning.

"I know, which is why I've been safe this time."

"Okay. Are you going to tell me? Drop a pin? Send me a pic of him?"

She giggled. "What are you going to do from the States?"

"I don't know, send Isaac."

Elle snorted. "Not an appropriate mission for the hot fuzz."

"Don't ever call my brother *the hot fuzz* again." I wrinkled my nose.

"Well, I don't need the police. I just..."

"You're nervous."

"Maybe."

"Your idiot ex was wrong about what he said to you. I'm glad you've found someone you can trust and are safe."

"I know," she breathed. "Anyway, gotta go. I miss you. Come home soon." She clicked off the call.

I stared at the blank screen in my hand as I joined the deli queue and prayed Elle would be safe. That girl needed a full-time keeper.

Back in Carol's office, the twinkling of the fairy lights on her tree made me smile. Everywhere looked much warmer and more inviting;

even Ben and Taylor had been impressed when I'd caught up with them in the breakroom. Dismantling the bullying culture would be more challenging, but Theo said he had a plan, so I'd leave the specifics to him.

I glanced at his door, and my thoughts drifted to our time together. Since waking up grinding on him, I'd kept things professional. He'd been working hard on his image, and I had to swallow my tongue from telling him how proud I was for handling the dipshit reporter the Gazette sent to interview him. It warmed my chest to see him putting in the effort. He looked so much tidier in his new tailored clothes with his beard trimmed.

It confused me, though, because my feelings for him had deepened despite the distance I had put up. Between that and Bowser, it felt like a good idea to wrap this styling process up as soon as possible.

"Abe!" Carol exclaimed, pulling my focus from the Christmas party to-do list.

A guy with sandy hair and an easy smile walked in and greeted her with a hug. He turned, and I noticed his eyes were the exact shade and shape of Theo's. He was tall like Theo but slimmer built.

"This must be the miracle worker my sister can't stop talking about." He grinned and came over to shake my hand.

"You must be Theo's brother."

"The one and only." He looked around the room with an impressed smirk on his lips. "I must say, I've never seen this place looking so festive. Theo usually complains about the state of my house in the lead up to Christmas. You must have some magic dust you've sprinkled on his brain." His eyes twinkled.

"It was just simple blackmail."

Abe roared with laughter, and Theo appeared in his doorway.

"Abe?"

"Bro." Abe bounded over and pulled Theo into a hug.

I noticed Theo wince, and so did Abe.

"You okay?"

"Garth came yesterday."

"Ah, the sadist himself. I didn't know you started seeing him again."

Theo grunted and looked at me. Abe followed his gaze and smothered a grin.

They disappeared inside his office, and Carol sat back, fanning herself.

"That boy is so good-looking."

I giggled, and she shot me a look.

"Not a word," she said sharply, and I saluted her.

I didn't want to get on the wrong side of Carol. Sweet, she may be, but I'd witnessed her fierce side. If she wanted to ogle a married man who was half her age, I wasn't going to stop her.

I threw myself into the last parts of planning, excited to kick off this festive party with a bang, trying not to feel sad that my time here was nearly over.

16

You're a fucking moron. Don't let that tramp Savannah ruin more than she already has. Abe's words rang in my ears.

He appeared midweek at the office, charming everyone in sight as usual, and I'd enjoyed seeing him and Zoe laughing together. He'd asked some pointed questions and then demanded we go out for dinner. He wasted no time in ripping me a new asshole after I told him I'd freaked out when I woke up with Zoe nestled against me. The connection I'd felt growing between us still scared me. What if I was wrong again? But I let those doubts lead me, and I'd been paying the price all week.

Abe pointed out Zoe was nothing like Savannah and went to pains to reiterate everything she'd helped me with. My weak argument about it being her job to improve me didn't sound believable even to my ears.

But she'd barely spared me a second glance this week aside from bringing the ice pack after Garth's visit. I had become increasingly desperate to spend time with her, and I missed our evening sparring the most. It felt like I was detoxing, which was a ridiculous concept. I'd done the anger management homework to impress her and the interview with the wet-behind-the-ears journalist without losing my temper.

Restlessness clawed at me as I dressed for the office Christmas party. It was the last place I wanted to go, but Zoe was leaving next week. The desire to snatch her up and keep her warred with my fear of letting someone in again. I respected her wishes to remain professional for her career, and we'd been lucky with the press as they didn't get a good shot of her face after the game, but once we weren't working together anymore, she would be gone. As I walked down the corridor, Christmas music blared ahead of me. Fucking hell, how did the elf get me to agree to such a thing?

I scanned the room, packed with employees in sparkly attire that ranged from classy to tacky and everything in between. The Christmas music made my skin itch, but I nodded to Carol, who waved from near the buffet table.

The party announcement caused a buzz around the office, and I could see its effect on the staff. They were much happier and, to my chagrin, more productive despite it being so close to Christmas. Concerningly, Vanessa was avoiding me. A mystery illness had prevented her from attending the last board meeting. She worked from home all week and didn't appear to be here.

"Fashionably late to his own party." Abe's voice had me whipping around.

Dressed impeccably, with a style I could never pull off, even with Zoe's help, he passed me a glass of champagne and sidled closer.

"I didn't think you'd come."

"I wouldn't miss this for the world. My big brother, the scrooge, at his first Christmas party. George says you are making a speech." He smirked, and I scowled at him.

"Fuck off."

"Teddy!"

"Jesus Christ," I muttered.

The last thing I needed was for my employees to hear my sister's pet name for me. How did my siblings both end up here?

"Pipsqueak." I greeted her one-armed as she jumped up to kiss my cheek.

"It looks so festive," she cooed and I rolled my eyes.

She produced a platter of mini sliders and my stomach growled.

"I made your favourites." She held them out, and I picked up two, stuffing one straight in my mouth as I scanned the room for the elf.

"She's gone to get changed." George elbowed me, and I turned to see both my siblings grinning at me.

"Best go mingle." Abe winked at me, and he and George snickered like children.

I sighed and pasted a smile on my face. The first employee I encountered shrank away from me, and I decided there was perhaps too many teeth for the expression to look friendly. Carol came and rescued me by towing me around to say hello to various people.

I fell into an easy conversation about the latest Giants game with a guy from accounting, which turned into a small crowd. My gaze snagged on the doorway and my breath caught in my chest. Zoe wore a black dress that hugged her curves, and the discussion about plays died on my lips. She spotted me and headed over.

"Theo, it's time for your speech." She smiled up at me and led me over to the microphone set up near the buffet table.

"You look great in that suit. Juan is a master." She adjusted my suit jacket.

I grunted. "You look stunning."

"Thank you." She blushed. "Have you got your speech?"

"I'll just wing it."

She smiled, then tapped the mic, motioning to the DJ. The music died away, and everyone turned our way. She stepped back, leaving me facing my workforce.

I cleared my throat.

"Thank you all for coming to the first Steel Ventures holiday party. I'll keep this brief because the bar is free and the food is excellent." I paused for the cheers, glancing at Zoe who beamed at me. "Thank you to Zoe, my consultant, and George from Delicious Catering for pulling the party together in a short time frame. And thank you to all of you for all your hard work throughout the year. Here's to another productive year. Happy holidays." I raised the glass Zoe handed me.

The room erupted in applause, far more than my short speech warranted. Perhaps Zoe was onto something about my popularity if I chose to lean into it.

The music restarted and I lost sight of the elf. George and Abe descended, giving me an excuse to quit mingling. The dancing grew more elaborate as the alcohol flowed.

"Er, Teddy. I think Zoe needs saving from one of your drunk employees."

I stiffened. "Where?"

She pointed over the far corner, and spots flashed in my vision. Zoe was wedged in next to a Christmas tree as she leaned away from a guy from marketing. I stormed over and clamped a hand on his shoulder.

"Leave," I snarled, breathing like a bull.

He winced under my tight grip. "Yes, of course, Mr Kelly."

He scampered off, and I backed my little elf into the corner.

She blinked up at me. "Theo, that was rude."

"Fuck rude. Were you lining up your next date?" I bit out, my gut churning.

"Why does it matter?" Her chin tipped up.

"Or was *he* your first date?"

My head was a mess; I'd never felt this strongly about anyone.

Zoe stared at me for a minute. "My first date was with a pizza and a Christmas movie. My competition date was crying and a pizza, after which I fell asleep on my client's couch and woke up in bed with his morning wood poking me. Things got weird, reminding me that I'd been unprofessional. So, no. I won't look for any more dates while I'm in New York."

Damn elf.

"And when you get home?" I demanded, as thoughts of her dating British schmucks crowded my half-deranged mind.

"I don't know what Elle has lined up, but I think she's started seeing someone, so maybe I'll have a dating reprieve until New Year." She shrugged.

"No dates."

You're mine.

The insane words formed on my lips, but I forced them down, scrambling for something else.

"Let me take you out this weekend. On a proper date."

Her smile faltered. "I don't think so, Theo. It didn't go well last time."

"I was an ass."

"Maybe, but I've moved my flight forward."

I reeled back as if she'd struck me.

"Why?"

"You don't need me anymore. Barking at drunk employees notwithstanding, look at the progress you've made." She gestured at my outfit. "Your interview, looking after your back, this party and speech. I'm so proud of you. You just need to clean up your management team and keep up the good work." She glanced away briefly. "Plus, Bowser isn't right since he ate those cookies. The vet has put him on a special diet and I need to be back for him."

Something swelled and simultaneously died inside me. She couldn't go so soon. I needed more time.

"When do you leave?"

"Tomorrow night," she whispered.

Something snapped inside me.

"Come with me." I grabbed her hand and led her out of the party room.

"Where are we going?"

I didn't answer her, leading her back to my office as if the hounds of hell were on our heels. I slammed the door closed and marched her over to my desk, crashing heavily into my seat and yanking her forward to straddle my lap. She stumbled, and her black dress rode high on her luscious thighs as she landed on me.

"Tell me to stop," I growled, my voice thick with lust but aware I was being a beast.

"I should," she panted, her pupils blown wide.

"You're leaving. I've graduated. You aren't my consultant anymore."

Her gaze dropped to my lips.

"Don't look at me like that. I need to know if you want this as much as me. That you feel this chemistry."

Something warred behind her eyes as her chest heaved. With a herculean effort, I released my grip on her, holding my hands out to the side, letting her choose.

She smoothed a hand down my shirt, making my muscles jump beneath her touch. "Don't stop," she whispered.

My control snapped, and I leaned down and slammed my lips on hers. I plundered her mouth, and our tongues slid against each other. The pent-up frustration and lust inside me threatened to explode. I was lost.

I yanked her dress up and over her head, and my gaze caught on her luscious curves encased in red underwear. Flicking open the lacy bra clasp, I cupped her ample breasts in my hands.

Motherfucker, they were so soft. I dipped my head, hunching over as I sucked a nipple into my mouth. My heart pounded out of my chest.

She let out a soft cry, and I wanted to hear more. Lavishing her breasts with my tongue, she squirmed on top of me, rubbing her pussy over my rock-hard dick.

She fumbled with the buttons, opening my shirt and smoothing her hands over my torso.

Too far gone to care, I tore her lacy panties on each side and ripped them away, running my hands over her soft skin. She felt like heaven. Dipping to her pussy, I found it drenched.

"Is this all for me?" I growled and she whimpered.

I returned to her breasts, nipping a trail up to her neck where I sucked at the skin, intent on marking her.

Dimly I realised I was being a beast, but her hands fumbled with my belt, and she opened the fly, drawing my dick out. My eyes rolled back at the feel of her small hand on my engorged flesh.

"That's it. Feel how hard I am for you."

She moaned again, and need thundered through me. I fumbled in my pocket for my wallet. I had to be inside her. This wasn't ideal for our first time. I wanted to worship her instead of giving her a dirty office fuck, but neither of us could stop now. We had denied this for too long. I ripped the packet open and rolled on the condom.

"Get up here and ride me."

She kissed me again and grabbed my cock, guiding me to her entrance. I groaned, my hands roaming over the lush curves. Perfection.

As she slid down on me, I swore that I heard angels weeping. Heavenly didn't come close. I gripped the arm of the chair to stop myself from climaxing like an inexperienced youngster.

"Theo," she said my name like a prayer, letting out breathy moans that drove me wild.

"Hold on." I stood up, my back protesting at the sudden lunging movement, and I laid her out on the desk.

"Hold on, my Christmas menace. This is going to be hard and fast."

She gazed up at me, panting, her lids hooded. I pulled back and slammed back into her, making her tits jiggle. Hoisting one of her legs high, I realised she still had her heels on, which was hot as fuck.

Relentlessly I plunged into her warm pussy, and the desk scraped along the floor as her moans rose. Sounds of flesh hitting flesh and the feel of her against me filled my mind as I fucked her in the way I'd needed to since we met. The pressure at the base of my spine was like a fist. I leaned over, finding her clit with my fingers and circled it as I thrust, almost mindless to the pleasure that boiled up inside me.

"Come with me," I commanded, and her channel rippled around me.

Huffing with the force of holding off my release, she finally cried out, and the tight gloving of my cock made the orgasm rip through me like a hurricane. I came longer and harder than I ever had. My movements slowed as I slumped over her. She encircled me with her arms and legs as we caught our breath.

Still inside her, I picked her up, hardly registering the twinge in my back this time, and took her over to my couch. She was relaxed and boneless, and her arms were shaky. I knew I needed to take off the condom, but I didn't want to leave her body. She draped over me, and the weight and warmth of her against me felt right.

"Say I can visit you in the UK?"

She lifted her head, looking ruffled up. "I... okay."

We snuggled as my cock softened, and regrettably, I pulled out of her and went to my bathroom. When I returned, she'd pulled my abandoned suit jacket around her.

The chilled air forced us to get dressed, although I smirked at the disgruntled look on her face when she picked up her shredded panties.

"I'll keep those." Snagging them off her, I stuffed them in my back pocket. "I'll buy you some more," I said, fully intending to trash future pairs.

Once dressed, I grabbed her to sit back on my lap, not wanting to be apart from her just yet.

"You said it yourself: our work together is over. It's okay if you don't want to visit the UK," she whispered as she doodled patterns on my forearm.

I knew what she was saying. She was giving me an out. But I was done denying this, especially now I'd been inside her. I wouldn't let her go easily. Hell, I'd already regretted letting her leave my house last weekend and hated the distance between us this week.

"I want to. I want to see where this goes. If you do?"

It was a hard admission for me. Letting myself be vulnerable with another person – with another woman. But Zoe was nothing like Savannah.

"When do you want to come over?" she asked, looking up at me.

I did some mental math about when I could feasibly be there. I couldn't let my mom down on Christmas day as much as I hated seeing the old man.

"The day after Christmas?"

She blinked at me, surprised. "Boxing Day? It's a big family day in my house. You are welcome, but you'll be mobbed."

"Will your brother handcuff me and read me my rights for defiling his sister?"

She giggled. "No defiling needed, but I might handcuff you instead."

"Bring it the fuck on."

17

Zoe

The guy next to me on the flight glanced at me as I clutched "Bowser Junior" to my chest. I'm sure I looked as lovesick as I felt. The dog in my arms was an almost identical replica of Bowser. I don't know how Theo got it made so quickly, but he gave it to me before he dropped me off at the airport this evening. My breathing slowed as I thought about spending the night in his arms.

It was a good job I'd packed before the Christmas party; otherwise, I'd have missed the flight, just like half the party I'd organised because the boss was blowing my mind on his desk, then cuddling me on the couch. I expected a wave of guilt, but as unprofessional as it was to have sex with my client in his office, I couldn't find it in me to be sorry. I only felt misery at heading thousands of miles away from him. My heart screamed at me to jump off the plane and rush back to Theo in some Hallmark moment.

I didn't know what shifted between us – aside from the earth with that orgasm – but things were different. Like we'd both silently agreed to stop pretending we weren't attracted to each other. But had it come too late? He'd become distant before, so maybe having sex with me had sealed our fate. What did I expect our fate to be, though? We lived on different continents.

I stroked the fur on Bowser Junior. How had I fallen for the grumpy, angry CEO I was supposed to be consulting? Deep down, I knew why: because there was more to Theo than his scowls.

The flight was a sleepless blur. My parents met me at the airport, and Mum instantly realised something was wrong, but she knew better than to mention it in front of Dad.

I'd arranged to stay with them until after Boxing Day. I had a perfectly good flat but wanted to spend as much time with Bowser as possible.

My boy came bounding over when I got back to my childhood home. I dropped to the floor, letting the tears flow for him and some for me.

"How's my boy?" I rubbed his belly, using the baby voice I reserved just for him. "I've missed you so much. You were naughty eating those cookies."

He rolled over and gave me a mournful look.

"The vet said it's gut rot from the stomach pumping. Been farting like a fucker," Dad groused.

"The vet actually said *gut rot*?" I asked sceptically.

"He used some fancy term, but it amounts to the same thing. Expensive fucking gut rot if you ask me. Bloody, mutt."

"Don't you listen to him. Who's my boy?" I rubbed his ears, and his tongue lolled out.

"I think he was just pining for you," Mum said, handing me a cup of tea.

Usually, I saw Bowser a few times a week when I popped into Mum and Dad's. My work schedule often had me travelling, so as much as I'd love to have him full-time, his living here meant my brothers could all drop in to see him, too. We all loved the big furball.

Mum followed me upstairs under the guise of getting me extra towels. Bowser at her heels.

"What's up?" she asked, closing the door.

I glanced about my childhood bedroom. I'd changed it over the years, but it remained a comfortable, familiar place. Bowser hopped up on the bed and settled on the end. I sat next to him and sipped the tea. Heck, I missed a brew while in the States. I loved coffee, but nothing beat a cuppa.

"I fell for him."

There wasn't any point trying to trick my mum. She was like a bloodhound.

"I thought as much." She plopped down beside me and pulled me against her. Her familiar perfume comforted me. "The way you talked about him was different. Isaac said he offered to fly you home when Bowser got sick."

"It's unprofessional."

My mum snorted. "Attraction doesn't care about what is supposedly professional or not. Neither of you are attached, and if you only worked with him briefly, what does it matter for the future?"

She spoke a lot of sense, and the sadness I felt leaving Theo behind told me more about how deep things had grown between us despite not knowing each other long.

"He's the grumpiest man I know." I sighed.

"Grumpier than your father?" Mum asked, and we both giggled.

"Maybe not," I said. "But underneath, Theo is much more."

Mum sighed. "The same with your father. That's why we fall for the cranky ones."

"We live so far apart."

"He's rich, right?"

I jabbed her in the side. "That's not the point."

She laughed. "I know it's not, but it makes a difference. Money moves things. Including people across oceans. New York isn't that far if you have the means to travel regularly."

I stared at her, shocked.

"Don't look at me like that. The last thing I want is for you to disappear to another continent, but I'd love to see you happy."

"I am happy."

"You are a cheerful person, sweetheart. You always were. My smiley, happy girl, but I'd love to see you with someone who cares for you."

"You mean you'd like some more grandbabies."

"I've got enough grandbabies to tide me over," she said too quickly to be believed.

A wry smile curved her lips. "Have you invited him here?"

I rolled my eyes. She was relentless.

"I invited him on Boxing Day."

She leapt up. "Oh, my goodness. How long will he stay? What does he eat? Does he like turkey? Oh dear. There is so much to do."

"He's not the King, Mum." But I knew it was pointless because Mum took her hosting seriously. "He might not even come," I said, picking at the bedcover.

"Of course he will. I need to check my lists." She disappeared in a flurry of movement.

My phone buzzed.

> Theozilla: Are you home?

> Me: Just got to my parents.

> Theozilla: Get some rest, elf. X

I stared at the single x like it might tell me everything I needed to know. I flopped back on the bed. My body didn't know what time it was. Eventually, I drifted off, daring to hope I might see him on Boxing Day.

18

Zoe

"Rise and shine, sleepyhead!" Elle's voice boomed in my ears.

I rolled over, gripping my pillow, groaning. Someone ripped the covers away, and cold air rushed over me.

"Ngh." I blindly grasped for the edge, but as the blurry room came into view, I realised Elle had pulled it off entirely and bundled it in her arms.

"You're back!" She screeched before jumping on me, the cover cushioning the blow of her body.

"Elle," I groaned.

"Why aren't you up?"

"You said ten." I rubbed my eyes.

"I was too excited to wait."

I glanced at the clock, and it said eight.

"Who let you in?"

"Your mum, of course. She gave me a cup of her hot chocolate, but even that couldn't keep me away. I can't believe you are back!" She began jumping up and down, making the bed sag and jolting me about.

"Missed you, Ellebear." I grinned.

"Missed you more," she sang, collapsing back against the head-board. "Oh, oh, I bought you something to wear today."

She scrambled off the bed, and I sat up, shaking off the last of my sleepiness. It wasn't easy as I hadn't fallen asleep until five. *Damn, jet lag.*

Elle unzipped a clothes bag, revealing a black dress covered in holly leaf patterns.

"I saw it on the rack at work. It's your size and everything. It's like Christmas fate."

I chuckled. Elle could access all the latest fashion at her work and could borrow samples, although I'm not sure they always got returned.

"It's gorgeous, Elle, but I'm going to need a truckload of coffee to make it to brunch."

"We can just chill here if you prefer?"

I blinked at her. "Who are you, and what have you done with my bestie?"

She giggled. "We don't have to go out. I'm just happy to see you."

"Okay." I'd accept that excuse for now, but I'd get to the bottom of it later.

Elle always took the chance to go out. Our plans were brunch and then shopping, so it was suspicious she would blow those off to chill around my parent's house, especially after she'd secured me a new dress.

"Come on, your mum said she would bring bacon sandwiches out to the snug if we wanted to stay here. We can still go shopping later."

Elle grabbed my hand and attempted to haul me out of bed. I looked at her, noticing the dark bags under her eyes.

"Are you okay?"

"Of course," she said with an overly sunny smile.

I grabbed my snowman onesie from the drawer and pulled it on. The snug was a garden room that Mum made into a comfy reading spot for when she or I needed to escape the testosterone in the house growing up. Dad upgraded it a few years ago by adding a mini log burner and extra bookshelves. Elle and I spent plenty of time between university terms, chilling and plotting our lives.

Once settled on the enormous outdoor bean bags covered in fluffy blankets, my mum brought us coffee and bacon sandwiches. The fire was already roaring, and Bowser had claimed the spot on the rug in front of it and had curled up.

"Spill it," I said.

"No, you first. Your mum told me you were upset."

I gave her a look that said she wasn't getting away that easily.

"Theo and I slept together at the office party."

Elle squealed, and I rolled my eyes.

"Was it as good as you imagined?"

"Yes," I breathed.

Despite it being a frantic shag over his desk, it was the best sex I'd ever had. Probably from the culmination of weeks of built-up forbidden lust.

"I want details."

I gave her a cliff notes version, and she fanned herself.

"I know you left out half the good stuff, but oh boy, that sounded fun. Maybe I could try that with..." she tailed off, grimacing.

"With who?"

She picked at the blanket on her legs. "You know I told you I was meeting a guy."

"The guy who dressed up as Santa?"

"What if there were two guys?" She squinted her eyes at me.

"You found two Santas?"

"Yeah."

"When did you meet the other guy?"

"The same night."

"What?" I sat upright.

"Ihadsexwithtwoguys," she said in a rush, colour tinting her cheeks.

I stared at her, my mouth gaping open.

"But... what about Santa?" I asked dumbly, trying to catch up.

"They were both Santa?"

She said it like a question and cringed slightly at the end. I realised she was expecting me to criticise her.

"Did you enjoy it?"

"Oh fuck, yes."

The tension burst, and we fell about laughing.

"Oh my god, Elle, you don't do things by halves."

"Nope, I'm a BOGOF girl here." She grinned, and we fell into hysterics again.

Oh my god!

My sides hurt as I tried to bring myself under control. Jeez, I'd missed this crazy girl. Eventually, we calmed down, and my stomach muscles ached.

"So why the long face? Shouldn't you be grinning like the cat that got the Christmas cream?" I giggled, and Elle threw a cushion at me.

"That was the worst joke ever."

"There is more where that came from, *Santa Banger.*"

She threw another cushion, but then her face fell.

"It's just that one of the guys—"

"Santa one or Santa two?" I interrupted.

She scowled at me and then cracked a grin. "Santa two."

"What about him? Did he not have a full sack for you?"

"That's disgusting."

I was already laughing again, the lack of sleep fuelling my hysteria.

"I'm serious. I like him, but..."

I sat up, wiping my tears and storing Santa's jokes for another time.

"But what?"

"But I thought he wanted to see me again. He even said, but then he rang me and told me it couldn't happen. And I guess it disappointed me more than I thought it would."

I reach out for her hand, understanding that feeling.

"I'm sorry, hun."

She blew out a breath. "Yeah."

"There's always the dating app?" I cringed internally, no longer wanting to go on a double date.

"I think I'll leave it. I fulfilled my biggest fantasy, and it was beyond anything I could have imagined, but I can't face dating douchebags again. I'm just going to focus on work for now." The corners of her mouth turned down.

I pulled her in for a hug.

"So I'm guessing it's the same for you and your hunky CEO. A bite of the forbidden fruit, and now you're sad too. We can eat chocolate together."

I cleared my throat, suddenly feeling bad that my issue differed from hers.

She stared at me, realisation dawning. "Theo wants more?"

I shrugged. "I invited him on Boxing Day, but he might not come. If he does, my family will probably put him off."

Elle studied me. "He'd be stupid not to come."

"Well, Santa Two is stupid, too."

She rolled her eyes. "Come on then, tell me about the New York fashions."

I was glad of the change of subject from heavier topics as we chatted about New York and caught up about Juan.

By the time Elle left, I felt better but exhausted. We never went shopping, so we rescheduled for later in the week. Now I was home earlier than planned, we had time to do more of our usual pre-Christmas rituals.

Much later, I lay in bed staring at the ceiling, attempting to count sheep. I mistakenly napped at five; now it was two am, and I was still very alert.

Theozilla: Are you still awake?

Me: Yes, jet lag is messing with me

Theozilla: I've got a cure for that 😉

Me: Oh yeah?

Theozilla flashed on the screen with an incoming video call. I glanced at the closed door and answered him.

"There you are." Theo's growly voice filled the line, and I shifted on the bed.

"Hi."

His handsome face filled the screen, and I realised he was sitting on the couch in his apartment.

"I've hardly got any work done today. I can't sit at my desk without remembering you stretched across it like a buffet. I gave up eventually and came home."

Heat shot through me at the reminder.

"It's the weekend. Why were you in the office?"

"There's still work to be done, but there's a streak on my desk from your pretty ass, and it kept distracting me."

"Why didn't you wipe it away?" I choked on a laugh.

"I'm going to frame it." He grinned wickedly. "What are you wearing?"

"A T-shirt. I'm in bed trying to sleep."

"Take it off," he commanded.

"Theo." I shivered.

"I told you I'd get you to sleep. Take it off."

A throb started in my centre as I pulled off my top. My large breasts spilt free, and Theo groaned.

"Fuck me, I've not had enough time with those beauties. Pull on those nipples for me, elf."

"I think you should take your top off too." My voice came out husky as I leaned into his game.

He swept his T-shirt off with one hand in the hot guy way, and his bronzed chest came into view, making my mouth dry.

"Show me my pussy."

"Your pussy?"

"Yes, mine. You let me have you over my desk, so it belongs to me now." His gravelly voice lit me up.

Excitement whipped through me. I'd never had phone sex before.

I panned the camera down to my underwear, which was an

uninviting pale pink, but Theo groaned, and his screen showed him palming his hard cock through his boxers.

"Take those pink panties off," he barked.

I wiggled and shimmied them down my thighs, tossing a self-conscious glance at my bedroom door.

"Show me how you like that pretty clit petted."

I slid my hand down to my centre as he pulled out his stiff cock and gripped it tightly. The sight caused a moan to slip free.

"That's it. Fuck, I miss those sounds."

I started circling my clit embarrassed by how wet I already was.

"Fuck I wish I was there. I'd kiss that pretty pussy."

It reminded me of the dirty dream. I'd had only days after meeting him.

"I dreamt of that once."

"You did, did you, dirty girl? Me too. You are the star of my dreams."

His hand shuttled along his cock, and I whimpered as my finger moved faster, my orgasm building.

"That's it, dirty elf. I can't wait until you are writhing under me again. I'm going to wreck you."

His filthy words spiralled lust through me and pushed me over the edge with a moan. Pleasure filled me, wracking my body with shudders as I bit down on my lip to stop from making too much noise.

"Yes," he groaned as I watched him spill over his hand, ropes of white cum painting his abs as he shuddered.

"Oh my god." I pulled the camera back up, noting my red face and wild eyes.

"That will help us both sleep, you naughty elf."

Indeed, I felt wrung out after that massive release.

"Night, night, elf. Christmas can't come fast enough."

"Night, night, Theo."

I cut the call and pulled my clothes back on. My limbs were now relaxed and heavy, ready for sleep.

19

*I*f my balls were blue before, they were the colour of the midnight sky now that Zoe was thousands of miles away. I averted my eyes from the spot where I'd fucked her over this very desk, and my eyes fell on Bob. The small Christmas tree cheerfully twinkled at me, mocking the lack of my elf. It was a cruel twist that she left this sad plastic tree for me. Instead of tossing it in the trash, I dutifully brought it back here after dropping her at the airport and set it up in my office.

It was Christmas Eve, and I could hardly muster enthusiasm for going home tomorrow. My flight to the UK was the only light at the end of the tunnel.

A knock at my door made me frown. Everyone had gone home for Christmas a few days ago, and Carol was already with her family upstate.

"Come in."

Vanessa pushed the door open and smiled at me.

"Hello, Theo. I figured I'd come and say Merry Christmas now that you're all for the season." She eyed Bob's sad, spindly limbs.

"I thought everyone had finished."

"That bug wiped me out. I had things to finish off before heading to the Hamptons."

I resisted the urge to roll my eyes. Vanessa's family was from old money, and I'd heard about the family beachfront property several times from her and her uncle.

"No rest for the wicked." I spread my hands, pretending that statement wasn't aimed at her.

My plan of catching her and her cronies bullying employees was on hold due to her mystery illness because she'd been out of the building for nearly two weeks.

Her long legs carried her to the window, and she stared at the city below us. I waited for her to say something, but she remained silent.

"I'm impressed with what the image consultant managed to do," she said, finally turning back and trailing her hand over one of my plants. "The staff seem happier since you let them put up a few plastic decorations." Her laugh was tinny and fake.

Why hadn't I seen her for what she was? She'd always been as efficient and reliable as my MD, and I never suspected her of being capable of what Zoe had unearthed.

"The stupid season means more to people than I realised," I muttered, turning away and powering down my laptop.

She laughed again. "I could have told you that, silly. But I do like the new look."

I grunted, and she tittered again.

Her condescending tone grated on my nerves, but I couldn't let her know I was on to her if I wanted my plan to work.

"I guess the image consultant will be off pandering to some new badly dressed CEO after Christmas."

My fist tightened at the idea of my elf styling other people who weren't me, but I didn't reply to her jibe about my image.

"I'll be off. Have a great time with your family." She finger-waved at me, disappearing back out the door.

I snatched up Bob, stuffing him into my briefcase, his fairy lights battery pack and tinsel included. Blowing out a frustrated breath, I focused on the flight at the crack of dawn the day after Christmas.

The doorbell echoed into our family home, and I pulled my jacket around me against the bitter wind as I waited on the stoop. The door opened, and my mom's short hair stuck up in all directions, and food smears decorated her apron.

"Darling." She kissed my cheek, and her perfume surrounded me.

"Close the door, for fuck's sake," my dad bellowed, and my mom jumped to close the door as she ushered me inside.

"You look well." She smiled at me, but her eyes looked tired. "I'm just getting the turkey out to rest. I hope you are up for carving."

In other words, my father wouldn't lift his eyes from the game screens to bother with the roast. The job had been mine since I was old enough to hold a knife.

I handed her the wine and some presents and followed her into the kitchen.

Dad was sprawled on his recliner, a beer in one hand and eyes glued to the screen as I passed the main room.

I rolled my sleeves up in the kitchen and began helping Mom trim up the dinner.

"Hey, Teddy." George bounced in and hugged my middle.

I placed a kiss on the top of her head.

"I wish Zoe could have come," she said.

"Who is Zoe?" Mom looked up from the counter.

I shot my sister a look that promised retribution, but she just stuck her tongue out.

"My girlfriend," I ground out.

"Oh, he's finally admitting it," George singsonged.

"I didn't know you had a girlfriend." My mom's face fell.

"It's very new."

"He's been pretending it's not a thing." George danced out of the way of my towel snap. "She's the one who got him to have the Christmas party."

"I thought he was helping you out." Mom frowned.

"Yeah, he was, but he was scoring points with his English rose." George made kissy faces,

"She's not American?"

"No, Mom. She's gone back to the UK, but I'm flying out tomorrow to see her."

"Really?" Mom looked more engaged in this conversation than she had in years. "That's great, darling, but will it work long distance?"

I sighed. "I don't know yet. It's early days."

"Well, I'd like to meet her."

"Meet who?" My father arrived in the kitchen, turning on the double screens above the dinner table and not looking at anyone.

"No one," I snapped just as Mom said, "Theo's girlfriend."

Dad scoffed, and George winced, grabbing some potatoes to take to the table.

"She another actress?" he asked.

"No."

Luckily, Dad got engrossed in deciding which sports channel to put on the second screen.

We set the table and filled it with food, and it wasn't until I began carving the turkey that there was a lull in the games, and my dad's focus fell back on me.

"What is this one's name then?"

"Zoe," I said through gritted teeth.

Dad shovelled food onto his plate, taking the first carved meat and grabbing the gravy. My eyes shot to Mom, who watched him with sad eyes.

Dinner was painfully quiet, like always, until Dad got onto his third beer, which probably meant it was number eight of the day.

"That could have been you." He pointed at the screen as a player walked off the field.

"Not today, Dad."

"Why not? Christmas is the only day I see your sorry face. You threw it all away. Not man enough to shake off that injury. Took the easy way out," he ranted, waving his can.

I ground my back teeth as the tired rhetoric beat against my skull.

"Micheal, please, let's just have a nice day," my mom implored.

"We could have had a nice day if he'd kept playing," Dad shouted.

"Don't fucking shout at her," I growled at him.

"I'll do whatever I like in my own fucking house, you washed-up piece of shit."

I laughed derisively. "Washed up? That's a laugh coming from you."

Dad stood from the table, swaying. "You got something to say, boy?"

"Please," my mom wailed, and tears slipped down her cheeks.

"I've had enough of this." I stood, throwing down my napkin. "Mom, if you want to leave this fucker, then there's always space at mine."

Mom gasped, and George pulled her away from the table as Dad roared, coming at me like a battering ram. But he was drunk and out of shape, and I dodged him, delivering a swift kick to his ass, sending him sprawling.

"Sober yourself up, you useless waste of air," I spat at him, finally done with his bullshit.

"Get out of my fucking house. I never want to see you again!" he roared, slipping in some fallen mash and crashing back to the floor.

"Come with me," I implored George and Mom, but they shook their heads, backing toward the kitchen.

"Get out," my dad roared again, launching a serving bowl across the room.

It crashed against the wall and left a dent. My pulse thundered in my ears. I didn't want to leave my mom and sister with him in this state.

"Please go," Mom said, tears falling freely.

My gut clenched, knowing I'd ruined today for her. I headed for the door and slumped into my car, breathing heavily. Unable to leave until I knew they were okay, I rang George. Dad had never been violent to anyone except me and Abe. He might be a bastard, but he'd never raised his hand to a woman.

"Are you okay?" I asked her when she answered.

"Yeah." George sighed.

"What's happening?"

"Dad's gone to the TV room, and I'm helping Mom clear up the mess."

"I'm sorry." I leaned my head against the steering wheel, shame filling me.

"Me too, but it's not your fault. Dad shouldn't speak to you like that."

"Is Mom okay?"

"Yeah, she'll be fine."

"I didn't mean to ruin Christmas."

"Well, it's on brand; you do hate it." She half chuckled. "I'll stay with Mom today."

"Why does she stay with him?" I asked, frustrated.

"No idea."

We said goodbye, and reluctantly, I drove away, twitchy from the leftover adrenaline. I hoped tomorrow would go better with Zoe's family, or I would definitely end up in her brother's handcuffs.

20

Smoothing my Christmas dress down, I paced the kitchen. It was Boxing Day evening, and despite my reservations over whether Theo would come, he was due to arrive anytime. I could barely believe it. Butterflies swarmed in my stomach.

"For Pete's sake, drink some wine and calm down, woman." David thrust a glass of bubbles into my hand.

"I am calm." I worried my lip.

"Tell that to the floor tiles you've killed walking over them five zillion times." David turned back to the cocktails he was making on the island.

I slumped onto a bar stool and watched him cut a fancy pattern into a piece of honeydew melon. My stomach dipped at the thought of seeing Theo again in the flesh. It had been a week, and somehow, I'd become a love-sick teen.

Not only had Theo texted and called me daily, but a massive box of Liquorice Allsorts and a box of high-end lingerie arrived for Christmas. He insisted I wear the lacy teddy in my room yesterday evening, and the memory of our video call still heated my blood.

"I knew you'd be good for that grumpy man. The *CEO Whisperer* strikes again, but I didn't think you'd fall for him," David said as he added various spirits to the shaker.

"I haven't," I lied and fiddled with my glass.

He coughed. "*Bullshit.*"

I threw a glacé cherry at him, and he squealed and jumped away.

"Kris! Your sister is trying to defile my outfit. It's sibling bullying." His voice went whiny, and my brother appeared in the doorway, rolling his eyes.

David was loud, gregarious and had no filter – the exact opposite of my quiet, creative artist brother. Kris was seven years older than me but still younger than Isaac and Dylan. Jay and I were Mum's bonus twins.

A pang hit me at another Christmas without Jay. Kris moved closer, reading my mood like the empath he was and curled an arm around my back, kissing the side of my head. I blinked back some tears, knowing he felt it, too. My grief mingled with my week of missing Theo. I could hardly compare the two, but they compounded each other.

"Right, you need one of these." David bustled over and swapped my untouched bubbles out for a bright orange cocktail with melon and umbrellas hanging out of it. It made me smile because it was less Christmas and more beach party.

Drinking the fruity and *very* alcoholic cocktail, I relaxed against Kris as he joked with David. I missed bantering with Theo and working at Steel Ventures with him. Although he'd made a lot of progress, things felt unfinished. I told David as much.

"I'm sure you could go back. I doubt the big guy would complain." He winked.

Would he, though?

Bowser came lopping in, looking for food.

"This furball is certainly fine now." David leaned down to scratch under Bowser's chin.

He wasn't wrong. Bowser had been perfectly okay since I got back, and I'd enjoyed days of snuggles and walks with him.

The doorbell rang, and I went rigid. Bowser began barking like mad. I lunged for him and wrestled to keep him in the kitchen.

David grinned at me and took Bowser's collar. "Better get the door before Isaac."

My eldest brother told me he "wanted a word with Theo when he arrived," which was code for threatening him, possibly with a gun.

I skated around the corner in the hall, and my eyes met Theo's over Isaac's shoulders. Heat flared to life in Theo's eyes before they flashed back to my eldest brother, who was crushing his hand and speaking in a low voice.

"Let go of him," I said unsuccessfully, trying to muscle past Isaac.

In a slick movement, one I assumed he had used more than once on the football field, Theo twisted past Isaac and picked me up.

"Hello, elf," he said and kissed me.

The world fell away as he pressed me into the coats hanging in the hall, and his familiar aftershave filled my lungs. The door slammed shut, and we broke apart. Isaac grumbled something about *Americans* under his breath.

"Listen. I've got a little sister. I get it," Theo said to my brother, who didn't look appeased.

Bowser rushed ahead of David, barking and jumping up at Theo's legs.

"Hello, boy." Theo returned me to my feet and crouched, rubbing Bowser behind the ears.

The little attention whore lapped it up and tried to give Theo more kisses than me.

"Mr Kelly," David crooned, appearing with a colourful cocktail adorned with Christmas candy canes. "Something sweet." He handed Theo the drink as he stood back up.

"Call me Theo, David. It's Christmas." He eyed the cocktail with a raised brow.

"And the Grinch's heart grew three times the size," David singsonged before wandering off back up the corridor.

Isaac shook his head and returned to the living room. I smothered a laugh into the sleeve of Theo's camel-coloured wool coat, which was one that I'd picked for him.

"I told you it was nuts here on Boxing Day."

He pulled me close and kissed my hair. "Bring it on."

"I'm so glad you're here."

"Me too." His arms squeezed around me.

"Come on, there's more crazy."

The introductions were a flurry of activity. My mum gushed over Theo, and my dad managed a smile. Dylan, my second eldest brother, started quizzing Theo about American football while my two nephews, Dylan's kids, tried to persuade him into a game of catch. We sat on the sofa, and the side that touched him felt electrified. I caught him watching me more than once.

We ate food and played games. My dad and Isaac were both surly types, so Theo didn't stick out as the quietest. He seemed pretty relaxed, considering he only knew me and David.

Eventually, everyone drifted home. Dylan took his kids first, and Kris herded a very drunk David towards the door. I got up to say goodbye. David leaned in, and his alcohol-soaked breath fanned my face.

"Make sure you get a good length of that dick tonight, girl," he whisper-shouted.

"Oh my gosh, take him home." I handed him off to my brother.

My parents went to bed shortly after, leaving Theo and me alone in the living room. The fire crackled in the now quiet room.

"You survived." I laughed.

"I avoided your brother's police cuffs but was promised some others." Theo wiggled his eyebrows at me.

I shivered as heat threaded through me. "You better come up to my room and get your present."

21

We headed upstairs, and I wished I'd taken him back to my flat. Thankfully, years ago, when my mum discovered one of the twins she carried was a girl, she made my dad build an extension over the garage so I'd have my own space. Mind you, Jay often ended up in here on the pullout. Even as teenagers, we didn't want to be too far away from each other.

Theo stepped inside and looked around.

"Is this the famous Elle?" he asked, pointing to an old picture of us on holiday in Greece.

"Yes," I said, shivering despite the warmth in the room.

"Did she go on the dating app dates alone?" He levelled me with an intense look.

"Did I tell you about the app?"

"You told Juan. It drove me nuts to think you might go on dates after you left me."

"What, even back then? You'd barely grunted at me."

"Grunting is a form of affection." His arms came around me as I giggled.

"I've missed you." I stared up at him.

"Me too, elf. The office has been too quiet."

I laced my fingers through his hair as he leaned down. "I bet you didn't think you'd be saying that a few weeks ago."

"You blew into my life, and as much as I tried to deny it, David's right, you made this Christmas Grinch's heart grow."

My own pounded in my chest at his words.

"So this Grinch doesn't want to steal Christmas anymore?"

"I'll settle for stealing your virtue."

I threw back my head and giggled. "You already did that."

"Practice makes perfect." He picked me up by my thighs and dumped me down on the bed. He came down over me, kissing me thoroughly.

"Wait, I have your present," I said, breaking the kiss.

He pulled back, and I scrambled to grab a little package off the nightstand. He ripped it open without looking at the label, and cuffs covered in fluffy red fur fell out.

"Do you expect these to hold me?"

"No, I just thought they'd look funny."

He rolled me over until I sprawled across his chest. "Cuff me." He held out his wrists.

I licked my lips. He made an inviting picture, staring up at me with heavy-lidded eyes. Desire pooled inside me.

"Let's get this off first." I pushed up his henley, exposing his muscular chest.

Last time, I didn't have long to explore, and my hands tingled with the need to do so. I couldn't resist kissing a trail across his pecs and sucking a nipple into my mouth.

He bucked his hard length against me and groaned.

"Tease."

Chuckling, I pulled his top off and then his trousers and socks, leaving him in his boxers. The fluffy cuffs barely closed around his wrists.

"Now for your second present." I stood up, climbing off him and admiring the picture he made with miles of skin on display, supposedly at my mercy. A late Christmas present gift half-unwrapped on my bed.

I loosened the halter top on my dress and unzipped it, letting it pool on the floor. My underwear was red and sheer, trimmed with white fluffy piping and bows. Theo's eyes went wide, and his cock jerked in his boxers.

My skin prickled at the attention. I was a curvy girl and comfortable in my skin, but seeing the reaction I drew from Theo was a boost of confidence that I could get used to.

"You cuffed me, then showed me a feast. Do you want to torture me?" Theo growled. "Get over here."

I shook my head and crept up his body, my skin brushing over his. Snaking a hand inside his boxers, I palmed his cock. It jerked in my hand as I pulled it out. Theo groaned as I lowered my mouth and took him inside. His salty flavour burst across my tongue. I worked him in and out of my mouth, growing wetter at the sounds falling from his mouth. His cuffed hands landed in my hair, and he gently lifted me off.

"Enough. I need to be inside you."

"Maybe I should tie you up, too." I grinned at him.

He glared at me, and I laughed. Truth be told, I wanted him inside me, too. A week was too long. I grabbed a condom from my drawer and rolled it on slowly as my own body throbbed with desire.

Hovering back over him, I felt how wet and eager I was as I sank down. The feeling of him inside me lit me up, and my eyes flickered shut. He was too far away to kiss in this position, but it felt incredible as I rose and fell, losing myself in the sensation. Frustrated noises erupted from Theo, and a snap told me the cuffs were history. He grabbed me and twisted us, flattening me onto the bed. The intense look in his eyes drove me wild, and he plunged into me with desperation. The weight of him and the exquisite drag of his cock inside me built me into a frenzy.

"I have something to ask you." He panted as he found my clit and circled.

My head felt fuzzy with pleasure. "Ask me after, I'm so close."

He picked up the pace and then halted. My eyes flew to his in frustration.

"I need an answer before you come."

"You're bribing me with my orgasm." I squirmed and tried to grind on the base of his cock.

"Call it an incentive." He collared my throat and pinned my hands.

Holy hell, that was hot. I clenched around him.

"My elf enjoys being restrained." He grinned like he'd won a prize while I unsuccessfully tried to lift my hips against him, desperate for him to move.

"Return to New York with me. See where this takes us." His eyes burned into mine.

"I can't believe you are asking me while you're inside me."

"Best leverage I have." He ground against me, and pleasure soared through me.

"Come on, elf. Agree. You can have this cock every day."

A furious laugh burst out of me. "I can't believe you said that."

"What? It's a selling point." He grinned.

He rocked into me, and the pressure to come was a clawing animal inside me. He released my throat to circle my clit again, and I rushed toward the edge of an orgasm, but at the last second, he stopped again.

"Motherfudger! I'm going to kill you," I growled.

"How about saying yes?"

Before I could agree, he brought me back to the edge twice, torturing me. My skin was on fire, and a fine layer of sweat covered me as I simmered like a pot ready to boil over. Our bodies slid together, and I panted on the verge of crying as I raced toward the edge again.

"Yes. Yes," I cried. "I'll come with you."

"Stay at my apartment."

"Yes, anything." My head spun as I agreed.

"Come for me now." He slammed back into me and pinched my clit.

My vision whited, and the rush of sensation stormed through me. "Theo!"

He let out a roar and continued to thrust until he shuddered to completion. His weight came down, crushing me as I wrapped my arms and legs around him, gripping him tightly. I gasped for air, and he rolled us onto the side. My limbs didn't work, and we lay panting for a few minutes. Everything inside me glowed like a Christmas tree.

"I can't believe you bribed me with an orgasm," I said when my brain came back online.

"I needed any advantage I could get."

"I would have agreed," I murmured, nestling into his chest, the sound of his heartbeat in my ear. "I need to be back early in the new year, but I want to spend time until then with you."

His arms tightened around me before he disentangled to deal with the condom. When he returned to bed, he gathered me onto his chest again, and I snuggled into his embrace. My body felt floaty and light.

Would this thing between us work out? I didn't know, but I wanted to find out.

22

Zoe

Warmth surrounded me, and a heavy weight pressed on my waist. Blinking my eyes open, I giggled at the sight of Theo's huge feet hanging off the end of my bed. The rest of him was firmly curled around me. His unique scent was everywhere, as was his heat, and my forehead rested an inch from the wall.

A groan issued from the giant gripping me. "Your bed is tiny. I think I only slept for ten minutes."

I shivered at his voice, which was extra growly this morning.

"You are just oversized."

"Everywhere," he rumbled, his large hand spanning my waist and dipping his fingers into the front of my sleep shorts.

He ground his morning wood against my butt. My core tingled with a delicious ache, reminding me why I'd slipped the shorts on. Theo was an insatiable beast, and we'd eventually fallen into bed, exhausted sometime in the early hours. I had tugged on my sleep shorts and top as a small barrier.

That small barrier was falling prey to Theo as he snagged them down. Tingles tracked across my skin where he pulled them off, and the movement jolted me dangerously close to the wall. My top went next, and a desire fizzled through me as he nuzzled and kissed my neck, his rough beard adding a layer of sensation.

"Are you sore?" He rolled me over and took my mouth in a kiss before I could decide how to answer.

His finger ran through my folds, and I arched into his touch as he circled my clit, pleasure curling through me. I winced as he pushed a finger inside me and pulled back from our kiss.

"You are sore." He narrowed his eyes.

"It's fine." I threaded my fingers through his messy hair and chased his lips.

"I've got just the thing." He lifted off me and moved down my body,

He grinned wickedly, and my heart danced at how handsome he was.

"Theo! I need a shower." I tried to scramble away as I realised what he was doing, but he pinned my arms and dropped his weight between my thighs.

"Don't interrupt my breakfast." He dived down to my pussy, and I squealed.

His hands pinned my thighs, and mine drove automatically into his hair. He wasted no time in focusing his warm, insistent tongue on a single spot, and I arched up into him as pleasure burst from my centre.

He groaned, and it sent shock waves through me as he circled and hassled my clit. I threw my head back, surrendering to the sensation completely. He shifted his hold on my leg, and I gasped at the stinging pinch to my nipple as his huge hand cupped my left breast. I moaned, and he chuckled against me.

"I love the sounds you make," he said darkly, but before I could answer, he resumed his task.

Pleasure built inside me as he forced me toward an orgasm with precision. I tightened my grip on his hair as my hips bucked to meet his talented tongue. His fingers brushed my entrance, and despite the brief sting of discomfort, it added to my building climax. He didn't push inside me. He just stared up at me with a wicked look in his eyes as I squirmed, trying to get him where I needed him.

"Come on my tongue." He sucked on my clit, hassling the bud with his teeth, and I was lost.

The orgasm washed over me, curling my toes and pulling a gasp from my lips.

Theo sat back on his knees with a satisfied smirk as he surveyed me. All the strength left my limbs, and I didn't even pretend not to be wrecked by him. His body was a work of art, and I got to ogle it unashamedly in the morning sunlight.

"I'm not that sore." I eyed the way his black boxers strained.

"No."

I propped myself up on my arms, which felt like noodles. "Let me take care of that for you then." I licked my lips.

He smirked at me. "As tempting as staying in bed all day sounds, if we are going to do that, we can relocate to the penthouse suite in the hotel I booked as the bed is human-sized."

"My bed is human-sized!" I threw a pillow at him as he got off the bed.

"It's sized for an elf. And my back can't take another night on it."

My outrage softened as my eye fell on the considerable scar along his spine. I scrambled upright.

"Let me give you a massage."

I jumped off the bed, and his gaze trailed heatedly down my naked body.

"You strike a hard bargain," he grunted.

"On the bed." I pointed back to where we'd been.

"Bossy," he muttered.

I opened the drawer next to my bed to grab a pot of baby oil, and my eyes fell on a present I'd forgotten. I grabbed a robe and pulled it on, snatching up the gift.

"I forgot your other present." I held it out to him.

Theo turned and propped his head on his elbow. "Another one?"

I'd given him a set of engraved cuff links at some point in the night between rounds of sex.

"It's just small."

"Is it more handcuffs because we can take those to the hotel?" He raised his eyebrows.

"I haven't agreed to go to your hotel yet, Mister."

Theo took the present from me, tearing off the wrapping paper. Meanwhile, I had to tear my eyes off his body to watch for his reaction. His brow creased, and I giggled.

"It's a football," I said.

"I can see that. It's a bit small."

"It's a stress ball."

His big mitt squeezed down on the foam ball that was probably less than a quarter of the size of a normal one.

"Your old one looks a bit worn."

"I burst the last one dealing with a little elfish menace at my office."

"Tough times." I rolled my eyes.

He grinned at me and it lit up his face. I loved that I'd finally broken through his grumpy façade. I grabbed the football back off him and placed it on the cabinet.

"You won't need that right now. I'm going to relax you."

Theo laid back down, and I squirted oil along his back.

"Holy shit, that's cold." He tensed.

"Don't be a baby," I teased him.

Straddling him to smooth the oil across his broad back, I realised my mistake as my pussy kissed the swell of his buttocks. He groaned as I settled on top of him and began to work the knots from his muscles.

A soft snore caught my attention, and I chuckled. Poor guy was probably knackered. I knew he'd work up to Christmas, then flew here just afterwards, and we'd not got much sleep last night.

I headed for the shower and pulled on some clothes, intending to grab breakfast for us both.

In the kitchen, I skidded to a halt as David's familiar face smirked at me over a coffee mug. His hip was propped against the counter next to my mum, who was chopping salad. The day after Boxing Day in our house was a feast of cold meat leftovers and salad accompanied by terrible Christmas TV. But it was rare to see my brother-in-law reappear before midday.

"What are you doing here so early?" I asked him.

"I want to snap a picture of a former grumpy CEO in the wild. It's my Christmas present to Liam."

I snorted. "I guess buying for a boss who has everything is tricky."

"Exactly, so piss-taking leverage over his business partner is a priceless gift money can't buy." David's eye twinkled with mischief.

"You might be waiting a while because he's fallen asleep."

"Exhausted and covered in scratch marks, I'm sure." He smirked, and I shot him a "shut your trap" look, glancing at my mum's back.

He waved his hand. "Catherine's heard it all before. She's had kids."

Mum turned to him with a bag of carrots and a grin. "Stop winding her up and peel these for me."

David saluted her and started his task. It wasn't a secret he loved my mum as much as the rest of us. His own family abandoned him when he came out, not being able to see past their prejudices. My mum welcomed him with open arms when he and Kris started dating, and he'd been part of the family for so long it was hard to remember when he'd not been in our lives.

I grabbed a coffee and put some bread into the toaster, frowning as I realised I didn't know what Theo liked for breakfast. My stomach swooped at the idea that I had the opportunity to find out, which scared and excited me in equal measure.

"Put marmite on it," David urged, pointing a carrot toward the open cupboard I was procrastinating in front of. "See if he has good taste."

"Marmite is the devil's poo juice, David. You will never convince me otherwise."

David gasped, feigning outrage like we didn't have this debate each time I saw him. He was pro-devils poo juice, and I was firmly in camp avoid. Why anyone would use yeast to create something that looked like it leaked from a rusty old car was beyond me, let alone eat it. I grabbed the jam and hoped Theo liked it because the only alternative was peanut butter, which was also disgusting.

I filled a tray with fruit, toast with jam, and coffee, but I paused, realising I needed to tell Mum about my decision.

"Mum?"

She turned and wiped her hands off, and David immediately abandoned his task and leaned back against the counter, biting his latest carrot and darting his eyes between me and Mum.

I took a deep breath. "I've told Theo I'd return with him for a while. I'll need to be back in the New Year for clients, but..." I ended lamely on a shrug.

I don't know why I was nervous; I was a grown woman who could do what she liked. Mum's face split into a big smile, and David whooped. He dived past me, shouting that Kris owed him money because he'd won the bet.

"Did he bet I'd be going back with him?"

"Yes. He's a force of nature, that boy." Mum smiled fondly after David, who was doing a victory lap around the living room. "I'm glad for you, though."

"Do you think it's the right thing to do?"

"It's always a risk opening your heart to love."

"I don't think that's..." trailing off as my pulse spiked.

We weren't there yet, but I had come to care a hell of a lot for Theo.

"No, but that's where it could lead." She smiled. "He seems like a good man. I saw how he looked at you last night, and no distance could quite smother the racket you were making, so it's clear you get on well." She raised her eyebrows at me.

Mortification flooded as I choked on air.

Mum patted my arm. "I kept your dad busy, so I don't think he heard."

I gaped at her as horror clawed up my throat, trying to decide which was worse. The fact my mother overheard me having loud sex or the fact she distracted my father by having sex themselves. *I am dead.* A hole needed to open in the kitchen and swallow my deceased body.

Mum chuckled as I floundered with my mouth open.

"Go and take him some breakfast. Don't let him sleep too long, else that jet lag will bite him in that fine butt of his."

"Mum!" I hissed.

She just turned towards the fridge. "Like David said, I've had enough kids to know how it works."

Unsticking my feet, I grabbed the tray and left the kitchen with cheeks so red they could have heated a small village. David finger-waved at me, and I decided he was a bad influence on my sweet mother.

23

$\mathcal{L}_{ot}$

$\mathcal{B}$uttoning my coat up to my neck against the cold wind, I gripped Theo's hand as we exited the cab.

"Are you sure it's on this street?" He looked around with a frown.

"Come on, if we are staying in your fancy hotel, I'm taking you to the best Italian in Sheffield." I led him to the pedestrian-only part of the road.

It was busier than expected. He stood head and shoulder above the other people around us, and it was a bit like towing a barge.

We had said goodbye to my family earlier, and I'd given Bowser some extra fuss. He whined when he saw my suitcase. I told him I'd return in a week, but he tucked his tail and slunk off like I'd broken his heart. I had a client booked early in the new year, so my time in New York would be limited.

Thinking about that sobered my magical mood, but I wanted to enjoy my time with Theo and not let the practical issues about where we lived settle around me too firmly.

Theo stopped me before we reached the tiny restaurant I'd been aiming for.

"Are you okay?" He stared down at me, and I realised I'd been lost in thought.

"Just trying not to let reality creep into our perfect bubble."

He frowned.

"But let's take it a day at a time," I rushed on, not wanting to bring in heavy topics despite me being the one who brought the mood down. "Prepare to be astonished by the best calzone you've ever had."

I pointed to my favourite restaurant. It was pure luck that they had a cancellation when I rang, as not everywhere was open today.

"You realise I grew up in New York, right?"

"Yes, and New York isn't Italy."

"Neither is this place," Theo grumbled as I steered him through the door.

Inside was the size of a large living room, with cosy tables packed together. There was an area upstairs for larger groups where I'd attended birthday parties.

The waitress showed us to a window table. Fake snow frosted the glass, and multicoloured fairy lights twinkled around the frame. Theo settled his big body into the small chair, and I giggled.

"This better be good," he complained.

I smiled at his grumpy personality peeking out.

The waitress took our drinks order and brought over some complimentary garlic bread. Theo's eyebrows rose at his first bite.

"I told you it was good."

"Have you been to Italy?" he asked.

"Are you asking a trained stylist if she has ever been to Milan Fashion Week? The answer is hell, yes. Elle and I ate our weight in gelato."

"I need to meet this infamous Elle," Theo muttered, hoovering up the bread.

I frowned. Elle had been avoiding me since our heart-to-heart before Christmas. She was more hung up on this guy she met than she'd admitted.

"What's that frown for?"

"She's a character, but I think she's got guy trouble."

Theo grunted, and I fell silent, wondering how to help her – deciding to hunt her down when I got back next week. The thought of my extended time with Theo being over sent a spike of anxiety through me, but I shoved it away.

Theo's phone lit up with a message, and he scowled at the screen.

"Is everything okay?"

"Abe got excited when I told him you were coming back with me and got us all tickets to a New Year's Eve party. It's an exclusive venue, and George is going, but we don't have to if you don't feel like it. I know New Year is tough for you. But he's been blowing my phone up, asking if we're coming for the ball drop, and I need to let him know."

The backs of my eyes prickled at Theo's thoughtfulness. I'd told him I didn't celebrate New Year's Eve often because of Jay. Of course, my twin would've been mad at the years of parties I'd missed out on in his name. He'd be angry because he loved a good party, especially a family one.

The familiar heaviness in my chest returned when I thought of Jay, and I considered Theo's offer. The sounds of people eating around us filled my ears, and Theo didn't rush me. I thought about the offer and made spending it with Theo's siblings seem like something I could manage, but my fingers twitched with the need to text him.

"There's no pressure."

"It's not that it's... it's silly."

"Tell me." He took my hand across the table, and I appreciated the warmth of his touch.

I looked up into Theo's face, etched with concern for me. "Do you mind if I text him? I mean, I know it's not him. And it's so stupid."

Theo reached up and cupped my cheek. "Do what you need to."

I nodded, a lump in my throat, and pulled out my phone, pausing over the picture of Jay under his phone profile. The picture was taken that final Christmas we had together, and he looked so young – frozen in time.

The tears flowed freely as I texted, and the letters blurred.

Me: I'm sorry I've not been texting you as much as usual. The truth is I've met someone. Remember that big grumpy CEO that I went to work with in New York? Well, it's him. I know, I know. I don't date people I work for, but I broke all my rules for him, and we aren't working together anymore. But I'm going to New York for New Year, and although I know that means I won't visit you on New Year's Day, it wasn't until Theo (yes, that's his name) asked me to go out that I really thought about it. I never want to forget you, but I also know you'd be mad that I've not been out and celebrated since you left. So I think I'm going to go. Theo loves his brother and sister, and it reminds me of us. I'm not asking you for permission because you told me it's better to ask for forgiveness than permission. I'll still be thinking of you and visit when I return. I love you always. Miss you. Xxxx Tink.

There was every chance that I had ruined my make-up and looked like a panda, but I wiped the worst away from my eyes with the napkin. Theo remained silent, but his pained expression told me he'd struggled to stay seated. Luckily, no one else noticed my meltdown. They were all engaged in their own food.

The waitress appeared with our calzone, and Theo had to move his hand off my arm where it had rested while I wrote my message. The food smelled lovely, and it helped me pull myself back together.

"I'd love to go out with you," I said, my voice a little scratchy but strong.

Theo scowled at me as he searched my face, so I decided to lighten the mood.

"But I didn't pack anything fancy to wear."

"I'll take you shopping, but only if you are sure?"

"I'm sure about the shopping." I managed a smile.

Theo rolled his eyes. "I'm serious. We can shop either way."

"Jay would kick my butt for not going out," I said as a rogue tear slipped out. "And I'd like to spend time with your siblings."

I realised how lonely I had felt without my connection to my twin. I couldn't control my grief over his loss, and it still suffocated me at times. No one would ever replace him, but maybe I could build a new closeness with Theo. As we held hands in the dimly lit restaurant, it seemed like the start of something big.

"What are you thinking now?" Theo wiped the rogue tear from my cheek.

"That you make me happy."

His face split into a huge grin, and his handsomeness turned up by a factor of ten.

"You make me happy too, elf."

24

Zoe

*P*anic flooded me as I bolted upright, and a fluffy blanket fell to the floor. My heart pounded as I blinked, and Theo's penthouse appeared. Theo mumbled something and then groaned. The TV played on low in the background.

"Fuck, I fell asleep too." Theo winced as he stretched next to me.

We'd put the movie on to stop us from falling asleep, but I must have dropped off first because the blanket had not been around me earlier.

"How long did we sleep for?" I croaked.

Theo looked at his watch and groaned again. "Four hours. No wonder my back is killing me."

"Do you want a massage?"

"No, I need to do those exercises the PT left me. I haven't done anything since before Christmas." He stood up, wincing.

I searched for my phone, disoriented as to what time of the day it was. We flew in on the fancy-pants jet yesterday, effectively going back in time, but neither of us slept well last night. It wasn't uncommon for me to lose track of the days between Christmas and New Year's, but this seemed particularly bad.

My phone had a message from Mum with a picture of Bowser

looking morose in the corner of the kitchen. It was entitled. *Missing you.*

After checking the date and time, I was relieved it was still a few days before the New Year's Eve party. I needed to shop for a dress, but it was well into the evening.

I sighed. Instead of making the most of Theo's days off, we'd just snored through half the day on the couch. I headed to the kitchen for water to relieve the headache that threatened my temples. Jet lag was a bitch.

"I might just add these exercises to my workout. Do you want to come to the gym?" Theo asked as he returned from his room, pulling on a workout top and hiding his enticing body from me.

What was the question?

He smirked at me. "Maybe it might be too distracting watching me work out."

I threw a couch cushion at him.

"Go to your fancy gym. I'll do some callisthenics here and put something together for dinner."

Theo bit his lip, his gaze raking down me. "Now I want to stay."

I laughed and shooed him off. As much as I'd like to work out that way, it wouldn't help Theo's back or my need for carbs.

My workout was minimal, mainly to stretch and wake me up, although doing the familiar exercises with a view of New York was pretty special.

I gathered my ingredients for the simple meal, and as I stirred the pasta sauce, I was struck by a sense of satisfaction. Preparing a meal for someone was domesticated in a way I didn't expect to enjoy, as I'd never seen myself in this role. I loved my work, but being a career woman had grown lonely. The idea of sharing meals and sharing my life with Theo made my heart beat faster. Could we make this work long-term? Could I move to New York? My heart twinged at the distance from my family, Bowser, and even Elle.

The pasta boiled over, and I rushed to pull it off the hob, stuffing away those thoughts while I prepared our spaghetti bolognese.

New York still took my breath away, and standing on the street surrounded by skyscrapers reminded me of the enormity of the world around me. I pushed into the lobby of the building where Steel Ventures New York was housed and nodded to the doorman. My shopping bags jostled each other as I swiped my employee ID and headed for the lifts. I wasn't employed here anymore, but Theo had reactivated it so I could meet him. I'd been out searching for the perfect pair of shoes to go with my new dress. He'd groaned when I suggested we try a few more shops, so I told him I'd meet him here if he wanted to get some work done. The relief on his face made me giggle.

Most employees were still off for the holidays, and I got the impression Theo usually took advantage of the empty office. Except this year, he'd been spending his time with me.

He'd given me his credit card and told me to buy anything I wanted. A girl with more self-restraint might not have taken him up on that, but the four boxes of new shoe babies indicated I wasn't, in fact, that girl. But I was a seriously happy girl, and I'd bought him a gift to unwrap as a thank you.

The lift door opened, and my heels clicked along the empty corridor, which smelled of pine and cloves, thanks to my seasonal air fresheners. I paused at the door of Theo's office, dropping my bags down and loosening my coat before pushing the door.

Theo's office smelled like him, and I smiled as he looked up, his frown lines relaxing.

"Did you need a truck to bring back all the shoes?"

"I only bought a few pairs." I batted my eyelashes innocently.

He pushed back from the desk and motioned for me to step around it.

"The bank rang me to check for abnormal spending."

My stomach dropped.

"The shoes weren't that expensive." I bit my lip, my chest tightening.

"True, but apparently, it's very out of character for me."

"That I can believe." I glanced at him, trying to gauge if he was mad. "I can take them back."

"Oh no." He grabbed my waist and pulled me in front of him. "Because they rang me about a string of transactions close together, including one at 'Secret Obsessions.'"

His hand snaked inside my coat, and I shrugged it off my shoulders.

Relief shot through me that he didn't seem upset.

"What if that was the thief's transactions? I only went out to buy shoes." I feigned innocence as I loosened the tie on my new wrap dress.

"Hmm. You're saying a thief stole my card from you and bought lingerie?" His thumbs brushed the material of my dress apart, revealing the electric blue teddy and suspender set I had bought for him.

Theo groaned long and low in his throat as his hungry eyes roved all over me.

"Did you buy this for me, elf?" His growly voice made my toes curl.

I slipped the dress off my shoulders, enjoying his full attention. His gaze settled on where my boobs threatened to burst from their cups.

Secret Obsessions was a lingerie store that catered to all types of bodies, including short and curvy ones like mine. This piece made me feel like a goddess in the shop, but seeing Theo's reaction confirmed it. I rubbed my thighs together.

"I thought this might take the sting out of the shoe bill."

"If you return looking as sexy as this each time you go out to buy shoes, I'll send you daily and fill a whole closet."

I moaned, turned on by him and the image of an entire shoe room.

Heaven.

Theo grabbed my thighs and sat me on the desk, pressing my legs wide with his body. The surface was cool beneath me, and the contrast to his heated mouth that feathered kisses down my neck made me moan again.

"I ought to worship you, but seeing you like this is sending me feral."

He took my lips in a rough kiss.

I pulled back, shoving him backwards. "Sit in your chair, and I'll treat you."

He raised an eyebrow.

"It's clear your back is sore, and as much as I'd love you to bend me over your desk, I want you to enjoy this too."

Theo opened his mouth to argue, but I placed a finger at his lips and pointed to his chair. He sat down scowling, but it faded as I sank to my knees. The floor was smooth and cold beneath my knees as I reached out and unzipped his fly.

"You don't know how often I've fantasised about this." He squeezed the seat's arms with a tight-knuckled grip as I unfurled his big cock from his boxers.

It sprang free, and I darted forward to lick the precum from the head. Theo sank his fingers into my hair and gripped the short strands.

"You look fucking amazing on your knees."

A thrill shot through me at having him at my mercy. I used the little pump on his chair to bring him to a better height for me. Theo's knees rose next to my head, and I leaned forward again, taking him into my mouth.

"Goddamn." Theo hissed, his muscles tensing.

Arousal pulsed through me as I sucked his cock into my mouth. It drew a delicious groan from his chest, and he panted as I took him to the back of my throat. My eyes were watering as I fought my gag reflex.

"Up." He grabbed me under my arms and yanked me upwards.

I landed awkwardly in his lap, straddling him.

"I need to be inside you. Tell me you brought a condom?"

"I actually had an injection just before Christmas."

We'd established we were both clean on testing, and I got the shot, but it took seven days to be active and it was finally working.

Theo groaned low in his throat. "Fuck. I can't wait to feel you."

He moved the lacy material of the thong that made up the bottom of the teddy aside and plunged inside me. The stretch was intense, and I cried out.

Theo gripped my arse as he thrust up from beneath me, and I grabbed the back of his chair for leverage as I met him thrust for thrust. His beard rubbed against my skin as we kissed, and pleasure bloomed inside me. This was everything I wanted, and I willingly lost myself in the sensation of our bodies.

He slipped one hand down to my clit and circled it. The chair squeaked and creaked, but neither of us stopped. I threw my head back, surrendering to the sensations rushing through me.

"Look at me," Theo barked.

His face was screwed up in pleasure as he panted and fucked into me. The intense look in his eye undid me, and the feel of him inside me sent me over the edge. My inner walls clamped down on him as I came. He groaned long and low, thrusting into me, prolonging my orgasm until his cum filled me.

We both sagged back into the chair. The leather stuck to my sweat-covered skin, and the air conditioner blew warm air across my back. I snuggled against Theo's bristly chin, laying in the crook of his neck as we both caught our breath.

"I'm never going to be able to concentrate in here again," Theo said, rubbing patterns up my back.

I chuckled, thinking this was the second time we'd defiled his office, but I couldn't bring myself to feel bad about it.

"Let's get cleaned up and grab some takeout," he said, tapping my arse.

The live music was loud enough to enjoy but didn't interrupt the conversation. The venue was intimate and dimly lit. After a fantastic meal, we moved to the extensive rooftop and settled beneath outdoor heaters. Fireworks dotted the sky in the distance, and the city's lights twinkled.

"It's nearly ball drop," George said, bouncing up and down.

She wore a glittery black dress, and her hair was up elegantly. I was sure she had her eye on a guy from a group nearby, but she hadn't ditched us yet. Abe and his husband were snuggled in a loveseat, giggling like teenagers. They were fun to be around and didn't take themselves very seriously. They brought out Theo's more playful side, and as I watched him interact with his siblings, I felt like I could see how he would be with our children.

I inhaled sharply, and the champagne shot up my nose, causing me to cough and choke. Where the hell had that thought come from?

"I know it's hard to believe he was ever that much fun." Abe grinned.

I realised I'd miss what he said as Theo rubbed my back.

"Are you okay?" Theo asked.

"I'm fine. I just inhaled instead of swallowing," I croaked, my eyes watering.

"I can give you something else to swallow later," he whispered in my ear, and heat trickled through me as I smacked his arm.

"Oh, look at that. Do you remember what it was like just after we met?" Abe asked his husband, who grinned and whispered something, making Abe laugh.

Theo pulled me into his lap just as a projected clock lit up the wall on the far side of the rooftop. We counted down and cheered at the stroke of midnight. Everyone toasted the New Year as more fireworks lit the sky. Theo turned my face to his.

"Happy New Year, elf. I can't wait to see what this year brings."

My stomach fluttered with butterflies. I couldn't wait either. He took my lips in a drugging kiss, eventually resting his forehead against mine, his eyes glowing with so many promises.

"Happy New Year, Theo."

25

T

The first of January had never looked so optimistic. Enjoying New Year's Eve with my siblings and Zoe made me realise how much I'd been missing out on by hiding myself away.

Unfortunately, Zoe's leave date was looming within a few days, and I wanted to beg her to stay. She'd been quiet this morning. I knew her being here was keeping her from visiting her brother's memorial today, like her family did each new year. Even in death, he remained an essential part of her life, and watching her text him in the restaurant as tears streamed down her face made me want to toss the table over and pull her into my arms.

I topped our mugs with whipped cream and marshmallows and returned to the couch. Although my cooking abilities were limited, I could make a decent hot chocolate.

Zoe took the mug with a brief smile, but her eyes were distant.

"Jay would have been furious if I'd cancelled this trip. He would think the whole ritual of visiting his ashes was pointless, but now I'm here, I can't help feeling guilty. Like I've let him down." Her voice hitched. "If I changed my life significantly, would I forget about him?"

I slid my arm around her and pulled her flush to my side. It seemed like she was talking about more than just her brother, and it was on the tip of my tongue to ask her to stay with me, but I couldn't be selfish right now.

"Do you really think you could forget your twin?"

She shook her head.

"I didn't think so. Visiting a grave isn't the only way to remember him. Although, I'm sorry being here has stopped you from doing that."

"I made this decision. I even text him!" She half laughed, half hiccupped. "I thought about everything, even leaving Bowser, the big faker, again." She gave a strangled laugh. "And I came anyway. So I'll have to deal with this guilt. I'm sorry I'm such a Debbie Downer."

I kissed the top of her head. "You are allowed to grieve."

I wished I could take the burden from her. She was always so optimistic, the exact opposite of my cynical ass, that seeing her sad was tough.

"Tell me more stories about him, and we'll have our own type of memorial, complete with hot chocolate."

"Jay would have liked this drink. He loved marshmallows. Once, I dared him to fit an entire bag of them in his mouth. He'd nearly got them all in when Mum caught us and started shouting about choking risks and demanding he spit them out. Marshmallows got banned from the house, and he blamed me." Zoe chuckled. "He's the reason I still don't curse. We started because Mum didn't like swearing, so we used to make up new ones instead, but after he died I just kept it up. Cursing doesn't bother me but it's another way for me to remember him."

I'd noticed she didn't curse, but I hadn't thought to ask her why. The reason pulled at my chest and I stroked her hair as she continued to speak.

"He was such a daredevil and adrenaline junkie. That's why he loved that bike so much, because of the freedom it brought him." Tears tracked her cheeks again, and I cuddled her close as she told me more of her brother's antics.

He sounded like pure energy and chaos, but Zoe's stories made it clear that he loved her as much as she loved him, and I wished I'd met him.

Did I love her? My thoughts shuddered to a stop.

At one time, I thought I'd been in love with Savannah, but looking back, it was superficial. Things were so different with Zoe. I wanted to know everything about her. I wanted her close, and I wanted a future together.

"Are you okay?" Zoe asked.

I stared at her heart-shaped face, taking in all the detail. *Holy shit, I'd fallen in love with her.* Damn it, I couldn't just blurt that out while she was grieving. I scrambled around for a reason why my mouth was open like a fish.

"I don't know what I'd do if I lost Abe."

She put down her empty mug and cuddled me. "Tell me about you guys growing up."

I took a deep breath, gathering my shattered thoughts.

"Growing up in the Kelly house, everything was a competition. Dad pitted us against each other and ourselves, but he never drove a wedge between us. We've always been tight.

"Abe was much more academic than me, and despite being a year younger, he was easily at my level in school. Dad tried to bully him into football, but aside from watching it, he had no interest in playing. After a while, Dad focused on me. Abe helped me with my homework, and I kept Dad's attention off him and on football."

"That sounds like a tough environment to grow up in." Her fingers feather across the back of my hand.

"In some ways, it was, but in others, it gave me and Abe the work ethic we have. Even George, who got off lightly being the youngest and a girl, has carved out a successful catering business in a competitive city."

"You said you fought with your dad on Christmas Day?"

I'd told her briefly that we'd fallen out.

"I can't hate him for his heavy-handed methods because it shaped me, but I can't forgive him for disowning Abe. The way he did it and the timing were beyond cruel, and to watch him gradually turn my mom into a shell makes him irredeemable in my eyes."

"Does he hit your mom?" Zoe asked, her voice shaky.

"No, but there are other types of abuse. I took Mom away once to stay with me, but within a few days, she wanted to go back. It tore me up inside to hear her begging to return to that piece of shit. Dropping her back at our house was hard."

My palms burned as I tightened my fists to the point of pain.

"You can't help someone that doesn't want it," Zoe soothed.

"I know, but this Christmas was the last straw. I can't see him anymore, even if he lets me back into the house. That only leaves George to keep an eye out for Mom."

Zoe didn't speak; she just held me tightly as I thought over the clusterfuck that was my family. Eventually, I dragged my miserable thoughts around and returned to the present. However, the joy of having the girl I loved cuddled up in my arms was tainted because she was due to fly an ocean away from me in a few days.

"Tell me where you see yourself in ten years," I said.

Zoe coughed a startled laugh. "Did we just start a job interview?"

I tickled her, and she shrieked, wiggling about. I took the opportunity to pull her into my lap. She straddled me, and the ridiculous kitty-covered onesie stretched, distorting the designs. The cats wore Santa hats, and I scowled because I hadn't even noticed the annoying seasonal reference.

"Are you frowning at the cats, Theozilla?"

"I didn't realise every item of your clothing was Christmas-themed."

"You've only just realised you let a Christmas elf into your house?" She bopped my nose. "Well, Mr Scrooge, it's time to move on to the ghost of Christmas future."

"All the more reason to answer my question." I gripped her ass, enjoying the weight of her on my lap.

"I have a ten-year plan, thank you very much."

"Is it in that huge planner you drag around? Does it have stickers and hearts around it?" I teased.

Zoe threw back her head and laughed. "You are just jealous that your boring spreadsheets don't have pictures."

"A digital backup might be a good idea," I muttered.

Zoe rolled her eyes. "What about you? What's your ten-year plan? World domination? Theozilla scaling the Empire State Building and banging his fists?" She dissolved into hysterical giggles, and I watched her with a lightness in my chest.

"My ten-year plan went out the window when a Christmas elf crashed into my life," I murmured.

Zoe's eyes caught mine, and the giggles fell away.

"Tell me this thing between us is just as intense for you," I demanded.

My heart thumped as if it might beat out of my chest.

She swallowed. "I never would have crossed a line with a client if it wasn't. I broke my number one rule."

I rubbed the sides of her onesie, relieved I wasn't alone in this.

"But where does that leave us, Theo? We live on different continents."

I opened my mouth to ask her to move here, but I knew that was selfish. The logistics were mind-blowing for me to move to the UK, but I knew it wasn't simple for her either.

"I have access to the company jet," I pointed out.

"That's what my mum said."

"Glad to see Mrs Barnes is on board."

We fell into silence, a gulf of questions between us as if the ocean of distance had already opened. When would I even see her again? Then I remembered what I'd been meaning to ask her.

"Will you be my plus one at a wedding in the UK?"

"Of course, I'd love to."

I told her the date, and she scrambled to dig out that scruffy-over-stuffed planner and scribbled it in. Inevitably it had hearts around the entry.

"There's something else written that day," I said, pointing at the entry over her shoulder.

"The awards ceremony is that weekend."

"What awards ceremony?"

"I'm nominated for 'Best Image Consultant' in Stylz magazine awards. The dinner is that evening, but I don't know yet if I've been formally shortlisted. They said they would let us know early in the New Year."

"That's incredible. We can go to the wedding in the day and leave for your awards dinner."

"Really? But whose wedding is it?" She put the behemoth planner away, and I settled her back on my lap.

"Oscar, my business partner. David's other boss."

"But you can't miss that. Where is it?"

"Some dusty old manor house that belongs to Oscar's family. Searcroft Hall. Your awards dinner is more important."

"Oh my god, it'll be like *Downton Abbey*." Zoe bounced in excitement, then paused and cupped my face. "It means a lot that you would leave the wedding for me."

"I hate weddings and parties, so it's not a hardship, but there's no question. If my elf is being recognised for being amazing, I want to be there. After all, you did the impossible with me." I held my arms out.

"Not impossible. Plus, I had a great canvas to work with." Her heated gaze dragged down me in a way I liked.

"I didn't make it easy."

"Where's the fun in easy?" She bounced on my lap again, giving all kinds of friction to my trapped dick. "I can't wait to go shopping for an outfit."

"Not more shopping." I groaned more due to her movement than her words.

She giggled. "Don't worry, I'll take Elle, or she might have something I can borrow."

"We can go," I rushed to say.

Shopping reminded me of slow torture, but the idea of her going with someone else set me on edge.

"I have an activity that you'll enjoy better than shopping," Zoe smirked, then leaned in for a filthy kiss on my mouth.

All my blood rushed south, and I pulled her up from the couch with me, ignoring my back's protest.

"That sounds like my kind of activity," I said, intent on claiming every inch of her.

26

*Z*oe

Cocooned in warmth, I avoided opening my eyes, ignoring the heaviness in my stomach. It was official: The CEO Whisperer and general boss girl I'd spent years perfecting was hiding today. Snuggled under Theo's heavy arm, surrounded by his scent and comfy sheets, I refused to face the fact that this was our final day today. My normal get-up-and-go had gotten up and gone.

Neither of us had spoken about the future. Sure, I had the date for attending a wedding slash awards ceremony together in my diary, but nothing else. Could I go that long without seeing him?

Theo shuffled behind me, tightening his grip. His hard lines pressed against me as his vast body dwarfed me. Maybe a distraction was just what I needed.

"Hmm." His warm breath fanned my ear as his hand snuck under the T-shirt I'd borrowed from him to sleep in.

Arousal pulsed through me. "Theo..."

The doorbell rang, and Theo growled, his hand stilling its descent.

"Who the fuck is that?"

He rolled over, grumbling, and picked up his phone. I flopped onto my back, watching him. He frowned and scrambled out of bed.

"What is it?" I sat up.

He yanked sweats over his boxers. "It's my mom. She's outside."

"Oh." My hand flew to my sticking-up hair.

"I need to let her in."

"Of course."

He disappeared out of the bedroom. Was she okay? I glanced around, grabbed my discarded sleep shorts and raced after him. I halted at the corner of the main room, realising that meeting Theo's mum for the first time, half-dressed in her son's clothes and emerging from his bedroom, wasn't ideal.

Theo's mum was slim and only a few inches taller than me. He guided her inside with an arm around her. Her eyes were red-rimmed.

"Oh, I didn't realise you had company." She halted, clutching a tear-stained tissue.

"It's okay, Mom. This is Zoe."

"Hi." I raised my hand lamely.

"I don't want to burden you…"

"Mom, it's fine," Theo said, steering her to the couch, although her eyes remained on me.

"I'm leaving today," I said, swallowing down the lump that statement brought to my throat.

Theo frowned as if this was news to him.

"I'll make some coffee," I said, feeling awkward. "Lattes?"

They both nodded, and I headed to the kitchen, relieved I'd learnt how Theo's fancy machine worked. It reminded me of the one at the coffee shop where I used to work while I was at university. I focused on frothing milk as Theo and his mum spoke quietly.

Bringing the drinks over, Theo lifted his anger-filled gaze to mine with a strained smile.

"Of course, you can stay for as long as you like. When you feel ready, I'll help you find your own place."

Theo's mum burst into tears, and he glanced at me in alarm. I didn't know what was happening but guessed she'd left Theo's dad.

"I-I'm so sorry you've had to see this." She sniffled, rubbing furiously at her face and looking up at me. "I'm Maria."

"Don't worry at all. I'm pleased to meet you, although I'm sorry you are upset. I'll put your drink here." I placed a hand on her arm, wanting to make contact but unsure if it was welcome.

She patted my hand and gave me a watery smile. "I've heard all about you from George. You've been making my boy very happy."

Theo grumbled something under his breath about giving George swirlies when he saw her next. I wasn't sure what that was, but it didn't sound good for George.

"I'm going to get changed and pack my suitcase." I stood and returned to Theo's room, wanting to give them space.

The sense of impending doom didn't lessen as I quietly showered and gathered my clothes to put back in my case. Luckily, I had space for all my new shoes. I procrastinated over a few items, wondering if I should leave something here or whether that was presumptuous. Theo had enough to deal with without finding a pile of my clothes in one of his drawers. I stuffed them in the slightly over-filled suitcase and closed the lid. My flight was a commercial one tonight from JFK. I insisted that using the company jet to take only me home wasn't necessary. If I considered the carbon emissions of keeping this long-distance relationship alive, I'd be planting trees the entire time we were apart.

My heart panged again at the idea of being an ocean away. How had I gone from career-focused to pining after a guy I'd not even left the house of yet?

Curling up on the couch in Theo's room, I decided I needed something to focus on, so I pulled out my Filofax to organise my calendar for next year.

"What are you doing?"

My head snapped up, my marker poise over March.

"Organising."

"You didn't have to stay in here." Theo ran a hand down his face.

"I wanted to give you time with your mum. Is she okay?"

"She's left my dad. It turns out he's been cheating on her." Theo ground his teeth, looking murderous.

My stomach lurched. The poor woman.

"Oh no." I got up and hugged Theo, even though my arms couldn't reach around him.

He gripped me tightly. "I should kill him."

"I'm so sorry."

"I don't know what to do for her." His voice cracked, and my heart hurt for him.

"Just be there for her," I said before an idea struck me. "Do you think she'd like ice cream?"

Theo barked a pained laugh. "Maybe later, she went to lie down in the spare room for now. Although I'm the worst option she had to turn to, I'm glad she came to me."

"She made a good choice." I reached up on tiptoes and cupped his cheek.

No matter what people thought of Theo's grumpy persona, he looked after his family, and they were lucky to have him in their corner.

"In any case, you said George's apartment is tiny."

"True. George knows she is here. I need to call Abe, though. Their relationship has been strained since Dad disowned him, but they still talk, and he'd want to know."

"Do what you need to."

"I'm sorry. I had plans for your last day. Goddamn it."

"It's okay, Theo. Family comes first."

"Yes, but..."

Theo's phone rang again, and he groaned low in his throat.

"What the fuck now?" He stalked over and snatched up the phone.

His conversation was terse with the person at the end of the phone, and he grew angrier.

"Fucking deal with it now," he barked, making me jump.

"What's going on?" I reached out to touch his arm.

"Fuck!" He tossed his phone on the bed and ran his hands through his hair.

My phone buzzed on the couch.

"Don't answer that."

"What, why?" My heart hammered in my ears.

"Because." He tipped his head back and glared at the ceiling. "Because I'll deal with it."

"You're scaring me," I said, my heart accelerating.

He snatched up his phone and began furiously texting, lost in his anger. I backed away towards my phone, and it went silent. The missed call was a UK number. But there were some text messages and email notifications.

I clicked into my email, and a wave of dizziness hit me. The contents contained words like *termination of services* and *company reputation*. They flashed before my eyes as I tried to make sense of it. As I read the first, more emails popped up, and my skin tingled.

My clients were cancelling.

Numbly, I listened to the voicemail message.

"This is a message for Zoe Barnes. Mr Colter no longer wishes to engage your services," the female voice said crisply.

I held the phone away from my ear with a fine tremble, stunned.

"W-what is going on?" I stuttered, moving jerkily to grasp Theo's arm.

"I'll have the pictures and video down immediately. My lawyer is on it." His face was cold and hard with rage.

"What?" I gaped up at him.

"Fucking hell. How did they get them? When I get my hands on them."

"Theo, my clients are cancelling. What's going on?" I shouted, desperate for him to help me understand.

"There are pictures of us having sex in my office and a video. Goddamn it, I'm so sorry."

"What?" Cold expanded out from inside me, chilling me from my core.

No, no, no.

"They've been leaked to a gossip site, and the media have picked it up." Theo ground his teeth.

"There are pictures of us having sex on the internet?" My ears were ringing as my heart pounded out of my chest.

Theo winced. "Not for long."

"How did my clients find out?" I whispered, sinking onto the bed, horrified.

"Fuck, fuck," Theo cursed, pacing back and forth.

"What site?" I swallowed a lump in my throat, appalled at the thought.

"Don't look."

"I need to see."

Theo told me the site, and my browser opened up. Dread pooled in my gut. Grainy pictures of us in Theo's office, me wearing that blue teddy, my head thrown back. A slimy, ugly feeling settled all over me. Against my will, I clicked on the 10-second clip, and my breathy voice filled the air between us, and I dropped my phone as if it had burned me.

"Turn that off," Theo growled.

Was this all over the UK press?

More messages came in, and a link to a US site with an article entitled "Theo Kelly Sex Scandal" and subtitled "Personal Stylist or Sex Consultant?"

"How did this happen?" I gasped.

"I don't know, but I will find out."

Oh my god, this was going to ruin me. My whole business was built on image, and now I was the consultant who slept with her client. My skin tightened as if it had shrunk ten sizes.

My breath came in pants. I needed to get home, retreat, and hide. No. I winced internally. I had to see what I could salvage. Stooping to snatch up my scattered sheets, I stuffed them inside my Filofax.

"What are you doing?" Theo held the phone to his ear but watched me intently.

"Getting my stuff. I must go home and sort this mess out."

"You aren't going anywhere. We will face this together."

I cringed at the idea of facing the press here.

"No, I need to get home."

"No."

"Don't tell me no!" I screeched. "My business will go up in flames." Tears sprang to my eyes. "I've been so stupid."

"Don't say that."

"It's true. I'm such an idiot." I swallowed rapidly.

He crossed the space and pulled me into his arms. "I don't regret a thing between us. I'll fix this."

I pushed him away, the nausea welling up my throat.

"It's not going to be that simple."

My life was disappearing down the drain. Everything I worked for.

"I'll deal with this." His voice was dangerously low, but I was beyond fear.

"No, Theo, I got myself into this mess. I need to get myself out."

"Don't call us a mess," he growled.

I shook my head. He wasn't listening. I didn't need him to ride in like a white knight. I needed to fix this. If that was even possible. There had to be a way. My heart pounded irregularly in my chest.

"I'm going to see if I can get on an earlier flight."

"Don't," Theo growled, reaching for me, but I lurched away.

"Just do what you can and get that video and those pictures down." I shuddered at the invasion of privacy. "I can't be here any longer."

Theo made a strangled noise and snatched up his phone again, calling someone and shouting directions at them.

I hunched over, frantically searching the flight app, desperate to flee home as quickly as humanly possible.

27

The doorbell rang, and I slammed my laptop closed with unnecessary force, surging to my feet. At the door, Abe took one look at me and embraced me.

"Fuck," he said as he pulled back.

"That's about right," I said, stomping to flick on the coffee machine.

"Is Mom here?" he asked, slipping off his coat and eying the paperwork explosion in my living room.

"She's gone for a walk."

I didn't make good company right now, seething in my rage and obsessively working to fix this before it blazed out of control.

We fell silent as I made us coffee.

"How long did the board say?" Abe asked, accepting his mug.

"No idea. They pressed Liam and Oscar to suspend me pending investigation. Whatever the fuck that means." I punched a couch cushion into shape.

Frank Cubit sounded positively gleeful when he rang to deliver the news.

"I'd have you back with me in a heartbeat. I hired two people to do half your old work."

"I took this position for a reason, Abe. And I'm not the quitter Dad always claims."

Abe paled. "That's not—"

"It's okay. I'm being an asshole. But I'm not letting this go. The pictures and videos are down, and the story is strangled. I need to help Zoe, But..." I hung my head in my hands. "She won't take my calls."

"She's probably just shocked."

"A few of her clients cancelled, and she left in a rush."

"Why? Did it even reach the UK press? Why would they even care?"

"I don't know." I ran a hand down my face.

What I did know was everything was a mess.

"And Liam and Oscar... I've let them down." The back of my neck tingled unpleasantly.

I'd joined forces with the Steel Brothers for various reasons but remained because we were a team despite the ocean divide. I loved the hustle and challenge of investment far more than the financial side of the hospitality business. While I felt terrible for failing my business partners, it was nothing compared to missing Zoe, and I would have jumped on a plane if the board hadn't demanded that I stay in New York.

"Bullshit. You have had your privacy invaded and splashed across the press. I can't see the Steel Brothers judging you for that."

"It was unprofessional, and it affects the company." My fingers rubbed over the edge of Zoe's panties in my pocket.

I didn't think Abe would appreciate me dragging them out and pressing them to my nose like I'd been doing every hour or two, so I suppressed that urge.

"You can't tell me neither of them has fucked their wives in the office."

"If you're going to tell me again about that blow job you got while you were on an international call, I'll punch you," I growled.

Abe snorted. "That was years ago. I've got better stories these days."

"Save it."

The last thing I needed was one of Abe's oversharing stories.

Abe sighed. "What's your plan?"

"I'm firefighting at the minute, working with the lawyers to keep those pictures down and trying to find the source."

The doorbell buzzed.

"Don't you have a doorman?" Abe asked.

"Yes, and Mom has a key." I frowned, heading to the door.

Freezing with the door half open, I gaped into the hallway. Liam and Oscar wore unreadable expressions and matching dark suits.

"How the fuck did you get up here?" I asked.

Liam waved his hand at me as if to say skirting the security in my building was easy. Oscar stepped forward and pulled me into a hug that rivalled Abe's.

We had spoken on Monday, and they weren't happy, but I hadn't heard from them since.

"We would have been here yesterday, but Chloe and Ivy had a check-up."

"Are they both alright?" I asked, shaking Liam's hand.

"Yes, it was routine, but we also wanted to clear the decks before we jumped on the jet to clear this bullshit up," Liam said.

I opened the door wide to let them through, then trailed after them into the living room, where they greeted Abe. They'd all met before, and something lifted inside me, having them all here like a team. My expansive penthouse looked small, filled with all of us.

Once everyone had a coffee, I dropped onto the couch and waited for them to open with a roasting.

"Before we get into it, here's your late Christmas present." Oscar handed me a large box.

I frowned, not expecting them to open with a gift. Ripping off the tape holding the box together, I opened it to find a leather box. Abe leaned forward and pulled the outer packing away as I grabbed the box. Inside, a polished metal football lay nestled in a satin lining.

"It's steel," Liam said as I lifted it out.

Abe whistled. "Bro, nice. Does this make you a Steel sibling now?" He grinned.

"More like a funny cousin," Liam muttered.

I smoothed my hands over the life-size replica of a game ball much heavier, and a lump rose up my throat.

"Thank you. This is incredible."

"It's fucking late. You'd think they could get something made in time for their biggest investors." Liam rolled his eyes.

"It was a last-minute order," Oscar said.

Liam scoffed. "Anyway, let's focus."

They began unloading paperwork, and I rested the stunning piece of metal back in its case. The significance of them bringing me a game ball made of steel wasn't lost on me as I caught Abe's eye across the room.

"*Onward and upward,*" he mouthed.

I nodded at him and refocused on the Steel Brothers.

"Were you aware Vanessa Cubit knows your ex-fiancée?" Oscar asked, pulling out glossy photos and spreading them on my coffee table.

My blood ran cold. The images showed Vanessa and Savannah meeting at a restaurant. Abe whistled under his breath as he picked one up.

"From what our private investigator can tell, the relationship is relatively new," Oscar said.

"I'm not aware they ever moved in the same circles. Savannah is a social climbing parasite, and Vanessa's family is from old money," I clipped, unease moving through me.

"Yes, we thought as much. Which means the common denominator is you. Namely, a dislike of you," Liam mused.

"How does that fit into all of this?"

"We aren't sure, but I think it has to do with bringing you down at any cost."

"The PI investigated your office and confirmed the camera used to capture the images had to have been inside the room. Perhaps nestled in a plant, but there was nothing to find."

"You've had a guy investigate in my office?"

"Of course. We arranged the clearance, and Carol let him in," Liam said.

A pang went through me at the thought of my secretary.

"Why?"

"You joined our partnership because we chose you to lead. Someone filmed you without your permission to make you look bad. If the suspected corruption exists, then we don't want that type of leadership infiltrating the top of our company. You earned your place there, and you are a friend. You're damn good at what you do. Even if you're a bit rough around the edges." Oscar grinned, but it fell as he became serious again. "We wouldn't let it stand in the UK, and we won't let it fucking stand here either," he said, his posh British accent making the curse sound harsher.

"It's clear the employees and board at Steel Ventures New York don't know who we are or why they shouldn't fuck with us. We built this company from nothing, and we didn't fumble when deciding its leadership, and we aren't swayed by bullshit," Liam added.

Emotion expanded in my chest at his words. I'd taken Liam and Oscar's silence over the past few days as anger, but they'd been preparing to come here instead and stand with me.

I swallowed past the lump in my throat. "It means a lot to have you here."

"Now we've sat around holding hands. Let's make a plan to clear this fucking mess up because I miss my wife and daughter already," Liam growled.

"I think Theo has something he'd like to collect from the UK too," Abe added slyly, and I shot him a "shut the fuck up look."

"David is looking after your woman," Liam muttered, examining some paperwork he'd scooped up from one of my piles.

"He is?"

"He's been around to see her. But that's another reason I need this cleared up. He's in a foul mood and staging a full-on mutiny. Almost as bad as when Chloe and I..." He trailed off, scowling. "He told me to tell you to fix it, or I quote, 'he'll personally chop your balls off.' That man is as vicious as a snake if you cross him, so I suggest, for all our sakes, we get this cleared up."

"But mostly for Liam's sake because he can't function without his PA." Oscar laughed.

"No one is irreplaceable," Liam growled.

"Sure, but it would be a tall order," Oscar countered and then turned to me. "We don't want to replace a trusted PA and a CEO partner just before I get married."

I nodded, guilt swirling in my gut, knowing this kept Liam from his young family and Oscar from his bride-to-be.

"Do you think David would take my call?" I asked, trying not to sound as desperate to hear news of Zoe as I was.

"I think you'd get an earful, but yes," Oscar said as Liam grunted, "Don't count on it."

I sighed. "Let's fix one thing at a time."

I didn't want to focus on the shit show here, but I needed to get it cleared up so I could return to Zoe.

We spent a couple of hours reviewing what I knew and the rest of the information from their PI. The plan they came up with was not legal but should be compelling enough to clear up our problems without needing a lengthy investigation. However, it would still take a few days to implement.

Abe took our mom back to his place for a few days and promised any support I might need. Liam called the PI to implement step one, and I rearranged the guest rooms for Liam and Oscar.

Once we'd finished plotting, they both disappeared to call their wives. When I tried Zoe's number again, it went to the voicemail, but the box was too full to leave a message. I texted her instead.

> Theo: My business partners are here, and we are clearing everything up. Then I'm coming for you, elf. I miss you.

The ticks turned blue, and my grip tightened on the phone. No dots appeared, and no reply came. I stared at all the unanswered text messages before closing my phone. If Zoe thought I'd go down without a fight, she was wrong.

28

Zoe

My eyes blurred, and my stomach rumbled as I wrote the last item on my list, then amended it.

Call a solicitor
Get a new phone number
Close socials
Electronic planner
Call Mum
Eat something ~~green~~

I didn't know how many days had passed since my life imploded, but it was more than a few. The list was the first positive step I'd taken, which wasn't curling up on the couch sleeping fitfully or staring blankly at the television screen. Unless I could count restraining myself from calling Theo as an action. Whenever I turned my phone on, the notifications overwhelmed me, and I wanted to call him, but the savage voice inside my head reminded me that I didn't get to have a relationship and a career.

Exhausted by my meagre attempt at organising myself, I retreated under a blanket on the sofa, closing my eyes.

When I woke later, the clock in my living room was barely readable in the twinkle of the fairy lights on the tree.

I should take those decorations down.

I checked my phone, but it was dead. Staggering to my feet, a wave of vertigo hit me, and I toppled back onto the couch. As the dizziness settled, I stood again, squinting at the clock, which read six. I didn't know what day it was.

Slowly, I made my way to the kitchen. Opening the cupboard, I found a packet of crackers. The biscuits were long gone, but thoughts of those pictures and that video caused bile to burn up my throat, so I put the crackers back. I grabbed my blanket from the couch and clutched it around me as if it could shield me from the shame. My bladder reminded me I needed to pee, so I went to do that and then grabbed a glass of water.

Maybe I could sort my life out now that I'd made my action plan. Returning to the couch, I grabbed my stuffed Bowser and curled up again. I stroked my chin on his fur, and the tears began to fall.

Banging awoke me with a start. My heart crashed against my ribcage as I stared around wildly. The clock read six again, but that didn't help me tell if it was day or night.

"Open the door, Zo," Isaac's booming police voice thundered from outside.

Untangling myself from the blanket, I shook my heavy limbs and headed toward the noise. Isaac glared down at me, his fist poised to knock again as I opened the door. Suddenly, I felt sympathy for the criminals he chased down.

"Do you have to be so loud?" I croaked.

"Fucking hell," he muttered as he pushed past me, clutching a bag.

"Come in." I waved my hand at his back, suddenly more exhausted than ever.

I loved my brother to death, but I didn't want to see him right now.

"What do you need a lawyer for?" he barked, gripping my list.

"Is nothing sacred?" My hand trembled as I snatched it from him and hid it down the back of the couch. "If you came here to tell me how stupid I am, just save it, Isaac. I know, okay. I get it." I averted my eyes and clutched my arms around myself.

And I did know. Every ounce of humiliation I suffered was of my own making. My one rule was not having a relationship with my client, and I broke it. I smashed it into a thousand pieces, and now I was facing the consequences.

Clients all gone; sick, humiliating emails; threats; name-calling; broken professional relationships.

And a new barrage added to my disgrace whenever I turned my phone on.

I flinched as solid arms grabbed me, squashing me into a broad chest that smelled like my big brother. It loosened a sob from my chest, and I trembled against Isaac. A wave of longing made me wish someone other than my brother was here with me.

"Zo," he said, cupping the back of my head. "Fucking hell. If you think I came here to tell you off, I've been a bad brother."

I clutched his jacket. He pulled me to arm's length and leaned down to my eye level.

"Listen, shortie, this wasn't your fault. It wasn't even that American twat's fault, even though I'll kick his arse if I ever see him again."

"It's not his fault."

And you probably won't see him again, I added internally, and a little piece of me shrivelled up inside.

"He was your boss," Isaac growled.

I shook my head, brushing away my tears.

"No. He was my client, which is why this has blown up in my face. I broke my own rule."

"Do you love him?"

I looked away. "I felt a lot for him."

"Does he feel the same? Even now?"

The question stung, but it was a fair one.

"I don't know. I've not taken his calls."

Isaac sighed. I glanced up at him, and he chewed his tongue, his jaw grinding.

"He's got his own mess to sort out." I closed my eyes, thinking of the text that said the board had suspended him.

I might not be answering his calls or messages, but I was still opening and listening to them.

"He's got his career to think of, too."

Isaac grumbled something about big boys and the consequences of their actions and steered me back to the couch. He picked up Bowser Junior and snorted, thrusting the cuddly toy at me.

"Why do you need a lawyer?" he demanded.

I sighed, wishing he wasn't as good at his job as an inspector.

"Because I'm being accused of breaching data protection. Someone contacted all my clients and shared those photos and links." My face tingled, and I swallowed thickly. "But they got those details from me."

"Fuck. I'll get Mike from the cyber task force involved."

"No."

I didn't need any more witnesses to my humiliation.

"Someone accessed my planner." I glanced at the big Filofax that made my stomach drop each time I looked at it. "I keep physical contact information."

"Where would they even know where to start in that thing?" Isaac eyed it.

"There is a contact section, thank you. It's well organised," I huffed.

"Of course it is." His big hand landed on my arm, and the backs of my eyes pricked again.

So much for my organisation skills. Look where they landed me.

"That's still a crime," he mused.

"One that's hard to trace and prove." I sighed, rubbing at the tension in my temples.

He grunted.

I'd spent time thinking about how this could have happened, and someone accessing my Filofax was the only logical explanation. Not that logic has been my friend since I returned to the UK.

"I'll ask Mike if he knows any good solicitors. He's familiar with all that data protection and GDPR shit. But you need to speak to that American twat."

"He has a name."

"Yeah, but I'm not going to use it. He can investigate that shit alongside where those photos came from."

"I'll ask him," I said, and Isaac narrowed his eyes.

My big brother could smell a lie from a mile away. But he dropped it, and I was grateful for his help because although finding a solicitor was on my list, I didn't know how to start looking.

"I bought breakfast, and yesterday I picked up cakes from Sweet Treats," Isaac said thankfully, changing the subject as he picked up the bag he brought with him.

I struggled to smile. "Thanks, I'm not that hungry."

My stomach rumbled, making a liar of me.

"Eat this before a cake." Isaac unwrapped a butty from the bag he'd brought in.

The greasy smell of bacon made my mouth water despite myself. He held it out, glaring at me until I took it from him.

"Bossy," I mumbled, biting down to a salty explosion in my mouth.

We sat in silence, munching on greasy food. I didn't realise how much I needed to eat something and speak to another human being.

Isaac opened a box with the familiar logo, and four multi-coloured cupcakes with unicorn horns and glitter sat there.

"You realise what it would have done to my reputation being seen buying these?" he grumbled.

I knocked my shoulder into him, but he didn't move. He was such a brick wall.

"You're manly enough to pull off buying glitter cupcakes."

He snorted. "I've been fucking worried about you, Zo. Call Mum, will you?"

My stomach churned. I'd been worried about how my family would react, but if Isaac, the most judgemental person I knew, was in my corner, I would be okay.

"I'll call her."

"I need to get to work."

"Criminals won't catch themselves." I smiled weakly.

I offered him one of the cupcakes from the box, and he eyed it before stuffing it whole into his mouth. A streak of blue and pink icing smeared the corner of his mouth, and I pointed at it. He scowled and rubbed his face. The action almost made me smile again.

"Most people take bites," I pointed out.

He rolled his eyes, chewing like a hamster. Eventually, he got up and walked towards the exit.

"Do I need to assign someone to your door to ensure you eat?"

"Do police do those kinds of jobs?" I followed him.

"They do if I pull enough strings."

"Yeah, don't do that. I'm okay. I made a list."

"The one you stuffed down the back of the sofa?"

I stuck my tongue out at him, feeling more like myself. Isaac pulled me into his big body for another hug, and I savoured the contact. He headed out, barking at me to lock the door behind him.

Returning to the sofa, I fished the list out. It looked long and daunting, but I fought the desire to shrink away from it.

How did someone function after being so exposed?

The ache to contact Theo flared as I stared at my dead phone. I took a deep breath and plugged it into the charger. It turned on, and notifications began pinging in, filling my screen. My skin tightened, and a squeezing sensation took hold of my ribs. Cringing, I lurched to turn it off and tossed it onto the floor, pulling the blanket back over my head.

29

he bitter wind blew through my jacket like it wasn't there, and a shiver wracked me. The wrought-iron bench in the remembrance garden was freezing underneath my butt. But no matter how cold I was, I hadn't moved, gazing without focus at the stone plaque with my brother's name.

"What am I going to do, Jay?" I asked him, the words lost in the turbulent air around me.

I squeezed my eyes tight and tried to imagine what he'd say. He was such a free spirit, but he was a protective brother just like all my siblings.

"Fuck them. Who cares what people say," Jay's voice said in my mind, his floppy hair dropping into his eyes.

A tear leaked out.

"It's not as easy as that," I whispered back.

"I thought I'd find you here." David's voice made me jump.

He dropped a thick blanket around my shoulder.

"It's going to rain. Come on, Kris has the heaters running in the car."

I went to open my mouth to ask him questions, but I closed it again and numbly stood up, my limbs stiff from the cold and lack of use.

David shuffled me into the back of the car, and Kris looked relieved as he restarted the engine. The warmth flowed over me, and I fumbled to remove my gloves and clip the seatbelt in.

"We're taking you back to ours."

"No," I said, my teeth beginning to chatter.

"No? We've been running around looking everywhere, and when I find you, you are half-frozen and moving like a zombie. Nuh uh, little sister." David pouted.

"I don't want to come to your house. My flat is fine."

The knot tightened in my throat because I didn't know how long I had left in my flat. I had savings, but I couldn't exist indefinitely without an income. One lone client left. I was lucky to have spotted the email request for a styling slot amongst the barrage of cancellations, threats, and abuse that filled my inbox. It was the only reason I left my bed this morning. I decided to come and visit Jay to tell him I wouldn't mess this chance up – like sharing it with him would help me stick to the plan when everything felt so hopeless.

"Is there even any food at your flat?" David demanded.

I gazed out of the window, avoiding his eyes. David huffed and tapped away on his phone. I was sorry they were trailing around after me.

Despite their threats, Kris pulled outside my relatively modern block of flats.

"Thanks for giving me a lift." I handed the blanket back to David in the front.

He scoffed. "Not a chance."

They both piled out of the car, and I sighed.

"There is a food delivery on the way, just the essentials."

My chest tightened, and I stopped short of the outer door, throwing my arms around David.

"Thank you."

Kris's warmth lined my back in a group hug.

"That's what family is supposed to do," David said as he pulled back.

I knew he was thinking of his family.

"Your family is so stupid."

He gave me a tight-lipped smile. "I know. That's why you are my family now. You're stuck with me. Now get your tiny butt inside."

I would have laughed, but my usual cheerful optimism had dried up with my client list. Trudging into my flat, I dropped my keys on the table and winced at the official letters.

"Isaac told me he was getting the name of a solicitor," David said.

I sighed. They were all talking about me.

"Why would someone target your planner like this? I thought this was about unseating Theo."

It was a good question as the internet didn't even have the images anymore. But that didn't stop the damage and decimation of my whole business, which had spread like cancer.

"I don't know." I shook my head. "It was never likely to hit the press here because I'm nobody, and the British masses don't care about American football dynasties or a prominent CEO from the States, not like they care over there. Someone wanted me gone, ruined."

They'd done a bang-up job of it, too.

"Does Theo know?"

"No, but I guess he'll get to know from wagging tongues." I glared at him, but it didn't really hold any heat.

"Hey, I'm on your side." He gripped his chest dramatically, and Kris rolled his eyes behind him.

"There aren't sides. There's Theo's mess, and there's mine. There's no us."

Pain twinged in my chest as I said words I didn't want to mean. But I'd learned the hard way what I'd always suspected. I couldn't have a relationship and a successful business. I needed to make my way out of the mess I'd made, just like Theo did, and because we lived an ocean apart, we needed to do that separately.

Kris made a noise at the back of his throat.

"What do you want me to say?" I asked Kris.

"Don't kill a good thing before it's started," Kris said.

I moved away from him because I didn't want to argue. The crushing weight of Theo's absence sat on my chest almost as heavy as the embarrassment and violation I felt over the pictures.

Theo's multiple texts and voicemails sounded angry but confident that he would sort everything out. I hoped he could deal with the board and fix things at work for himself, but he couldn't sort out the mess I was in.

My business was nuked, and my life was a mess. The only flicker of hope was the one new client I'd clung to like a life raft. I was due to meet them next week. Despite how effective the campaign of humiliation against me was, the lack of widespread media meant not everyone knew.

The doorbell rang, and Kris went out to collect the shopping bags from the food courier. David set about putting the things away and making cheese on toast. Only the sound of him working in the kitchen filled the flat as Kris and I sat in silence. David passed me a plate of gooey cheesy bread and offered me Worcestershire sauce.

I wrinkled my nose at him. "Disgusting."

He snorted, splashing it all over his and my brother's food. I shuddered. I needed to get these invaders and their weird food tastes out of my house.

"Mum is worried," Kris murmured after we finished eating.

"I know, but it's humiliating."

Despite promising Isaac the other day, I'd only texted Mum, not called her, and even worse, I'd not been back to see Bowser either, but then I'd barely fed myself this past week, so looking after a dog wasn't a good idea.

"Do you think your mum cares about some compromising photos?" David asked, taking our plates away.

"Maybe not, but I do."

"Just call her. She's worried," Kris said.

"Okay."

"Is your phone even charged?"

"I turned it off."

David grumbled something and pulled out a phone box from his bag.

"This is a new number and handset. Don't bother telling me you'll pay me back as I charged the company. It's the least they can do. I'll get it set up with everyone's details. And add you to my family locater so that we aren't chasing around the city after you next time."

I thanked him, incredibly grateful that he'd ticked something off my list that I'd made no headway on. Kris placed the blanket around me, and I curled up on the sofa, watching David fiddle with the new phone. Exhaustion rolled over me, and I closed my eyes. I'd barely slept since I returned due to a combination of jet lag and anxiety.

The buzzer sounded, jolting me awake. It took a minute to remember where I was.

"Darling!" David cried into the intercom. "Did you bring wine and ice cream?"

Elle's laughter cut off as he buzzed her up.

I sat up, shaking off the fuzziness from my nap and patting down my hair.

David answered the door, and she breezed in, wrapped in a shawl and her full-length wool coat.

She rushed over and embraced me. "I'm so sorry I've not been here."

"It's okay. You had work." My breathing hitched.

Elle had been negotiating with a fashion house in Paris, so I had not seen her since I returned.

She pulled back and studied my face. "I bought a present for you to wear." She produced a fluffy onesie covered in dancing strawberries from her bag.

I choked on a sob, so thankful that she was back.

"And you two. I'm glad you've been here feeding Zoe, but it's time for girl talk."

"We can do girl talk." David pouted.

My brother pulled his husband up from the couch. "Come on, reinforcements have arrived."

David grumbled something under his breath.

"Answer my messages, or we'll be back." He pointed his finger at me. "And I'll finally agree with Isaac about getting you a police guard."

"Oh my god." I buried my face in my hands.

Kris bent over and kissed the top of my head.

David ruffled my hair. "Get a shower, sweets. You're a bit smelly."

"Thanks," I said dryly.

"Always." David made a "watching you" gesture, and they left my apartment.

"Go on, we've got a date with Ben and Jerry." Elle ushered me towards my bathroom.

I shuffled off, and the hot water spray woke me up a little. Reality seeped in as I wondered for the millionth time what to do, but I was profoundly grateful my bestie was back. The onesie was incredibly soft and smelled of strawberries as I pulled it on after drying myself.

When I returned to the main room, Elle was flitting about the kitchen making popcorn. The *Pretty Woman* opening credits were on pause.

I sat down on the sofa and glanced away. I wasn't sure I could watch that movie right now. My eyes fell on a piece of paper with the Stylz logo. There was no need to print the email I received, but I was in self-torture mode, and I decided that seeing concrete proof of my broken dreams might spur me into action.

"Oh, hun." Elle threw herself down next to me, and the floodgates broke.

A single sob turned into a torrent wracking through my body as Elle hugged me. Sadness swallowed me whole. How had I lost everything I worked for in one single swoop? The worst thing about my situation – which shouldn't have been my biggest concern as my life fell apart so profoundly – was missing Theo. So badly. Just as intensely as I had before, but this time, it was tainted with finality. An unbearable hole in my chest opened up without him.

"I miss him, Elle, so much."

Elle stroked my hair and let me ramble. I told her how stupid I was for breaking my only rule and how mad I was at myself for falling in love with him. Because that's what this was – the only thing deep enough to hurt more than losing everything I'd worked for.

"He didn't say it was over, though."

"We can't be together after this." I wiped my face.

"Why not?" Elle leaned away from me, studying my face.

"Because you can't have a successful career and a great relationship."

"Bullshit. Tell me that's not what you believe?"

"It's what experience tells me. Men are intimidated by career women. It's a known fact."

"It's a generalisation. Has Theo ever indicated your career intimidated him?"

I snorted because the idea of something intimidating Theo was funny. His grumpy face was pictured in the dictionary under intimidating.

"Exactly," Elle said, taking my snort as agreement.

It was true he'd never made me feel that way. I moved on to my other arguments over our doomed relationship.

"It doesn't matter because he'll sort things out in New York, but I can't return there. Now, half the staff in his office have seen pictures of us having sex. I can't tarnish his image worse than I already have. I was supposed to be improving it." My voice rose to a screech, and Elle raised her eyebrows.

"We live on different continents. Plus, I need to focus on rebuilding my reputation and my brand. If I even can."

"Is that what you want?" Elle cut off my rant as I drew a deep breath.

"This business is all I've wanted for years." My frustration rose.

"Yes, but when did you last do something just for yourself? I try to get you to date, but it's always like dragging a stubborn mule, because you've decided what they'll be like before you meet them." She glared at me.

I avoided her eyes. Was I that transparent?

"You've told me you feel lonely," Elle went on in a softer voice.

"When?"

"All the time when you're drunk."

"Drunk Zoe doesn't make good decisions."

"No, but at least she is honest with herself."

I frowned at Elle. "You're supposed to bring ice cream and sympathy, not hard truths and common sense."

She rolled her eyes. "I know what it's like to want to do well in a career, to be recognised, and to do a good job, but at the same time, feel lonely and long for a connection to someone. I've wanted a proper relationship for a long time, and I know you have too."

As I picked at a thread on my sofa cushion, I thought about her words. She was correct; I did want a connection. It was one thing I'd reflected on at Christmas.

"But that doesn't make all the issues magically disappear," I said, my chest squeezing.

"No, but it's a starting point, and you know the end goal if you get out of your own way."

"When did you get so wise?"

"I've always been wise." She grinned. "Now, come on. There are two yummy guys in the freezer waiting on us. Ben and Jerry won't lick themselves."

I giggled for the first time in days, wiping the tears from my face.

"I missed you, Ellebear."

"Same."

We agreed to put on a spoof zombie movie and dug into the ice cream tub with two spoons. I was so lucky to have Elle and my family. Everything had gone to hell, but they were still in my corner, and because of that, I would find the strength to face whatever was coming.

30

The office block in the centre of Northampton loomed ahead of me as I parked. Exiting my car, I gathered my jacket around me, reminding myself not everywhere could be like New York. This job was a simple restyle with a social media update, not a whole corporate image overhaul.

The CEO needed my help, and I was grateful for the work. Thankfully, he hadn't been in my planner. He knew one of my old clients but didn't seem aware of my recent troubles.

Anxiety knotted my belly as I stepped inside the building. The receptionist directed me to the eighth floor, where McKenna Ltd. took up three levels of the multi-use office building.

Mr McKenna's secretary directed me to wait in the chairs by his office. Without my Filofax, my bag felt light, and I tried not to fidget with the strap. After discussing things with Elle and creating an action plan, my mental state was better, but I was still nervous.

Don't mess this up.

The first step in the objectives list Elle helped me formulate was to focus on this client. Next was rebranding and moving toward corporate styling packages rather than individuals. I'd miss working directly with the top people in companies and getting to know how they worked alongside the styling side, but it was a trade-off.

Despite promising Elle, the only thing I'd not put into action was texting Theo, who had magically acquired my new number courtesy of David, the meddler.

The office door opened, tearing me from my guilt over avoiding Theo.

"Miss Barnes." The CEO took my hand in his sweaty fist. "I'm so glad you are here."

From my research, he had just turned fifty, was recently divorced and, by the state of his current suit, in need of a serious makeover.

"Hello, Mr McKenna." I smiled at him, projecting more confidence than I felt.

His gut hung over his belt, and it was clear his jacket wouldn't close around it. Plenty of businessmen carried weight, but many didn't realise how clever tailoring could improve their overall look, just like the correct shape of a woman's clothing could.

Not everyone can look like Theo.

An ache flared inside my chest, and I forced my thoughts to the present.

"Please come inside. And call me Thomas." His hand landed on the small of my back as he led me inside.

Cringing away, I walked rapidly to look out of the window. The cityscape sprawled beyond the windows was a far cry from the New York skyline.

"The view can be distracting." Mr McKenna's breath fanned over my shoulder.

I turned to the side, plastering on a smile as I moved toward a seat. The guy didn't seem to understand the concept of personal space, and he was setting off my internal creep-meter.

He settled behind his desk and gave me a broad smile as I batted away my thoughts, reminding myself again that I couldn't be picky with my clients.

Beggers can't be choosers, Zoe.

I pulled out my tablet, unlocked it with my face and fingerprint, and opened my notes section. It felt unnatural to work this way, but everything would have CIA-level cyber security from now on.

"What goals would you like to achieve with these styling sessions?"

He smirked, and a shiver passed down my spine again.

"The long and short of it is that I need a new look. The poison witch left me, and now that I'm not footing the bill for her shopping addiction, I can afford it."

I declined to ask after the *"poison witch,"* whom I assumed was his ex-wife. We reviewed a few more things, and I drilled into the specifics to ensure we had some SMART goals planned.

"Are you ready to shop?"

He groaned. "Yes, I guess I am."

We were right in the city centre here, and I'd set up some appointments, including one with a tailor. I didn't always know outfitters in the client's area, but I had a lot of contacts. Luckily, they were spared the embarrassing photo distribution because their information had been in a different part of my planner.

We headed out, and Mr McKenna, who I refused to call Thomas in favour of remaining professional, stuck close to me. At the suit shop, he began undressing, and my stomach knotted – memories of Theo in Juan's fitting room ran through my head like a premium version of this experience.

Would it always be a constant comparison?

Despite needing to do his colours, I left the changing room, leaving him with Guy, the tailor.

"Zoe?" His voice called out a little while later.

"Are you all done?" I asked, heading back in, unprepared for the expanse of pudgy-white flesh on show.

For some unknown reason, he was wearing a bright yellow jock strap and had twisted his leg out to allow measurement of his inseam. Guy turned to me and caught my eye before standing and declaring himself finished.

"Did you need to do my colours?" Mr McKenna said, moving closer.

"Yes, but you can get dressed first, then we'll talk styles and fabrics." I swallowed thickly.

"It's fine. You've got them ready." He pointed to the swatches tightly fisted in my hand.

"Oh yes, okay." I forced away my unease and moved closer, holding colours against his sallow skin, which was nothing like Theo's golden tones.

You are being unfair comparing him.

Refocusing on my task, I flipped through a few bold swatches that I thought would do him a favour and glanced up to compare to his eye colour. His gaze was on my chest, and he smirked while adjusting his jock strap.

Urgh.

I whirled around, my stomach churning. Motherfudger. He was precisely the type of client I would have ditched at the first opportunity; however, he was my only client.

Fleeing the changing room, I swallowed down a bitter taste in my mouth and forced myself to focus on speaking to Guy.

"Have you fixed me all up?" Mr McKenna's hands gripped my hips.

I sidestepped, breaking his hold. He was crossing a line, and I might be desperate for clients, but I didn't need a lecherous one.

We finished up with Guy, agreeing on a timeline, and I led Mr McKenna outside before whirling around on him.

"I'm grateful you chose me as your stylist, Mr McKenna, but please keep your hands to yourself."

"Call me Thomas. I'm sorry, but I'm a tactile guy. No harm, no foul." He held his hands up.

Heat warmed my cheeks. I didn't want to overreact, but it was hard not to after everything that happened.

"Thank you. Now we know the boundaries." I plastered a smile on my face.

"I'm sorry if I offended you." He looked genuinely apologetic, and I felt bad for snapping at him.

"Would you still be willing to do my wardrobe assessment? Or have I blown my chance?"

"I..."

Wardrobe assessments involved assessing a client's current clothes and picking out pieces to enhance their collection. Although it was an option, I didn't remember seeing it ticked on the application.

"You didn't request that."

"I didn't at first, but I remember you offered it, and I thought perhaps you could come around on Friday evening. I have a date. It's my first date since my wife left." He stared at the floor, and I felt nasty for judging him.

Don't blow it with your only client.

Stifling my reservations, I cleared my throat.

"Friday works. I'll pick pieces for a date now that I have your measurements. Then, I can tailor the rest of the suggestions around what clothes you have." I injected fake enthusiasm into my voice.

"The psycho ex burned half my clothes before she left, so starting afresh would be good." His shoulders slumped.

I made a sympathetic noise, reminding myself the guy was trying to get his life back in line after his divorce. I agreed to meet him on Friday afternoon and bring Guy's adjusted suits and other key pieces.

By the time I returned to my apartment, I was exhausted. It seemed returning to work had wiped me out. Part of me desperately wanted to call Theo, but I decided I was too tired. Instead, I face-planted my pillows when I reached my bedroom, immediately falling asleep.

31

T HEO

The January sunshine poured through my office window, and I straightened the jacket on one of the suits Zoe picked out for me. Once we tackled this problem, I was heading to confront my girl. She couldn't avoid me forever.

Wiping my sweaty hands on my pants, I reminded myself not to be such a pussy. I'd faced worse opponents than these on the field, but somehow, the stakes today were exponentially higher. Not because I didn't have options but because I played to win.

Despite being unkeen to be away from their loved ones, Liam and Oscar were still here a week later as we brought all of this to a head. They wanted to ensure we knew how deep this went, which meant dissecting all the high-level employees' lives and all the board members. Liam and Oscar were relentless and fucking ruthless. The speed with which they uncovered information told me Liam's PI was using less than legal means. Besides dirty detective work, we got a lot of other work done this week mapping out our trajectory for the year, and despite the circumstances, working closely united us and the vision for the company.

Our investigation at the firm also caused us all to look long and hard at how we'd structured Steel Ventures New York. Liam and

Oscar admitted they'd been distracted when they set everything up here, and I realised I'd trusted too many things at face value. One of the original mistakes was using a recruiter who seemed to be the sole source of the problem employees – none other than a long-time family friend of Frank Cubit.

"Are you ready?" Oscar strode in, fixing his cuff links.

Liam stalked in behind him. "Because I'm ready to knock some fucking heads together."

I glanced at the steel football they gifted me in pride of place in my office, and a sense of justice rose inside me. This was my rightful place.

"Let's do this," I nodded curtly.

A thrill raced through me, anticipating these fuckers going down. Standing from my desk, I gripped both their hands firmly in a shake, my muscles tightening in readiness. I led us through my outer office, where Carol gave me a thumbs-up and approached the conference room. As we entered, every eye turned to the two founders.

"I thought this meeting would be conducted without Mr Kelly's presence." Frank Cubit's wiry moustache quivered as he spoke.

I resisted the desire to punch his smarmy face.

"Well, you thought wrong, didn't you, Frankie-boy," Liam said, baring his teeth.

Frank turned red and spluttered for a few seconds.

"Mr Reid, with the greatest respect—"

"Mr Cubit, with the least respect, shut the fuck up," Liam growled, and the room took a shocked gasp.

"As Liam *eloquently* requested, please refrain from questioning us until we have finished our presentation," Oscar said, his cultural voice broking no more arguments than Liam's rough cursing. "What I'm about to demonstrate is both unfit conduct and a severe breach of fiduciary duties of several board members, not to mention other illegal activities. Please also note that Vanessa Cubit has already resigned as Managing Director." Oscar clicked through the preloaded presentation.

The hush that fell over the boardroom was palpable, even as

Oscar read out Vannessa's statement framing Frank as the spearhead of the campaign to tank Steel Ventures New York shares and then take over the company for a significantly reduced price.

My pulse pounded with rage as Oscar recapped the conniving bullshit Frank had tried to pull. Oscar clicked the presentation off, and I itched to lay into the backstabbing snakes around the table, but we agreed that Oscar and Liam would take the lead, presenting a united front. That didn't stop my fist from curling as I slid my jaw from side to side.

"As for the three board members in cahoots with Mr Cubit and the illegal wire tapping and violation of Mr Kelly and Miss Barnes—"

"I'm not staying to hear this slander. You'll be hearing from my lawyer." Frank leapt to his feet, spittle flying from the corners of his mouth.

"Feel free to see our lawyers now. They are at the door with your papers," Oscar said.

I grinned at Frank, his red face paling, and satisfaction settled in my gut. Did I want to punch him? *Absolutely.* Was this better? *Probably a close second.*

The other three implicated members scrambled to stand, too, heading after Frank.

Silence greeted their absence.

"As shocking as this is, it doesn't clear up the media scandal surrounding Mr Kelly," Deborah, the grey-haired former banker, finally said.

She'd turned up squeaky clean in our investigations but was a known hardass.

"True. While it wasn't wise of Mr Kelly to have relations on company property, I'm sure the knowledge Miss Barnes is his fiancé changes the narrative," Oscar replied.

Only years of control of my facial muscles stop my jaw from dropping at that statement. What the fuck was he talking about? Zoe wouldn't even take my calls. Liam stared at me as if daring me to contradict Oscar's words.

"I suppose this mess with Frank will create a far bigger scandal than some amorous congress in the office, but the share prices will be hit." Her face pinched.

Liam shrugged. "We will deal with it."

The meeting went on as we hammered out plans for everything from handling the media to restructuring and recruiting for the board. By the time we left the building, we were all dragging ass.

Flashes and noise slammed into me like a wall.

"Mr Kelly!"

"Mr Reid. Sir Russell. What are you here in New York for?"

"No comment," Oscar shouted.

"Where is the fucking car?" Liam growled at me.

The car Carol booked was further down the road, swamped by paps. No one was here when we arrived, but someone must have tipped them off.

"Is it true you had relations with your employee?"

"Sir Oscar, do you support Mr Kelly's seduction of a junior assistant?"

"What do you say to claims you are a predator, Mr Kelly?"

My head whipped around, and my vision tinted red at the edges. The junior reporter Zoe had set me up to speak to thrust a microphone into my face, his eyes alight with malice. My fist tightened, ready to slam into the side of his face.

Breathe. Use your calmness anchor.

The voice of my elf ran through my head, giving me the split-second clarity to hold back.

"The woman I was pictured with is the love of my life," I growled at him, baring my teeth.

The teenager recovered quickly from his shock and sneered.

"She was your employee."

"She was an independent consultant hired by the firm, and we fell in love. Those pictures were a gross violation of our privacy, and a suit has been filed against the perpetrators."

"Who filmed you?" another pap shouted as more microphones were shoved in my face.

"No further comment." Oscar grabbed my arm, and we pushed our way toward the vehicle.

Once inside, I released my fist and blew out a breath.

"I must say, I'm impressed," Oscar said once the door closed.

"That's because you are well known for punching the press," Liam said, running his hand through his hair.

"Piss off," Oscar drawled.

"Why did you tell the board we're engaged?" I asked, remembering their bombshell from earlier.

"Because we needed some excuse for you shagging on the desk. We support you, Theo, but as Deborah pointed out, you were caught in a compromising position," Oscar said. "Plus, we all know where this is heading with David's sister-in-law."

"Thank god there are no cameras in my office," Liam muttered.

"That's more information than I ever needed," Oscar replied.

"Fuck off. You are telling me you never banged Eve in the office."

"Don't talk about my wife and sex in the same sentence. And the point is I've never been *caught* having sex in my office." Oscar's eyes flashed to me.

"Neither have I." Liam grinned, also turning to me.

I wanted to ream them out. They'd saved my ass, but then they'd thrown me to the wolves.

"She won't even take my calls. How do you suggest I follow through on being engaged to her?"

"It's just a formality," Oscar said.

I gaped at him. Did I want to ask Zoe to marry me? *No, yes, maybe?* But not as some cover for all this bullshit.

"Pfft, you're gone for her. Are you going to lie down and take her silent treatment?" Liam asked, cracking open a can of soda from the minibar.

"No, but—"

"No, buts, you've been pining over her like a lost dog this week. Apologise, and if she needs longer to forgive you, kidnap her, put her on the plane back here." Liam tossed peanuts into his mouth as if he hadn't suggested committing a felony.

"Did you just suggest I kidnap Zoe?" I asked.

"I have some rope," he added.

I stared between them, and Oscar shrugged as if to say, "He's crazy, but what can you do?"

"Let's get some food before we organise the jet. I'm starving," Liam grumbled.

I shook my head, but somehow, the idea of kidnapping Zoe and bringing her back here didn't seem as terrible as it should.

Back at my apartment, I unpacked the takeout, and Liam called David to arrange things for our return.

"Yes, I realise what time it is. I told you we'd be returning today," Liam growled. "Of course he is." He sighed deeply, pinching his nose and holding the phone to me. "He wants to talk to you."

"Why are you coming back with them?" David demanded.

"Zoe won't take my calls. She reads my messages but doesn't reply."

"She changed her number because she was being harassed. I didn't send you the new one to make it worse. Are you trying to get her to sign an NDA?" he demanded.

"What?" I glared at the phone. "No."

"I thought not, but I had to check."

Tightness fisted my heart at the thought of her facing harassment alone; I had worried that might be why she'd changed her number.

"I saw the sound bite from your press ambush earlier. Are you trying to save your arse by saying you are in love with her?"

"No, David. I love her. I miss her. And I'd like to tell her to her face. This whole situation is fucked up, and I wish I hadn't let her go. Maybe I won't next time."

Jesus, now I was sounding as crazy as Liam.

"Good luck trying to keep her against her will," David said.

"There go the kidnap plans," Liam muttered, and I realised he was listening over my shoulder.

"I did not hear that," David said.

"Is she okay?" I asked, ignoring the crazy bastard breathing down my neck.

David sighed and went quiet. "She's eating again and started an assignment with a client. It's possibly the only one she has left."

"Why have all her clients cancelled?" Liam asked.

"Why are you still listening in?" I shoved him, but he didn't move.

"You're on my phone."

"Someone took the contacts from her Filofax and contacted them with those pictures," David said, returning my attention to him.

"What!" I growled, my anger surging back to the surface.

"I thought you knew?" David said.

My skin prickled with discomfort.

"How would I know? She won't talk to me."

"She's got letters from solicitors about data breaches. It's a mess. She told Isaac she would speak to you about it."

"She didn't." I ran a hand down my face.

Fuck, things were so much worse than I realised.

"Now you know. I'm sure you can all combine your big steel brains and determine who targeted her, but it doesn't change what happened."

"We'll deal with it." Liam squeezed my shoulder.

"I need to see her, David."

I needed her back in my arms. His comment about her not eating shook me. Sorting everything out here paled in comparison to her life's work falling apart. She needed me.

"Tell Liam the plane will be ready for ten," David said.

"Good," Liam said, heading for the takeaway boxes.

"I had a key made for her place. I'll have it couriered to the airstrip for when you guys land. To be clear, I'm only trusting you, Theo, because I believe you want what's best for her, but if she calls the police on you, you're on your own with Isaac."

I would deal with Zoe's cop brother if I had to because I needed to speak to her.

"Thanks, David."

It was time to go and get my girl.

32

*T*he winter sun hung high in the sky on the drive from the airport just outside Sheffield. When I arrived at her apartment, there was no reply to my rap on Zoe's door, but the key David left me turned silently. Her apartment was modern and clean, with colourful trinkets and abstract paintings. Pictures of family and friends were dotted around, along with some strange pottery.

I sank onto the sofa, gathering a blanket and pressing it to my nose like a weirdo stalker. It smelled like her.

A muffled noise from down the hall alerted me to her presence. I wanted to head straight into what I assumed was her bedroom and gather her up in my arms, but there was every chance she would freak out, so I kept my ass on the seat.

The shower started up, and I groaned, thinking of her wet and naked. I was officially moving into creeper territory. The water turned off, and shortly after, the door opened. She emerged with a towel around her lush body and one cutely curled around her head.

She spotted me and released an ear-piercing scream. I jumped to my feet, and pain flashed up my spine.

"Hey, hey, it's me." I held my hands out.

She clutched her towel, her heaving chest. "What are you doing inside my flat?"

"David gave me a key."

"What? Where the heck did he get the key?"

"He's been worried about you."

"So he's giving out my key to random people?" Her voice was screechy and her comment stung.

"I'm not a random person. What was I supposed to do? You've been refusing my calls. I needed to see you." I took a cautious step forward, and she backed up.

"When people don't answer calls, it usually means they have nothing to say."

"I don't believe that."

She shook her head, looking away. "I need to get some clothes on. Make yourself at home, I guess."

She walked back to her bedroom and closed the door. I collapsed back onto the couch, dropping my head into my hands.

"That went well," I muttered.

"Theo." A hand touched my shoulder, and I lifted my head. I'd gotten lost in thought while she dressed. She looked gorgeous in an oversized hoodie and leggings. She was so tiny I wanted to scoop her up, but I curled my hand into fists.

"I'm sorry," I said.

"No, stop. I don't want your apologies. I chose to have sex with you. You didn't record us, and I know you've been battling your own problems. It's my fault. I should never have been so unprofessional."

"No," I growled, losing the battle not to touch her as I yanked her into my lap.

"Theo?" She landed with a yelp.

"Hush, woman. I've fucking missed you." I buried my face in her neck, and she sagged against me.

Minutes passed as we soaked each other in.

"I don't think it's a good idea—"

"Stop. Many things are a bad idea, but you and I aren't one of them."

I pressed a finger to her lips, but she pulled my hand down.

"How is this going to look with your work?" Her eyes pleaded with me, and I hated the pain and sadness there.

"We'll work it out." I cupped her cheek, and she closed her eyes.

"It's not as easy as that."

"Firstly, work will expect to see me with my fiancée, so that's one less thing to worry about," I joked.

She frowned. "What?"

"Oscar told the board we are engaged." I held my hands up. "It blindsided me, too, but I'm not opposed to the idea."

She gasped and scrambled back off my lap.

"Is that why you are here?"

"What? No. That's..."

She was backing away with an expression I couldn't read. "I want you to leave."

Shock rang through me.

"Why?" I spluttered.

"Because this isn't a good idea."

"Why not?"

"Because I'm not your beard." Unshed tears shone in her eyes.

"My beard? What are you talking about? Aren't beards for gay men? Look, never mind." I shook my head, realising this wasn't how I thought it would go. "You are mine. Of course, I'd be here; it's been driving me nuts not seeing you."

"Is this driving you nuts? My business is obliterated. Gone. Everyone except for one client. I'm glad your business partners have helped you fix your issue with a convenient marriage proposal, but you must find someone else to fill that role." Her voice hardened.

She didn't sound anything like the woman I knew, and I was scrambling to backtrack.

"I'm so sorry about what's happened, and we will find out how they got hold of your planner and make things right, but the engagement thing came out wrong."

She laughed hollowly. "There's no making this right, Theo. Not for me. I need to rebuild brick by brick."

I stared at her. Gone was my happy, cheerful elf.

"Get out of my apartment, Theo."

"What?"

"You heard. I must get ready to go and see the one client I have left. Leave the key my brother-in-law stupidly gave you." She stormed over to the door and held it open.

"No." I closed the gap.

"Yes." The fire sparked behind her eyes but didn't blot out the pain there.

"This isn't over." I shook my head, backing out.

"Yes, it is." She slammed the door in my face and left me in the hallway, my chest cleaving apart.

"You didn't tell her like that?" Oscar shook his head. "Christ, you're worse than Liam."

"What?" I asked, still reeling.

We were in Liam's office, and both the Steel Brothers were there, along with Chloe, Liam's blonde-haired wife, who sat rocking his sleeping daughter Ivy.

"Where did I go wrong?" I asked Chloe for her female opinion.

"You made it sound like the engagement solved your problems, and you'd returned to tell her to play along. It's not exactly a romantic prospect."

"I never said that!"

"No, but that's what she got from what you said." Chloe shrugged.

"Fuck me. I should go back there."

"I suggest letting her cool down first," Chloe replied.

I still had her key, and I debated Liam's suggestion of kidnapping, but keeping her from her only remaining client didn't sound like the way to win her back, even if the instant pounding in my chest demanded I do just that.

"What can I do to fix it?"

"You've heard my suggestion," Liam said from behind his desk.

I groaned, staring up at the ceiling. "This is both your faults."

"Fuck off. We didn't force you to shag her at the office. We sent you an image consultant to help you be less grumpy, not for a happy ending."

I thumped my fist down on his desk.

"Don't fucking speak about her like that."

"Don't wake my daughter up," Liam growled.

I apologised to Chloe.

"Maybe it's time for my original suggestion," he said.

I was beginning to think he might be a psychopath. Ivy woke up fussing, and Liam gave me a dirty look. Chloe excused herself to go and feed her.

"Call David," I demanded.

"Call him yourself."

"My phone is dead."

I'd drained the battery between everything yesterday, flying and racing to Zoe's. Liam tossed a charger and his unlocked phone over to me. I plugged mine in and scrolled to the phone book of his device to find David. Catching sight of Chloe and his daughter on his wallpaper caused my chest to tighten.

"You raaang?" David said in an impression of Lurch from the Addams family.

"David, it's Theo. I fucked up."

"I'm sharing your location with Isaac," David huffed.

"I'm serious."

"So am I. Zoe is going to be pissed at me for giving you a key. I'll end up with itching powder in my shorts."

"David," I snapped.

"Okay, okay. What happened?"

I gave him a rundown.

"You cavemen are all the same. Why would you say that to her?" he sighed.

"It came out wrong." I ground my teeth.

"You think?"

I growled.

"Keep your ridiculous noises to the bedroom. I'll check on Zoe tomorrow; she is working later."

I growled again, not liking the idea of her styling someone else.

"Listen to me. Everything is gone. Her award nomination, her client base. She's got lawyer letters. She's even considering giving up the lease on her flat."

A lump tightened my throat. It was so much worse for Zoe than I realised. If only she'd contacted me. But I was thousands of miles away dealing with my bullshit.

"She doesn't need to work. Especially if she has only one client left. I'll take care of her, and we can sort it out together."

"You need to dial that caveman back because as simple as you think that sounds, it won't fly with Zoe," David said.

I blew out a breath. It seemed simple to me. I had plenty of money, and we could sort everything else out.

"Who is her remaining client?" Liam interjected, reminding me I was on his phone.

"Thomas McKenna at McKenna Limited," David answered, having heard him.

I relayed it to Liam, who made a noise in his throat.

"What does that mean?" I frowned at him.

"Yes, what does that mean?" David asked, picking up our weird three-way conversation.

"I'm not sure. Let me make a call." Liam held out his hand.

"Call me back," David barked before hanging up.

"Who is this McKenna guy?" I asked, passing his phone back.

"Someone I've heard of," Liam replied evasively.

Something in his tone caused an unpleasant sensation to crawl across my nape. A male voice answered his call. Liam relayed the name, and his face grew grimmer as he listened to the person on the other end of the line. My palms started to sweat as I waited, trying to hear parts of their clipped conversation.

"Call David." Liam looked over.

My phone was still attached to the charger, but it had turned back on, so I dialled David.

"Theo. What's going on?"

"Ask him where Zoe is," Liam asked, remaining on the phone.

My pulse thundered in my ears.

"Do you know where Zoe is?"

"Let me bring up her location," David replied.

"Does she know you are tracking her?" I asked.

"She's on my friend and family finder," he replied.

David read the address out, and I relayed it to Liam, who spoke to the mystery person on the other end of the phone.

"She's at his house," Liam said.

"What the fuck?"

"It's nearly forty minutes from here. Sean is closer. He knows the place."

"Who the fuck is Sean?"

"My cousin."

I scanned my memory, and my pulse pounded when I realised who he meant.

"The Irish mobster?" I hissed.

Liam had never confirmed the rumours but hadn't denied them either.

"Yes."

"Eve is at work until the evening. Do you want me to come?" Oscar asked.

"No. Let Chloe know I'll be back," Liam said, and they shared a look before Oscar marched out.

My gut swooped. Why would a mobster know Zoe's client?

"Tell me what Sean said," I demanded

"I'll tell you in the car." Liam grabbed his keys, and we raced out of the office, dread pooling in my stomach.

33

Still panting from lugging my clothes rack up the steps and avoiding taking a chunk out of the honest-to-god columns on the porch, my hand hesitated over Mr McKenna's doorbell as I tried to project a calm facade.

My encounter with Theo earlier had shaken me. First, he appeared in my flat, practically giving me a heart attack, and then all the relief at seeing him gave way to horror at his words. It almost tore me in half when he casually told me about our surprise engagement. The longing that ripped through me stole my breath, only to be replaced by devastation. It was cruel, and it exposed the depth of the feelings I still had for him.

Stupid, stupid woman.

Before I could tap the buzzer, Mr McKenna opened the door and greeted me with a wide smile. I pushed the clothes rack before me to avoid taking his hand.

"Would you like a drink?" he asked as he led me into the sitting room.

The casters on the rail clattered against the stone tiles.

"Yes, please. A coffee would be nice." I didn't want a drink, but this would take at least an hour. "What time is your date?"

Mr McKenna ignored my question and disappeared into the kitchen.

The living room was a riot of onyx and gold, and my eyes fell on a plaster bust of him. My stomach churned, and I wondered if this flashy and garish style was his ex-wife's.

Mr McKenna returned with cocktails complete with slivers of pineapple and umbrellas. They looked like something David would have prepared.

"I'm fresh out of coffee, but we should celebrate my new look."

"I don't drink on the job." I shifted my feet.

He smiled at me indulgently like he didn't believe that for a second. I took the proffered drink and placed it on the side.

"I've picked out a few options for your date."

"Don't you need to see my wardrobe?"

"Not for date outfits. Did you separate your favourites from your collection?"

He sighed dramatically. "It's just not my thing. My ex did a lot of my shopping, and then she destroyed a lot." He looked away, and I felt terrible for him.

"Show me what you have left," I said, and my scalp prickled.

Quelling the worry that twisted my gut, I decided to grab his relevant wardrobe pieces and bring them back downstairs. I followed him upstairs and into the main bedroom, where a four-poster bed was draped in black silk sheets. I looked away, suppressing a shudder. The whole space smelled of his overpowering cologne. He headed for the dressing room, and I tried to breathe through my mouth.

Inside the walk-in, the rails were reasonably empty. A few suits hung limply on unsuitable hangers, and the cubbies were haphazardly filled with T-shirts. His ex hadn't left him with much. I leaned over to rifle through the piles. He might be better starting afresh.

Heat lined my back, and I froze the hair lifting on the back of my neck.

"What are you doing?" I straightened, but firm hands gripped my hips.

"Oh, come on. Don't play coy with me." His bulk pressed me uncomfortably against the in-built shelving.

"Get off me!" My heartbeat raced in my chest.

"It's okay. You can drop the act now. I know you are a cock tease, but you knew where this was going."

My stomach rolled with dread, and I bucked against him.

"Get off me—"

He pressed his hand to my mouth, stifling my protest, and my fear racketed up tenfold. He was so heavy. Bile lurched up my throat as the hard length of him pressed against my back.

"Come on. I saw that video. You like seducing powerful men. That's what a whore like you gets off on."

No!

Panic clawed through my veins. Isaac's voice shouted in my head: *Instep, nuts, solar plexus, nose.* I slammed my foot down on his and twisted to nail my knee into his balls, but he moved his leg at the last second.

"You like it rough, do you, whore?"

I bit his hand and he screamed, releasing me. Slamming my palm upwards into his nose, it crunched, and he wailed. I jerked as his backhand hit my cheek, the force sending me flying into the wall. My head smashed against it, causing a bright light to pop before my eyes.

"You fucking bitch." He dived for me, grabbing a handful of my short hair.

My scalp burned, but it barely registered.

Get away. Run. Get away.

I rammed my elbow up, right in his groin. He screeched, doubling over, and his grip loosened. I scrambled around him, pulling boxes and suitcases from the other side of the closet down on him to stop him from following.

Stumbling, I bolted out of the closet and towards the doorway. My pulse thrashed in my ears. I didn't stop, taking the stairs two at a time. I slammed into the front door and rattled the handle. It was locked. I searched wildly for the key as footsteps thundered upstairs. A fierce need for Theo ripped through me, but he wasn't here, and I needed to get away. I ran toward the back of the house and shrieked as I collided with a hard body. Massive arms grabbed me, immobilising me against a broad chest.

"Jesus fecking Christ, she got some pipes on her." An Irish accent cut through my panic, and I swung my head wildly to the side to see a man in a three-piece suit.

He looked terrifying, but the massive guy holding me was worse. He had a bald head and a dead-eyed stare, and his freakish strength efficiently cut off my struggle.

Mr McKenna stormed into the kitchen, blood pouring from his nose, and I flinched violently.

"I-I... What?" he stuttered, halting.

His eyes widened as he took in the two guys.

"You do that, *Clíodhna*?" the first guy asked me.

"Just let me go." I struggled pointlessly against the bald giant as my vision swam.

I had no clue what was happening, but the need to flee was strong. I wished that with every fibre, Theo, Isaac, or anyone else was here. The first guy pulled out a gun, and I whimpered.

"You're not leaving, you piece of shite," he said, pointing the firearm at Mr McKenna, who had backed toward the kitchen door.

"Mr O'Sullivan, this has been a mistake." He raised his hands as I struggled with the behemoth holding me.

"Sit down, or I'll shoot you in the back, you spineless feck," the Irish man commanded, indicating a seat.

I shrank away as he edged closer, but the giant moved me further away, and I glanced up at him.

"He won't get near you," he growled, his voice low, also accented.

The gunman's phone rang, and he spoke briefly into it before clicking it off. I sagged into my captor's hold to conserve my energy. Four men appeared in the kitchen, all dressed in black, and Mr McKenna shouted as they dragged him away.

The first man crossed the kitchen and bent down in front of me, and I froze.

"I am a friend of a friend. My name is Sean, and this is Loch."

"Let me go," I croaked, my voice hoarse from screaming.

"No can do, *Clíodhna*. You are in shock, and I can't let you run off."

"That's not my name."

"I know." He motioned to the guy, Loch, who scooped me up bridal style.

"Wait! Let me go. I won't say anything."

They weren't cops, which meant they were probably shady. Although they'd saved me from Mr McKenna, my fate could be worse if I remained with them.

"We're taking you to your brother."

"My brother?"

"Detective Inspector Barnes." Sean grinned, and it didn't reassure me.

"How do you know Isaac?"

He ignored my question, and Loch carried me to a blacked-out Range Rover outside. The warmth inside the car rolled over me.

"Where are you taking..." My voice choked up, unable to say his name as bile rose up my throat, remembering his hands on me, his intentions.

"Don't worry your little head about that piece of shite."

Shivering broke out all over my body as my adrenaline crashed. Loch buckled me in and sat a seat away, although he was still close because he was so freakishly large. I curled my legs beneath me, and tears blurred my vision as the street flashed by. Was this how I was going to die? Theo's face flashed in my mind, and a million regrets bubbled up. But then I recognised a familiar street, and suddenly, we were pulling into Isaac's driveway, and a sob loosened from my chest.

Isaac threw open his front door. "What the fuck are you doing on my property, O'Sullivan?"

Sean got out of the car and walked around to my door.

"You should be a little nicer, considering what I brought you."

Fumbling, I released my seat belt and stumbled out of the car. Isaac roared with fury as he spotted me.

"You fucking bastard!" Issac thundered.

Sean drew his gun, and the big guy Loch suddenly had one

pressed on the back of Isaac's head. I screamed, my pulse rocking again.

"I don't think you want a scene on your front lawn, do you, Inspector?"

Isaac's face was bright red with fury, but fear lanced through me. He might get hurt doing something stupid.

"They didn't do this, Isaac." I indicated my swollen cheek. "They helped me."

"He doesn't help anyone unless it benefits him." His eyes spat daggers at Sean.

"While this is true, if you ever insinuate I would hurt a woman in that way, you won't know the meaning of pain by the time I'm through."

Isaac just glared, and then he gestured us inside. I bolted into my brother's arms, and he swept me up.

"What the fuck happened, Zo?"

"My client. He tried to..." My voice cracked. "He said he knew I was a... whore."

"Who the fuck is he?" Isaac growled, coming to a stop in his living room.

"No need. We have him," Sean said calmly.

"And what do you want from me to hand him back over?"

"Inspector, you impress me. But I have other plans for him. He already owes me a considerable debt, and tonight's events moved my collection timeline up."

"I'll kill him," Isaac growled.

"There are other things more painful than death. Not that I've ever caused anyone's death, Inspector." Sean gave Isaac a sly smile.

My mind shut down as they argued back and forth.

"What *do* you want then?" Isaac demanded.

Sean smiled, and it was a frightening thing.

"Just a favour for future use."

I shuddered against Isaac, closing my eyes. This was all my fault.

"Just get out of my house."

"Take care, *Clíodhna,*" Sean said to me, then dipped an imaginary hat to Isaac and left us in the living room, his retreat covered by Loch's colossal frame.

Isaac collapsed on his sofa with me in his arms. "Do you need the hospital?"

I shook my head, burying my face in his chest. "I'm sorry."

"Don't say that, Zo. I'd do anything for you, even owe a favour to the mob."

I pulled back. "The Irish guys are gangsters? But Isaac, your job."

"Fuck my job. Family is more important."

My muddled thoughts swamped me, and I wished Theo was here. How had everything gone so wrong?

34

T HEO

y knuckles whited under my grip on the door handle as Liam drove like a bat out of hell on the wrong side of the road. Liam's cousin told him Thomas McKenna was a sack of shit – massive gambling debts, battered ex-wife, and hushed-up harassment claims at work. My fist clenched and unclenched as rocks smashed around in my stomach. The same kind of rage-filled helplessness I'd felt after my injury threatened to overwhelm me.

Liam's phone rang. My heart drummed in my ears as he answered through the in-car speakers.

"I've dropped her off with her brother," the thick Irish voice said.

"Which brother?" Liam asked.

"The copper."

"Fucking hell, Sean."

"Two birds with one stone." The lilting voice chuckled.

"Is she alright?" I bit out.

"That must be the footballer. Yer mots a fighter."

"What the fuck do you mean?"

"Thomas tried to take what wasn't his, and your girl nailed him good."

The fucker tried to assault her?

"We need to get there now. I'm going to kill him," I barked at Liam.

"Fair play, but he's not home." Sean chuckled like this was amusing. "I'll send you the pig's address because I doubt you eejits have it. Go see your girl. Then I'll drop you a location. Liam, he can't go all the way because I need the little shite for now, but it'll help him feel better." The call went dead.

I glared at Liam. I didn't have a fucking clue about half of what the Irishman said, aside from the fact some fucker had laid a hand on my girl. Liam cursed under his breath and pulled over.

"Why are we stopping?"

"Because Sean took Zoe to her brother's.

"Isaac?"

"If he's the policeman."

"How the fuck does your mob family know Zoe's cop brother?"

"There's no fucking mob family. It's just Sean. He's useful at times. Other times he's a pain in the arse," Liam sighed.

His phone beeped, and he plugged a new address into the GPS. Restless fury burned in my veins, but I needed more answers than I'd got already.

"So what? He does your bidding? Like a pet mobster?"

Liam snorted. "Sean is like having a feral tiger on a leash. Don't ever assume he's domesticated despite the smiles and jokes. He's already twisted today's situation to suit his own needs. That's how he works, but he'll have looked after Zoe. He might be a lot of things, but he's not like that piece of shit McKenna."

"Why did you call him in the first place?"

I rubbed my face, and fears for Zoe crowded my mind.

"I recognised McKenna's name. Sean mentioned a CEO getting in deep with his poker games. I rang him because I knew he had information on him. Turns out poker debt was the tip of the shit storm."

"Fuck." My blood boiled.

Was Zoe okay?

"Why was she at his house?" The words burst out of me in an angry flood.

Liam shrugged. "Best guess? She was desperate for work and ignored the red flags."

"Fuck. Fuck!" I slammed my hands on the dash.

Isaac's place was close, and in ten minutes, we were pulling into a suburban street and Zoe's brother's drive. Tall trees lined the front lawns on this street, which was a good thing because Isaac stormed out with a gun in his hand.

"Get off my property," he snarled.

"I've come for Zoe." I slammed my door, facing him off.

"And you've got some nerve after your *family* dropped her off," he snarled at Liam.

"It never quite sat right all that business with Mark Reynolds. You're fucking crooked, the lot of you."

I had no clue what he was talking about, but Liam shrugged, looking bored.

"Fuck off before I put a bullet in you."

"That would be an awful lot of paperwork, Inspector." Liam leaned against his car door.

"I'm not letting you take her. I've just got her to sleep. She's traumatised."

"How is she?"

"Physically, he only hit her."

I growled.

"From what I gather, that bastard tried to assault her, but I taught her to deal with fuckers like him. O'Sullivan came upon her running from McKenna inside his house."

Blood roared in my ears. The need to kill rose inside me.

"Let me see her," I gritted out.

"Not in this state," Isaac snapped. "She just got to sleep."

"Get in the car," Liam said.

"Fuck no."

I would wait right here until she was awake.

"Sean has him," Liam said.

I whipped my head around. "Who?"

"McKenna."

The need to see Zoe warred with the need to eradicate the fucker who laid hands on her.

"I'll be back," I bit out.

"Don't bother. You ruined her life. Fuck off back to America, and don't come back here," Isaac spat, storming back into the house and locking the door.

"Come on, let's pay that fucker a visit," Liam said.

I stormed back to the vehicle, barely registering Liam's words or the journey as fury burned through my thoughts. The next thing I knew, we were climbing out of the car in an abandoned warehouse area, and I followed Liam, a rage like nothing I'd felt before burrowed inside me.

A guy in black greeted us at the side door and ushered us down a long corridor to another room.

"It's like old times," the Irish accent from the phone greeted us.

Liam's cousin, Sean, was dressed in a fitted suit with a pocket square and looked out of place in the dingy warehouse. Behind him, tied to a chair, was a weaselly looking man with a swollen nose and dry blood across his face.

"Is that him?" I growled.

"You must be Theodore," Sean greeted me. "Yer mot did a good job on his face."

I still didn't know what he was talking about, but my vision was tinted red at the edge, and I was itching to push past him.

"That wasn't you?" Liam asked Sean.

"I wouldn't waste a punch on him. I'm happy for you to get things started, but I can't have yer killin' him."

"Why not?" This fucker put his hands on my girl.

"Because I have plans for this sack of shite before I put a bullet in his miserable skull. However, I know the blood lust you are feeling needs to be satisfied, so I'm feeling benevolent." He gestured to the bound man.

"Unbind him," I growled.

"I'll let that slide because of how upset you are, but that's the last order you give me, big man." He patted my shoulder, smiling in a way that bared his teeth.

Unease knifed through my fury, remembering Liam's comment about the feral tiger. I glanced at Liam, who shook his head minutely. A big bald guy who looked like he'd make a hell of a defensive player unbound McKenna, and the fucker shot out of his seat.

A burst of speed launched me forward, and I collided with him. My back twinged, but I barely felt it as I tackled him to the cold concrete. He twisted with a cry and sucker-punched me. The pain burst through my lip, and I relished it.

"You sick fuck." I slammed punch after punch into his face.

He caught my kidney, winding me, but none of his feeble punches stopped me. My vision tunnelled on him, and a haze tinted my vision. My knuckles split across his cheek again, and strong hands pulled me off. I bellowed at them to release me, lost to the red rage.

"Let me kill him," I spat at the big bald guy and two others who'd wrestled me away.

My body shook with the effort of fighting the restraining hands.

Sean crouched before me, blocking my singular vision of the motionless McKenna.

"To be sure, that was a thing of beauty, but I can't let you kill him." He patted my sweaty face.

"Why not? He doesn't deserve to live."

"Because he's useful to me for now. I want my money back."

"Then you'll kill him?"

"For sure." He stood up and barked orders at the men who picked the fucker up and dragged him back to his chair. I took satisfaction in his swollen face.

"Up you get, Rocky." Liam hooked a hand under my arm as the restraining hands fell away.

I stumbled to my feet, my adrenaline draining. My back hummed with pain, and a dull ache flared in my knuckles.

"Take a shower, boys. You know the drill, Liam."

I glanced at Liam and wondered how he knew *the drill*. He caught my eye and shook his head.

Perhaps I didn't want to know.

35

"Oh my god, Zo," Elle said.

The vibration of her call had woken me. I had been tempted to decline it, but I answered and blurted out what had happened instead.

Swallowing the water that had filled my mouth, I blocked those thoughts out again.

"I don't know what to do, Ellebear," I said.

Aside from the banging headache, I felt numb. As much as Isaac could keep me safe, I rejected the idea of staying here for days. There was one person I wanted to see and curl up in his arms.

"Have you called Theo?"

"He didn't pick up. It's probably karma." I stared at my lap.

Everything felt like karma; I must have done something terrible in my past life.

"Come and stay with me. Isaac can drop you off," Elle urged.

"I should go home."

But the thought of returning to my flat alone made me cringe.

"We'll both go then. I'll drop my Nana's shopping off and come and get you."

"Okay." I dismissed the call, hoping she would arrive soon.

"Go and grab a shower, Zo. Take these to put on." Isaac's voice startled me.

I opened my mouth to ask about evidence but dismissed the thought, remembering Thomas being hauled off by dark-suited men. Instead, I sidestepped my brother, taking the clothes from his outstretched hand.

The hot water didn't fully relieve my shivering, and afterwards I dressed my heavy limbs in oversized clothes, folding up the hems multiple times. Sitting back on the couch, Isaac brought me some painkillers and a heat pack, and I closed my eyes against the thumping in my head as exhaustion crashed over me again.

Raised voices stirred me from sleep, and my limbs were stiff and slow at responding to commands from my brain. A pulse pounded behind my eyes as I dragged myself off the couch and shifted Isaac's blinds across. My chest tightened at the scene on the lawn. Theo and Isaac were angrily squared off, and Elle was shouting at them.

My breath caught as I spotted Theo's split lip. Had Isaac done that? I scrambled towards the front door, almost tripping over my blanket as it got tangled up in my legs, but I got to the door and pulled it open.

"Back up, Zo. He's leaving," Isaac shouted, spotting me.

"Did you hit him?" I croaked, squinting in the bright lights illuminating the lawn.

Isaac scoffed. "No, but I will shoot him if he doesn't get out of here."

"Zoe!" Theo's face twisted in horror as he looked me over.

"Don't you go any closer," Isaac snarled and slammed a restraining hand into the centre of Theo's chest.

My lip trembled as I stared at Theo. The fury on his face should have terrified me, but only relief slammed into me.

"Theo," I said, my voice hoarse

Theo threw off Isaac's arm and ducked past him.

"Zoe." He hit his knees in front of me, his eyes filled with anguish.

"Who hit you?" My voice wobbled.

"No one that matters." He cupped my swollen cheek, making me wince.

"I should have killed him. Did he...?"

I shook my head, and my vision wavered.

"I'm so sorry," he said, his voice cracking.

"This wasn't your fault."

"As endearing as this is, big guy, the front porch isn't the place," Elle said as she came up behind Theo.

"He's not going in my house. Get back inside, Zo."

"Isaac, don't be a bellend," Elle said, rounding on my brother with her hands on her hips. "You might be able to order criminals around like that, but Zoe is your sister."

"I..." Isaac spluttered, his eyes bulging.

"Zip it." She made a pinching motion with her fingers. "I'm taking Zoe home. If the big guy has grovelled enough, he might be allowed along, too, but the jury is out." Elle popped a hip, glaring at both men.

"I like her." Theo half smiled, then opened his arms.

I fell into them, and the sense of safety I'd been missing washed over me.

"That's settled. Into the car." Elle clapped. "Whether the big guy will fit in my Fiesta remains to be seen."

"I don't think this is a good idea," Isaac argued.

I rolled my head to the side, remaining in Theo's arms and watching in a detached way as Elle handed my brother his arse.

"It's not up to you. I'm pulling best friend rights, and they trump brother ones. Zoe needs to be somewhere she's looked after. How long until you are back on shift for hot fuzz patrol, leaving her to fend for herself in your bachelor pad?"

"Hot fuzz patrol? Jesus Christ, you're nuts." Isaac ran a hand through his hair.

Elle sniffed and walked off. I might have found it funny if I had any emotional capacity left, but I felt like a hollowed-out shell. Theo stood with me in his arms.

"I'll take care of her," Theo told my brother.

"If you hurt her, there's no place on earth you can hide."

Theo nodded, and Isaac visibly deflated as he searched my face.

"Thank you." My voice cracked, knowing I was lucky to have a big brother like him.

"Anytime you need me, shorty." He ruffled my hair. "And good luck with Elle. You're going to need it," Isaac muttered to Theo.

He carried me to the car, and Elle opened the rear door.

"Put her in the back. You'll need to go in the front. I've put the seat back as far as it'll go."

Theo gently placed me in the seat, and a wash of cold air stole over me as his body heat was removed. He shrugged his jacket off, tucked it around my shoulder, and clipped my belt in.

"He *is* a hottie," Elle whisper-shouted when she closed the door.

I couldn't manage a smile, but I appreciated her not acting weird around me.

Theo folded himself into the tiny car and reached back to take my hand, which wasn't hard as he was practically seated in the back.

"Your British cars are tiny," he muttered.

"Don't hate on Dolly." Elle stroked the dashboard, scowling at Theo.

I stared out the window and gripped his hand, holding on for dear life.

⁘

"Elle, you must go to work tomorrow. I can't have you losing your job." I sighed, rubbing my sore neck.

At least my headache was finally gone.

Elle was curled beside me on my sofa, arguing about staying with me this week.

"I don't want to leave you. It's not that the big guy isn't taking good care of you, but…"

She trailed off, but I understood the last part without her saying it. Theo needed to go back to the States at some point.

He was in my spare room taking a call despite it being Sunday. I knew he still had a lot of things to sort out. Selfishly, I didn't want him to leave. I didn't want Elle to either, but they both still had jobs.

"Are you going to go with him?" she asked tentatively.

"I-I'd not thought about it," I admitted.

"Listen, I don't want to force you into anything, but I think it might do you good. Get away from here. I'll keep an eye on the flat."

"I probably need to give my notice." I swallowed thickly.

"Don't do anything hasty. And don't be mad, but I kinda spoke to my boss. She told me she would take you on in a heartbeat. She's always liked you."

"Until she finds out from someone that I bang my clients." My shoulders curled in.

"She would listen to your side, and I doubt she'd care. She's not like that."

Was that what my future employment would be like? Would I always be in a dilemma of whether to disclose my past in case they found out?

"I appreciate you doing that for me." I squeezed her hand.

"Of course. But I didn't think you'd take it because I figured I'd lose you to the Big Apple." She bumped her shoulder with mine. "I want to visit, though."

"I'm not in the right headspace to decide."

"So don't decide forever. Decide for now. Life gave you a shit ton of lemons, and it's time to make the Limoncello. You've got a hunky rich man doting on you. Don't get in your head about it."

I sighed. Could it be that easy? After years of self-sufficiency, it felt wrong to rely on Theo coming in to sweep my problems away.

"It's not going to magically fix things by running away," I said.

"Nothing magically fixes things, babe. That's for Disney movies. But you've got two options. Pull things back together alone, or do it with a hot guy who's in love with you by your side. I'll be with you either way, but it's not the same. I'm not saying it's a no-brainer, but it kinda is."

I thought about how he'd held me both nights we'd been home and soothed me when I woke up screaming. Frowning, I tried to imagine staying here alone once he left, and my stomach dropped, and an image of me curling up on Theo's sofa entered my mind.

"Okay." I leaned against her.

She squealed, making me jump. She leapt up and rushed towards the spare room, bursting through the door as Theo paced, arguing into his phone.

"Prepare the jet!" she declared.

Theo frowned and said something into the handset, clicking it off.

"I'm allowing you to take her back with you. However, Isaac might look scary, but it's me you should be afraid of if you fuck this up, big man." She poked him in the chest before letting him pass her in the doorway.

"Do you want to return with me? I don't want to force you. I'll stay here as long as you need."

Despite his best efforts, I heard the strain in his voice. He needed to return to the States.

"I'm not sure I'll be much help to you with everything you have going on," I confessed.

"Don't worry about that." He crossed the distance and sat beside me.

I wet my lips. "I'd like to stay with you if you want me to?"

"Yes," Theo said instantly. "When would you feel ready to leave?"

I shrugged. "When I've packed."

"I think you should get someone she can talk to as well," Elle added.

"Of course," Theo said.

"I am right here, you know." I pulled a face at her.

"I'll help you pack." She pulled me up, and I allowed her to tow me over to my room.

Was I running away or finally going in the right direction?

36

*T*HEO

*M*y back popped as I stretched, waiting for my final appointment. The week since I brought Zoe back to the States with me had been rough on us both, but knowing she was in my apartment waiting for me to come home drove me out of the office as early as possible.

Carol knocked and opened my door, frowning as she introduced my next appointment.

Savannah's heels clicked on the tiles as she swept inside, dressed in flashy designer clothes, her fake tits spilling out of her skimpy top. As she approached my desk, a cloud of perfume slapped me in the face, and my heart rate quickened.

"I knew you'd come to your senses." She batted her huge eyelashes, which seemed to have grown an inch since we were together.

"Have a seat." I gestured to the guest chair.

She sat down, arranging her hands demurely as if she were a lady rather than a vindictive bitch.

"I'm willing to forgive you. But I want a summer wedding. There are several trendy event spaces large enough and available for the dates I'm thinking of, and if we sell press rights to it, it'll practically pay for itself—"

"Stop." I threw up a hand. "Do you think I brought you here to rekindle our toxic relationship?"

"Why else? Your press has been so negative I knew you needed me back."

I forced a laugh. "And why has my press been so negative? Is it because my office was infiltrated, and an intimate moment between me and the love of my life was filmed, then released to a gossip site?"

Savannah snorted. "Love of your life? Don't make me laugh. That video was straight-up porn. You're still an animal in the sack, Theo. That's what I miss about you most." She dragged a manicured nail down her cleavage.

She made me sick. I squeezed the football-shaped stress ball Zoe bought me, forcing down my rage.

"Enough. I called you here today to see your face when your life implodes, just like you set Zoe's up to." I bared my teeth at her.

Her eyes went wide. "I don't know what you are talking about."

"You were so eager to sell Vanessa Cubit out to that private investigator that she was only too keen to do the same. She says your price for handing over sensitive corporate information was to get rid of, and I quote, 'his new English whore'."

"I did no such thing," she scoffed and fidgeted in her seat.

"Because you had a camera in here since before we broke up, eavesdropping on me. That's how you knew where to turn up and meet me to make a scene, and that's how you knew about Zoe. But the Christmas decorations dislodged your perfect angle. That's why you had Vanessa place a new one for your mutual benefit. You sold confidential information to my managing director in exchange for her replacing your camera and copying information from Zoe's planner. You systematically destroyed Zoe's client base to get rid of her so that you could weasel your way back into my life because you couldn't bear to see me happy," I spat, and her face flushed as her mask began to slip. "You are so desperate for your five minutes of fame you don't care who you fuck up in the process of getting it."

Savannah sneered a cruel look, twisting her features. "I was the best thing that ever happened to you. You have no proof, and if you go public, I'll say you forced yourself on me."

I shook my head, unable to believe I had ever fallen for her. My old feelings paled in comparison to what I felt for Zoe.

"You could try, but I followed your example, Savannah." I pointed over my shoulder at a small camera placed roughly where Liam's PI decided the camera had been.

"You can't accuse me of trapping you when you've done the same!" she screeched.

"This isn't trapping. It's my backup for your bullshit. Everything coming for you has nothing to do with that. You're broke, you've lied to, stolen from and manipulated one too many people, and it's all about to go public. Good luck getting your Z-list celebrity gigs after that all comes out."

Savannah's bottom lip trembled.

"Save it. The police are outside waiting to take your statement about those embezzled funds you persuaded that poor schmuck of an accountant that you've been secretly banging for years to steal."

She reeled back in her chair. I pressed the buzzer on my desk, and her head wheeled around as two cops entered my office.

"What! No! That had nothing to do with me. I had no idea what Geoff was doing with the money!"

Warmth spread through my body as they read her rights and hauled her away, screeching, mascara running down her face as she sobbed. I relished every moment of her downfall, hoping she felt every inch of Zoe's pain and more.

Mamoru

The apartment was dark as I dropped my keys and the mail from the front desk on the side table near the door.

"Zoe?" I called.

Navigating the space by the city's lights beyond the windows, I scanned for signs of her, finding her wrapped up like a burrito on my bed, staring out the window. She'd had her second therapy session yesterday, and they seemed to wipe her out. The therapist told us it might make things worse at first. She insisted I go in today, but maybe that was a bad call.

"Elf?"

She lifted her eyes and smiled faintly. "It's not Christmas anymore."

"Does that mean I can't use it?" I sat on the bed next to her.

A selfish part of me loved having her here, but the rest wished it was under different circumstances.

"No, I like it," she said eventually.

I smoothed my hand over her cheek, which looked silvery in the half-light. The mark that the bastard had left on her had faded.

"David sent me a video today," she said.

"Another cat video?"

"No, I sent him a cease-and-desist notice for the cats."

I snorted. That man was a law unto himself.

"It was of you, Mr Reid, and Sir Oscar leaving Steel Ventures." She unlocked her phone, and I noticed multiple unread messages from her family and Elle.

She pressed play on the snippet of us wading through the press, caught on shaky camera work. I rubbed my beard, wondering if I usually look that rough. The little fucker that interviewed me started spewing his questions, and my face went red, nostrils flaring and my jaw sliding.

Was that what I looked like when I was mad?

"There." Zoe paused it, pointing to my angry face. "What were you thinking about?"

"Punching him?"

"I didn't ask what *Theozilla* was thinking. I asked what went through your head to stop you?"

"Your voice. Telling me to use my calmness anchor."

She blinked up at me, tears filling her eyes. "I did help you."

I brushed away the first droplet to fall and cupped her face. "Of course you did. I'm irrevocably changed because of you."

"Did you mean what you said next?" She clicked the video on, and we listened as I declared her the love of my life.

"Every word." My fingers tingled where they touched her face.

"It wasn't just a sound bite for the board?"

"Fuck no," I growled.

"Thank you." She closed her eyes.

"What are you thanking me for?"

"For loving me."

I pulled her closer, stroking her skin. "There was never any question."

"I love you too."

My heart hammered a drum beat against my chest. *Fuck yes.*

"I love you so much, elf." I lowered my mouth to hers, pressing our lips together.

Hers were salty from her tears.

"Don't treat me like I'm broken, Theo," she murmured as I pulled away.

"I'm treating you with the care you deserve."

She wasn't ready for me to show her just how much her words meant to me, even if my dick didn't get the memo, straining against my slacks trying to reach her. I needed a plan that got us out of the bedroom before I forgot to be a gentleman.

"How are you feeling right now?"

"Tired. I'm not sure why because I slept most of the day." She sighed. "I should have done something productive."

"Taking time to heal is productive."

She gave me an unimpressed look.

"What about food and brainstorming, or food and a movie?"

I didn't want to push her, but Zoe liked a clear action plan. She was the queen of lists, so I thought it might settle her mind, and selfishly, I wanted to be included to encourage plans that kept us together.

"Can we have Thai food and see how I feel?"

"That sounds perfect. I've got a present for you, too."

"Really?"

"Come on, let's get the food ordered, and I'll show you."

I subtly adjusted my rogue dick and unwrapped her from her blankets. Scooping her up, I carried her into the living room and placed her on the couch, where she burrowed under the weighted comforter I bought her. I clicked on the dimmer lights and retrieved the parcel from the entranceway before ordering the food.

"What's this?" Zoe asked as I placed the courier box in her lap.

"Your present."

It took a few minutes to get inside, but she gasped as she drew out the heavy planner and a handwritten card.

> *Theo,*
> *I hope your wife enjoys our SecurePlan360. Thank you for your investment.*
> *Terry*

"Wife?"

I shrugged. "Terry got the wrong idea, and I didn't correct him."

It was a formality I intended to rectify soon.

"What is it?"

"It's a prototype just out of beta testing. Even though the crowd-funding campaign had closed, I contacted the inventors and persuaded them to include me. It's a secure planner with a combination lock and fingerprint scanner. It's one hundred percent tamper-proof. They are pitching at the commercial market, but there's enough interest from individuals who still want to use pen and paper but need security," I rambled.

Maybe I did the wrong thing, aggressively investing in the start-up company to get my hands on this for her.

"I don't know if I can return to a physical planner." Her bottom lip trembled.

"I wanted you to have the option."

"Thank you." She threw her arms around me, and I let out a relieved breath.

"While we are on the subject of planners, I have some news about the investigation into your information theft."

She stiffened against me. I took a deep breath and told her everything I'd held back since I contracted Liam's PI to find the person who tampered with her planner, how he obtained weeks of video recordings of my office, which he returned to me unwatched. Vanessa was on tape "borrowing" the planner from Zoe's bag on the night of the party and putting it back shortly before I dragged Zoe in there. The PI returned to Vanessa and got the rest of the story. It was a story she conveniently missed out on her "confession" because she knew I wouldn't have let her take immunity from the corporate charges for testifying against Frank if she had. But that didn't mean I wouldn't circle back and ruin her.

Zoe grew still beside me as I spoke about my meeting with Savannah today.

"Everything should hit the press by tomorrow. All of Savannah's schemes and crimes. No one will hire her for so much as a celebrity yard sale, and she'll be lucky to stay out of prison."

The minutes ticked by as Zoe stared straight ahead, and I wiped my sweaty hands on my knees. The buzzer startled us both, and I reluctantly left a blank-looking Zoe to grab our food. I brought it inside and hastily shoved it into the warmer to return to her.

"Are you okay?"

"You met with Savannah today?" She traced a circle on the arm of the couch.

"Yes, do you want to see the recording?"

"What?" She blinked up at me.

"I recorded it just in case, and I thought you'd like to see her face when her world fell apart."

Zoe flinched.

"Talk to me, elf. Did I do the wrong thing?"

"I don't like that you met with her," she muttered.

"You're jealous?" I blew out a relieved breath.

"No, I... Maybe?"

I threw the blanket off her and hauled her onto my lap. "Listen to me, elf, as sexy as your jealousy is, it's wholly unfounded. She already repulsed me, but seeing her today made me wonder if I'd taken a bump to the head while we were together. She's poison, and if I didn't already hate her, I would for what she did to you. If she'd been a man, I'd have done far more than ruin her reputation and get her sent to jail."

The battered face of Thomas McKenna swam into my memory and my recently healed knuckles ached.

Zoe sighed and sagged against me. "Is it weird that I hate her more for thinking she had another chance with you than what she did to me? Hearing her life is wrecked doesn't make me happier. I think it just makes me doubly sad for us both."

"Is that how you felt when I told you about McKenna?" I asked, and she stilled at his name.

When we returned, I gave her the cliff notes on what had happened in that warehouse, but she went quiet on me. I thought I'd fucked up. Not that I could honestly say I would have changed my actions.

She buried her face in my neck. "No, that made me feel protected."

"Really?"

She nodded and we fell silent.

"How did it feel for you to get your own back?" She stroked her fingers through my beard.

"Satisfying," I replied. "Maybe your satisfaction about Savannah will come later. Perhaps you should watch the recording as she turned a special red shade."

"You are so bad," she huffed against my skin.

"I'm not bad for you."

"Theozilla, my personal demon slayer." She giggled quietly, and it was music to my ears.

"Damn straight."

I'd slay whatever she needed me to. My elf would always be safe.

37

"*You* look stunning," Elle added the final touch to my lipstick and stood back with her lips pursed. "You just need a post-orgasmic glow to top it off."

"Shut up." I tossed a tissue at her.

We were in Elle's tiny apartment, where she'd dressed me and done my make-up for Sir Oscar's wedding – or just Oscar, as he insisted I call him when I finally met him on a video chat with Theo last week.

"I'm just saying this outfit will get you laid."

"I wished I'd never said anything."

Elle scoffed. "As if you could ever keep something from me."

I grinned at her. "True."

Almost as soon as I'd arrived, she'd ferreted out my main worry like a sniffer dog. It should have been about my ongoing career situation, but it was, in fact, my growing sexual frustration.

"The final touch." She spritzed a small bottle of perfume over me.

"Oh, that smells nice."

"It's a pheromone spray. The big guy won't be able to keep his hands off you."

"Oh my god, is this like the ones they use on dogs when they want them to mate?"

"I don't think that's a thing. You just got paranoid for Bowser after that article about that weirdo spraying random dogs in the street."

I dissolved into a fit of giggles at the memory.

"How are you feeling, though? Other than horny."

"I feel better. It's weird because I still have nightmares, and I don't know if I can go back to one-on-one styling with men, but overall, I feel calmer than I've been in a long time."

Therapy was helping me process what happened, and although it was rough at times, I'd come a long way. I'd even embraced the idea I could have a career and a relationship, but my current focus was heavily on the physical side of that relationship, or lack thereof.

"Relaxing in a penthouse with a big hunky man is probably helping."

"Not helping my libido," I muttered. "But I do want to get back to work. I can't be a lady of leisure forever."

"Why not?"

"Because I think my brain would turn to mush."

"Let's hope the plan 'get Zoe laid' works, and you might not care."

"I'm fairly sure having sex isn't a substitute for contributing." I snorted.

"But it would be nice, though." Elle sighed.

I was grateful for all the care and attention Theo gave me. And at first, his idea of taking things slow physically was good. It wasn't just the assault I needed to unpack in therapy but the systematic unravelling of my life. But weeks had passed, and my need to be intimate with Theo had grown.

Elle was moving forward with the big guns for Oscar's wedding, and now I was dosed up in pheromones from who-knows-where with a killer raw silk dress she "borrowed" from work and the tiniest underwear I could find on our shopping trip yesterday.

"Did you sort all that data breach stuff out with the solicitors?"

"David and Theo dealt with everything, and both refused to tell me how much the fine they agreed on was, just saying it was tiny." I sighed. "I'm not sure I'd ever get used to someone else sorting things out for me."

"Tough times." Elle rolled her eyes.

"Shut up." I threw a tortilla from the bag she'd opened at her, and she snagged it with her mouth. "Show off."

"Have you decided what to do next?"

"I've made a list."

"Of course you have."

The heavily brainstormed list was locked away in my secure journal – it was the only thing I'd put in there so far, and it filled me with hope. Even today, when sadness threatened to settle in the pit of my stomach about the award ceremony I never got formally invited to.

"Do you think you'll get the bonus?" I asked her, staring at her goals list pinned to the mirror on her make-up table.

"I better bloody get it. I've worked my butt off."

"You deserve it."

"Yeah." She looked away.

"What's wrong?"

"I just really want it."

"What will you spend it on?"

She packed her make-up, avoiding the question.

"Ellebear?"

"Okay, okay. You know that kink club I went to at Christmas?"

"The one where you met the Santas and their sacks?" I snickered.

"Stop that. You keep making it weird."

I didn't want to tell her it was a bit of a weird story.

"Okay, go on."

"I want to pay for membership there."

"But what about Santa Two? Doesn't he go there?" I asked, confused.

"Fuck him."

"You did," I quipped.

She growled at me, and it was cute.

"He told me he's not interested in me, but other men attend the club. I can go by myself."

"Is it safe?"

"Yes, very safe."

"I'll keep my fingers crossed for your bonus then."

"In the meantime, you need to get banged to make up for us both."

The doorbell chimed, and a thrill shot through me.

"Come on, Cinderella, it's time to go to the ball." Elle clapped her hands.

Theo's mouth popped open as I opened the door to Elle's flat.

"Fuck me."

"That's the plan," Elle murmured in my ear, leaning against my right shoulder and bouncing lightly on her heels.

I elbowed her, and she cackled. "You two are so cute."

That snapped Theo out of his goldfish mode, and he swept forward, kissing me. His beard brushed my face, making me shiver in the circle of his arms.

"Alright, alright, leave that for later." Elle laughed.

"You smell delicious." He ran his nose up my neck, and I made big eyes at Elle.

Her snickering turned into belly laughter. Theo didn't seem to notice as his hands roamed my side, his face still buried in my neck. Heat rose in my body, and my nipples puckered. I stepped away from him before things got more inappropriate in Elle's doorway. Theo's hot glare followed me.

"Right, time for you kids to go have fun." Elle handed me my bag with an exaggerated wink.

Theo said a gruff goodbye to Elle, his eyes not leaving me. He moved closer, his hand across my back, tucking my more petite frame into his side.

I twisted to wave at Elle and found her making rude "finger in the hole" gestures, so I stuck my tongue out.

Oscar's childhood home was like something out of a period drama. The fashions on show at the wedding were fascinating, too. A vast marquee dwarfed the main lawn, and flowers dripped from every surface. The service was lovely, and seeing how in love Oscar and Eve were brought a tear to my eye.

"I bet you could do a better job dressing half these people," Theo leaned down and commented in my ear.

It was clear that money didn't always buy knowledge of dressing for your shape.

"Maybe I should write a book on it."

He nuzzled me. "That sounds like an amazing idea."

"There are other books out there for that."

"You'd need to put your spin on it, then we could market it hard."

I chuckled at him already plotting to promote this imaginary book I'd not written. But it made my stomach flutter at his support for my ideas.

After photos in the garden, the happy couple reappeared, and I stared openly at Oscar's beautiful wife. I hadn't met Eve in person yet. Theo told me she was a doctor, and I was surprised. I thought Liam and Oscar might have socialite brides, but I'd met Chloe a few days ago on a video chat, and she was down to earth. When we spoke, she had some exciting ideas, which inspired my brainstorming of the list inside my impenetrable planner.

"Can you see Chloe from your vantage point up there?" I asked Theo.

He'd not removed the arm from around my back since we arrived.

"It's not my fault you're elf-sized. I saw Chloe take the baby back into the house," he said. "Why?"

"I wanted to talk to her."

"About?"

"Girl things," I said evasively.

The idea she'd given me wasn't fully formed, and I didn't want to tell Theo yet and have him try and plan everything out. I might have learned to accept help and was comfortable thinking of our relationship as permanent, but I wanted to keep ownership of some things as I regained my sense of self.

"Fancy seeing you here." A familiar Irish accent sent a fizz of fear down my spine.

Theo spun us to face Sean, greeting him gruffly. He was wearing another three-piece suit, this time with a yellow pocket square, which matched the beautiful creature that hung off his arm. Dark hair and olive skin set off her lemon-yellow gown. A pretty fascinator topped off her look.

"You must be, Zoe. I'm Amy." She smiled widely. "I love that dress. Sean told me you're a stylist."

I grimaced, and her sympathetic look told me she knew at least a little of my past.

"I'm sorry. I got excited because I'd love your help sometime, but only when you feel ready. I spend most of my time in my work uniform or sweatpants."

"Your dress is lovely."

"The woman in the boutique picked it out. Honestly, I'd just finished a full clinic and probably would have said yes to anything. Luckily for me, she knew what she was doing."

"My wife is a dentist," Sean said; his gaze was intense and worshipful as he stared at Amy's profile. "She's the best."

"He's exaggerating. I'm not even qualified yet."

He yanked her close and whispered something in her ear that made her blush. I watched his interaction with his wife with fascination.

"Can we exchange numbers?" she said, pulling out her phone.

I was too shocked to do more than swap contacts before Sean led her away.

"The mob boss and the dentist. I don't even want to know how that happened." Theo shook his head and steered us over to the bar.

The wedding breakfast flew by, and I was hyperaware of Theo's presence at my side. Liam swore during his best man speech, and I chuckled at the look on Oscar's mum's face. The well-dressed staff seamlessly transformed the marquee into a dancefloor. After mingling and chatting, Theo led us to a table in the corner and pulled me into his lap, burying his face in my neck.

A tipsy David persuaded me onto the dancefloor for a while. His dancing grew increasingly erratic, so I headed back towards Theo and my brother Kris to avoid injury from David's crazy arm movements.

"Kris, you need to cut your husband off," I told him.

He sighed and went to wrangle his crazy man.

"Will you dance with me?" I said to Theo.

"One song." He scowled and climbed to his feet, stretching out his back.

I pulled him into the crowd of dancing wedding guests. He was taller than everyone around him and looked uncomfortable. Turning, I moulded myself against him. His arms encircled me, reminding me how much bigger he was. We swayed, and being surrounded by him filled me with heat. His hardness pressed into my lower back, and his hands roamed my sides as we moved together, causing my breath to quicken.

In my haze of arousal, I rubbed myself against him, making him grunt.

The music ended abruptly, and Oscar's voice shouted something about lining up, but I couldn't see through the people around us. A few people squealed, and the crowd pressed against us. Theo snarled, straightening at my back, his arms tightening around me. Something flew into the air, and we were jostled. Theo grunted, twisting me behind him as his arm went up.

The crowd drew back, and I realised Theo had a bouquet of tropical flowers in his hand. He was scowling at them as if they offended him. He said something about reflexes and then held them out to me.

I blinked at him dumbly. Had Theo just caught the bouquet? I took them, and everyone clapped.

Some people said congratulations, but Theo grabbed my hand and pushed through the dancers toward the back entrance to the marquee, forcing me to run in heels to keep up.

We burst into the cold night air, and I shivered, gripping the flowers.

"Theo, what's wrong?"

"I had champagne and roses back at the hotel," he muttered as he dropped onto one knee, and I gasped.

The ring inside the box he opened held me spellbound. It was a beautiful square-cut diamond that sparkled in the lights from the marquee.

"Zoe Barnes, my elf, my personal sunshine, will you make me the happiest grumpy man and become my wife?"

I giggled at his words, but the earnest look on his face made my breath catch.

A nasty thought occurred to me.

"This isn't to do with the board?"

"Fuck the board. This is me and you forever. Come on, elf, don't leave me down here. You know this old man's back is busted."

"Yes, Theo. Yes." I threw my arms around his neck.

He lifted me as he stood, and my feet dangled. A laugh bubbled up my throat, and my stomach fluttered. He set me down and slipped the ring on my finger.

"My fiancée." He bent and kissed me.

I grabbed his tie. "Did you say there was champagne and roses?"

"Come on, elf, let's go."

38

The diamond on my finger glittered as I rolled my hand back and forth, admiring it as the taxi drove us back to our hotel. Oscar's ancestral home was not in Sheffield, and Theo had booked a nearby hotel.

"I'm guessing you like it then?" Theo leaned in.

"It's so pretty." I watched it sparkle, enthralled.

"George helped me pick it."

"She's got great taste."

"She said it was elegant and classy, just like you."

"I've always wanted a sister," I said, and my throat grew thick.

"She's so excited. Expect a visit as soon as we return."

"Are you asking me to move in, too?"

"Aren't you already?"

I rested my head on his shoulder. "I was taking it one day at a time."

"We can still do that."

"And be engaged across an ocean?"

He frowned. "That's not happening."

"You didn't think that through," I teased.

"I was thinking about making you my wife. But if you want us to move back here, we could always find a dusty old mansion like Oscar's mom's crib."

I chuckled at his description, but my heart felt full at his offer.

"I like your apartment, and I like New York. But I want to come back here often."

Maybe I'd purposely avoided thinking about the future, but Theo's proposal clicked things into place for me, and I knew it was the right decision.

"That's easily arranged."

"Although I'm still not a fan of jet lag."

The taxi pulled up in front of the large hotel, and we headed inside. Theo tucked me under his arm, and excitement hummed to life under my skin. The conversation fell away, leaving only a charged kind of anticipation that filled the lift and prickled the back of my neck. My breathing turned heavy.

Theo swiped the key to the penthouse, and his warm hand against my back shot tingles through me as he led us inside. He helped me out of my coat, and his fingers trailed my arms, making me shiver. Moisture slicked my core, and my eyes fluttered shut, anticipating his kiss. The moment lengthened, and I opened my eyes. He stared down at me, his jaw ticking.

"Do you want a drink?" He turned abruptly toward the minibar.

I almost stumbled at the loss of him. My eyes chased his retreat across the room. He began mixing a drink with jerky movement, and I decided to take matters into my own hands.

I unzipped my dress and let the raw silk caress my skin as it slipped to the floor. The cool air in the hotel room brushed my skin, heightening my need. Leaving my sparkly heels on, I walked towards Theo.

He turned with two gin and tonics in his hand and froze. The scorching path of his gaze pebbled my nipples.

"Fuck," he cursed, his knuckles whiting on the glasses. "I'm hanging on by a thread, and you look... you look like sex and sin."

"That's the idea."

He stepped forward, then faltered and didn't come any closer.

"You need to put some clothes on because I don't think I can be a gentleman."

I closed the gap, placing the drinks back on the bar.

"What if I don't need a gentleman?" The fluttering in my chest was almost painful as I burned for him to touch me.

"You've been through a lot." He gritted, his eyes trailing over me.

"I know that, and you've been careful with me for weeks. I love you for it, but now I need my Theo back."

He groaned long and low in his throat. "If anything upsets you, you've got to tell me."

I ran my hands across his broad chest, flicking open buttons and sliding underneath the fabric.

"You would never hurt me."

Theo snatched me up, forcing my legs around his waist, and slammed his lips down on mine. A buzz flew through me at his rough, possessive touch as I met his intensity in the kiss. Pleasure throbbed through me.

"I need you," I whined as he pulled back

"My fiancée, my wife." He gazed at me reverently.

"Yours," I replied, needing him badly.

He walked us towards the master suite, and I undid his tie and final buttons, peppering kisses along his neck below his beard and sucking on the skin. He groaned, pressing me against the wall just inside the bedroom.

"Elf." He boosted me up and took my lips in another searing kiss, our tongues mating with each other.

Desire zipped through my body, and I restlessly ground against him.

"I want to kiss you all night, but I need to fuck you."

We'd realised there were quite a few positions we couldn't kiss in, and as much as I loved the feel of kissing him, I wanted him inside me.

"Need to worship you first." He tossed me onto the bed and descended on me.

Pulling the peak of my nipple into his mouth through the lace of my bra, his hands were gripping and massaging me everywhere. The ache inside me reached fever pitch, and I arched up to meet his mouth as the rest of him pressed me into the bed.

This was what I'd been missing – his intensity and the feeling of him consuming me.

His beard pricked my overheated skin as he feathered kisses down my belly, not stopping for my underwear as he ripped them down and away. He positioned his wide shoulder between my thighs, pausing to stare down at me before lunging. The friction of his facial hair on my skin, combined with a long lick, had me bowing off the bed with a moan.

"That's it. I want all those sounds," he growled.

He focused on my clit, circling and harassing the bundle of nerves, causing pleasure to zip out of my centre and unintelligent ramblings to fall from my lips.

"Theo." I gripped his hair as he teased my entrance with first one, then two fingers.

The combination of his movements inside and the suction to my clit had me racing to my peak. It felt monumental, like a dam threatening to burst, and I thrashed my head from side to side, the sensation growing too much and not enough all at once.

Moaning, I writhed beneath him as he pinned me with an arm over my stomach.

He nipped at my clit, and the bite of pain threw me over the edge. Pleasure filled me, and my toes curled with the intensity. A tear leaked from the corner of my eye as I panted through the sensation that washed through me.

"You're so beautiful when you come." Theo's hair was wild, and his lips shone with my release.

His half-opened shirt brushed my skin, and the tent in his dress trousers told me he enjoyed it, too. I sat up on my elbows as he stripped and squeezed my legs together as he removed his boxers, making his long thick cock spring free. He circled the bed and climbed beside me, reclining against the pillows.

"I want to see you riding me." He gripped himself with a smirk.

I scrambled up and crawled towards him, throbbing with the aftershocks of my orgasm but greedy for more.

"Face the door," he barked.

A thrill passed through me. I'd *accidentally, on purpose*, left a magazine article open on sex positions for short girls that he must have read.

Twisting around, I threw my leg over him, popping my arse toward his face.

"What a fucking view." He gripped my cheeks and kneaded them, making me yelp.

I wrapped my hand around his dick, guiding him to my entrance, which was drenched from his incredible efforts. I sank down on him, and the exquisite stretch made my eyelids flutter shut. I moaned as he filled me and steadied myself on his outstretched legs.

"Fuck. You feel so good," Theo ground out.

I rose and fell once, and Theo's hands guided my arse. Picking up the pace, I tossed my head back and lost myself in the sensation. But Theo's hand snuck around to play with my clit, and he bent his knees to add power up into me. We smacked together, and each impact bottomed him out deliciously inside me. This angle was different, and it set off a deep ache inside me that pushed me toward another release. Theo's other hand supported my hip as his thrusts grew faster, and my legs trembled with the intensity.

"Look at you riding me like a cowgirl. Fuck, the view is incredible, but I miss seeing those tits bouncing."

I realised I hadn't even removed my bra as Theo flicked the clasp open and palmed my breast as he continued to play with my clit. I bucked against his punishing upward drive as pleasure flooded me. He pinched my nipple and clit at the same time, and the zip of pain triggered me to orgasm, forcing me to scream his name. Theo's movements grew uncoordinated, and he roared with his release and warmth filled me. I slumped forward, spent. We panted, catching our breath. Theo crunched and curled forward, his cock still inside me, as he held me tightly.

"That was incredible," he said, and I could only nod.

Once we'd caught our breath, he carried me to the shower, and we cleaned off before he took me against the wall in another frenzy. He was insatiable, and I wasn't mad about it.

My chest felt light as he curled around my back when we were finally dry and tucked back into bed.

"Are you okay?" he asked.

"More than okay. I've missed that with you." I stroked his arms.

"I didn't want you to feel pressured, but fuck, it's been hard to keep my hands off you."

"I made a plan with Elle tonight to seduce you. I guess it worked."

"Devious woman." He nipped my earlobe, making me squeal a laugh.

"I love you, Theo." I basked in the feeling of warmth inside me.

"I love you too, elf."

EPILOGUE
10 MONTHS LATER

*T*heo's warmth lined my back as I grinned up at the twinkly lights, gripping the paper cup filled with hot chocolate.

"I don't see what all the fuss is about. It's just a big ass tree," he grumbled, resting his head on the top of mine.

I smiled at my grumpy Grinch.

"Hush you. Don't spoil the magic."

He snorted.

His anti-Christmas views had gradually improved, and our apartment was fully decorated, but he still rolled his eyes at some of my Christmas antics.

"What a difference a year makes," I said, my chest warming as Theo's arms encircled me.

"True."

I sipped my drink, savouring the moment as people bustled by, thinking over the rollercoaster of a year since I met Theo.

For one, New York had become my home. I loved the city, but we travelled home most months, sometimes more than once. Thankfully, Theo invested in green projects to offset our giant carbon footprint.

I drained my chocolaty goodness and handed Theo my phone.

"I want a selfie with us both in front of the tree."

"Let me guess, your little arms won't get us both in."

"My little arms won't get your massive bulk in." I poked him affectionately.

He tickled me, making me shriek and drop my empty cup.

"You don't seem to mind my *massive bulk* when it's drilling you into the bed," he growled in my ear.

"Stop!" I laughed, twisting away inside his embrace.

"Mmm. That's not what you said last night." He leaned down, kissing me.

The world fell away as I went up on my tiptoes to deepen the kiss. A wolf whistle caused us to pull apart. The twinkle in my husband's eye told me what I was in for when we got home, and a thrill zipped through me at the thought.

"Picture." I poked his bicep, and he spun us around to face away from the tree.

Beaming, I adjusted his arm to get the right angle, and he snapped the picture. I sent it to my family thread and Elle.

> Elle: Argh! That will be us next week. I can't wait.

> Me: Me too. You are going to love it here at Christmas.

Elle was flying over at the weekend, and I couldn't wait to show her around again.

Theo groaned, looking over my shoulder. "I'm going to lose my wife to twelve-hour shopping sprees."

"Shut up. You love Elle."

"That woman is dangerous."

I giggled. He wasn't wrong.

> David: Does Theo have gas?

"That smart ass," Theo growled, trying to grab my phone, but I hid it from him.

David always ribbed Theo if he saw him smiling. More messages vibrated through.

> The Old Bill: Mobile phones are easily stolen by pickpockets in large cities. Put it away safely.

I rolled my eyes at his message. Dylan, Kris and Dad just sent thumbs up.

> Mum: You both look lovely. I can't wait to see you for Christmas. Bowser is getting his outfit ready.

She sent a picture of Bowser wearing a bowtie, which made me smile. I did miss my boy, but Mum sent regular texts, and I always visited Mum and Dad's to give him fusses when I returned to the UK. He wouldn't be suited to the life here, and I couldn't deprive him of the rest of my family.

I scrolled to Jay's profile and texted him.

> Me: What a difference a year makes. Miss you always. Xx Tink.

Wiping away a tear, Theo squeezed his arm around my back in support. I didn't think I would ever stop texting or missing my twin, but I was happy now, and I'd like to think wherever he was, he was happy for me too.

"Is Maria still coming for Christmas?" I cleared my throat, returning to the present.

Theo and his siblings had moved their mum into an apartment nearby, and none of them had spoken to their dad this year. We'd invited Maria and George to the UK as Abe and his hubby usually jetted off to one of Abe's hotels over Christmas.

"She's excited to visit the UK with George. Hopefully, it'll get her away from that sketchy fucker."

Maria had a new male friend that Theo took an instant dislike of as soon as she mentioned him.

"Do you have any evidence he's dodgy?" I asked, tucking my phone away as per Big Brother's instructions.

We walked away from the Home Alone tree towards the taxi rank.

Theo grunted. "What kind of guy goes to a flower arranging night class?"

"A guy who likes flowers?"

Theo huffed. "More like a guy trying to pick up women."

I laughed. "Why not go to a bar?"

"Because women like my mom don't hang out in bars."

"Your mum says they are just friends."

"She talks about him enough."

"She'll introduce us if it turns into something, then we can see what he's like."

"I already know what he's like." He scowled, but it was his papabear one with no real heat.

I paused at the cab door as Theo held it open for me.

"What do you mean?"

"I had Liam's PI dig into his background."

"Theo, you can't do that," I said as I climbed inside the cab.

"Yes, I can if he's putting the moves on my mom. Abe agreed."

"Did Abe agree, or did you just tell him afterwards?"

Theo directed the cab driver to take us home instead of answering.

"Did you find something dodgy?" I pressed, not wanting something bad for Maria.

"No." Theo frowned.

"Isn't that a good thing?"

"It still seems shady."

"Is it possible you might just feel protective of her?" I snuggled into his side.

"Maybe?" he grumbled.

I smiled as I watched the people and buildings slip by outside in a blur of Christmas lights and shop signs. My grumpy CEO had come a long way in a year, but he was still a bit cranky sometimes, and I still loved him for it.

"I am a bit jealous of Abe this year. They are off to his resort in Hawaii," I said.

We held our wedding there a few months ago. Abe hadn't long acquired it, and we took over the whole thing with our close friends and family.

"Maybe we should go next year?" Theo suggested.

"That sounds amazing."

I spent the rest of the drive cuddled up, thinking of white sand beaches and cocktails.

Back at the apartment, we heated one of the dinners the chef service sent each week and curled up on the sofa.

"How is the book going?" Theo asked.

I groaned. "Slowly. Every time I write something, I delete it again as I don't like what it sounds like."

"Isn't that what an editor is for?"

"I guess. It's hard because I want it to be relevant and useful. I write blogs and articles all the time, but this feels different."

"Treat it like one of your articles, and you can always tweak it later. It's going to be amazing," he assured me, and I sank into his strong belief in me.

After pressure from everyone, I caved and began writing my book. There were styling elements for individual shapes and styling on a budget.

After holding several corporate styling sessions, I realised it wasn't for me. Private small group stylings were fun, like the one I did for Chloe, Eve, and Amy. That one was memorable.

"When is your next class at Chloe's retreat?"

"January. We figured many women with kids would be busy in December, plus the New Year is a great time for new looks."

I spent time soul-searching this year, and David pointed out that contributing and giving value didn't have to be exchanged for money, especially if we weren't struggling without my wage. That's when I took Chloe up on the offer of styling classes for her domestic violence charity. We focused on thrift and charity shop shopping and where to pick up bargains online or in sales to pull together a look on a budget.

Helping women whose lives had fallen apart lit a fire underneath me and was more fulfilling than anything I'd ever done.

I helped Theo occasionally at work, which was also fun, although we'd never had sex in the office again. The staff at Steel Ventures eventually forgot about the scandal despite the occasional leg-pulling by Ben and Taylor in the break room. Brandy was working on her plan B and was nearly ready to set up her own company. She'd come a long way from the mousy intern I met on my first day there.

"Maybe we'll be busy next December too." Theo looked at me heatedly.

I flushed at his words, throwing a leg over him and straddling his big thighs.

"Are you still keen?"

"To make some mini elves? Fuck yes."

We agreed I would come off my birth control in the New Year and begin trying for kids. The real reason for designing my new career in a portfolio way was to slot around a family. My therapist encouraged me to consider what I wanted for my life outside of my work, and the more I thought about it, the more I wanted to be the type of mum mine had been to me, and I wanted a big family.

"We should start practising now, just in case." He buried his wiry chin in my neck, making me laugh.

"We can't have forgotten since last night?" I raised my eyebrows at him.

The man was insatiable.

"I think I might have." He gripped my arse in his hands and ground me against him.

"I could be persuaded," I said as lust speared through me.

He stood with me in his arms, carrying me towards our bedroom, and the giggle I released was pure joy.

I never imagined coming to New York to consult a grumpy CEO would land me here. Things happened that I wouldn't wish on anyone, but despite all the odds, I got my happy ending.

AFTERWORD

If you're wondering who **Elle** found to fulfil her naughty Santa desires, then you can read all about it in her story entitled *Christmas Desires* https://books2read.com/u/bQnxQ6

Or also inside the collection of BDSM stories in *Seasons of Desire* https://books2read.com/u/bz8O5E

Would you like to read about Theo's business partners across the pond? Then start with **Liam** in *Steel Vengeance* (fair warning, he's an arsehole). https://books2read.com/u/b5qGVk

ACKNOWLEDGMENTS

This story was originally part of an anthology last year, and the less said about that car crash, the better. This version has been expanded, and two-thirds of it is new. When I first thought I could make Theo and Zoe's story into a novella, I was soon sorely wrong. I packed in what I could within the word count limit to the anthology piece, but it's been fun expanding it into the book it always was meant to be.

Thanks to my original alpha readers: Nicole, who taught me all I know about American Football (my knowledge is still sketchy at best), and Noor, who provided me with insider New York knowledge! I've visited the city, but never at Christmas—unless you count watching Hallmark movies.

Nina, thank you for the speedy and ever-accurate beta read of the original novella.

Tanya and Noor my main alpha readers who have been keeping pace with me as I expanded this version, and I am always grateful for your insight.

Allie Bliss of Blissed Out Editing, thank you for the full beta of the final book. And to my fantastic editor, Chloe, who always has my back.

Thank you to my writer friends in my "Queens of Peen" group and my writing "Tits" group, who helped with my blurb. Especially Aurelia, the *blurb whisperer* who helped finesse it.

Thank you to my Advanced Arc team: Christina, Logan, Trude, Denise, Alix, Petra, Beth, Katie, Elizabeth and Monika, for your eyes and to my main ARC and Street team for your unending support and hype.

To my Ream flock, who support me in so many ways. Especially my wise Flamingos Georgina and Tara.

ABOUT THE AUTHOR

CC Gedling is a mother, wife and doctor alongside her writing.

She uses her medical background and interest in psychology to build complex characters. Her books contain a mix of romance, suspense and a dash of spice.

Her British dry sense of humour allows her to survive the dreary UK weather and the chaos of being a mum.

For all her social media links https://linktr.ee/ccgedlingauthor

Website – www.ccgedling.com

Printed in Great Britain
by Amazon

51082081R00152